MAVERICK
JETPANTS
IN THE CITY
OF QUALITY

Black Balloon Publishing
www.blackballoonpublishing.com

ISBN-13: 978-1-936787-02-9

Black Balloon Publishing titles are distributed to the trade by
Consortium Book Sales and Distribution
Phone: 800.283.3572 / SAN 631-760X

Library of Congress Control Number: 2012933626

Designed and Composed by Kyle G. Hunter
Printed in the United States of America

9 8 7 6 5 4 3 2 1

MAVERICK JETPANTS

IN THE CITY OF QUALITY

BILL PETERS

BLACK BALLOON PUBLISHING

NEW YORK

CONTENTS

THE ROCHESTER
CLASSIC DRIVEAROUND

The night before our friendship ends and the city burns down and the Colonel Hellstache begins forever, I change out of my Bills pajama pants into my Bills sweatpants and drive Mom's car into the snow crust to find Necro—my last friend left even when I first met him. Past the Main Applebee's, past the Irondequoit Applebee's, past the Dollar Theater, I slow down to see if Necro's Vomit Cruiser is in any lot, anywhere, before giving up on Rochester's outside towns and heading to the city.

In a field along 490, the moon's reflection spreads out on a long layer of ice. Downtown, the skyline's five buildings are lit up and deserted. But my Joke Rolodex is stocked. I have one-liners Necro will totally crack up at if I find him tonight, jokes worth a Holy Grail Point for every message I've left on his Robot Voice Message Machine the last thirteen nights. In other words, 71 Holy Grail Points.

Down Monroe, past Mark's Texas Hots, where it's crowded enough to fog the windows but early enough not to need a door guard, I keep driving. Past a man sleeping outside the theater entrance of Monroe Show World. Past the McDonald's That Is Sometimes Out of Hamburgers where, for a second, I think I see him—Necro's tall mantis-lankfest, his wreath of unponytailed hair, the cardboard-colored Necro Parka—but it's some frizz-haired lady, wearing snowpants and Reebok Pumps, standing at the drive-thru speaker, ordering.

So no Necro tonight. And when I can't find Necro, I drive past the Bills bars I can't get into yet to look for Toby, who I go find when I want to see him Go Off the Top Ropes on someone. But I see no milkbag neckfat, no shaven heads or moonman Bills jackets, no Toby.

And when I can't find Toby, I drive past the 7-Eleven Powered Only by an Iron Lung to look for Lip Cheese, who at least I can rip on, although it's way better when it's me and Necro and Toby ripping on him. And when I can't find Lip Cheese, I look to see if I'll finally do it: the Sadness Custard Montage. Because I can feel some dials turning in my tear ducts, because I am probably Friendship Dead Weight now, and now I can cry myself out of Colonel Hellstache Nate and maybe into Platinum-Murman-Card Gold Membership Nate, who has Plans beyond doing Rochester Classic Drivearounds every night, who isn't afraid to apply for jobs and wouldn't be embarrassed about messing up the cash register subtotal in front of everyone, and who could remember, at night, to set a vitamin on the counter for the next morning, and wake up early enough to eat breakfast like a man if needed.

I pull into the lot of the Blockbuster on Goodman. The store is bright in my mirrors. I turn off the car and shorten my breath—You're finally ready! says the Sadness Custard flight attendant—and I try to find a way to let the Sadness Custard Montage happen. Because, Sadness Custard Montages are rare as comets. I'm still 0 for 5 going through with one; I couldn't even cry when Norwood missed that kick in 1991. And right when I start to really get amped—like I don't even care who sees me, like this is a goddamn Mountain Dew commercial—the inside of my chest turns into sealed Tupperware.

Fortunately, me and the Tupperware Feeling go way back. So as a detour, I look for the guilt-like feeling I get whenever I look at Mom's coffee mug with the Golden Retriever sketched onto it, but all I do is grind my teeth. So I tell myself: Someday your parents will be dead, asshole, and if you can't feel Sadness Custard Montage then how long are you going to wait until some woman who maybe you could have married, who I can't picture, finally takes me aside and says: "Oh my God. You *sociopath.*"

And when I can't find any of that, I lean forward and hug the steering wheel. Outside the store entrance, a man with a gray buzz cut and a white Dolphins jacket is straddling a BMX and looking at me. So I drive home.

The one-floor houses in Gates have muddy front yards and longish driveways. The kitchen light is off in my house— a shingly juice-drink carton on Gillett—and the TV is on in the living room. Mom doesn't look over when I untie my shoes.

"Home?" I say.

She's still in her rib-high work pantsuit, pouring the one

glass of Sam Adams she allows herself each night. She sets the glass underneath the paper towel rack in the corner of our tree-fort-sized kitchen, like she's hiding it. Then she goes into the living room, so when she wants a sip she has to go back into the kitchen, creating a hassle for herself.

I check the refrigerator for Post-its—No "Nate: Necro called," no "Toby called," not even "Lip Cheese called." I step down the single step into the living room and sit on the carpet, which is marbled blue, as if to imitate water maybe.

Mom leans back on the Woolly Mammoth, which she calls our sofa, stretching the punctures in the leather. Her work loafers are still on, hanging above the carpet in a way that makes her stomach look inflated.

"Hey, Mom?" I say.

She keeps her eyes on the TV, where on Letterman, which she takes in like news, a robot with Bill Clinton's head shoots lasers out of its eyes at a bag of French fries.

So I go: "I don't know. I just wanted to ask. I'm just worried that. It's just. I'm just worried that, I don't know, I just feel sometimes like, I don't know. It's just that I'm worried that . . ."

"You're worried *what*?" she says.

I don't bother finishing, and I take the cordless phone to bed with me in case it rings and it's Necro. Lights on, I stare at the glow-in-the-dark stars I pasted to my ceiling in fifth grade and try to form constellations—the Bright-Nippled Astronaut; the Talking Sump Pump; a constellation that looks like a bird, then a mustache, then a bird, then a mustache, then a bird. Then I get mad, because I can never concentrate, and whenever I can concentrate, it's during times like when

I'm brushing my teeth, and I'll splash water on a moth in the sink until it squirms down the drain, like I just killed something, on total cruise control, like I might blink my eyes one afternoon while mowing the lawn, and when I open them, I'll be in a Friendly's, with a knife in my hands and a waiter on the floor. So I roll over.

The next morning, the phone is twisted up into the corner of my pillowcase when I wake up. But there's freshness in my muscles and eyes, like the first day back from the flu, like I could call somebody Colonel Hellstache and mean it.

Which thank God, because I will need it today. Because hear that noise from one bedroom over, like metal train gears? It's Mom and Fake Dad No. 3. Their lovemaking sounds angry, like slapped mozzarella and ground teeth—a real Alaskan Meteor Shower. The reflection in my framed Machine Gun Kelly poster—his arm right-angled to throw the football—is vibrating.

Alaskan Meteor Shower, Somerville Catcher's Mitt, Twin Cities Yogurt Bowl: Real Dad's phrases. The idea being that if you combine any geographic location with any item, it'll sound like a sex term. Which he came up with after he moved out and blew all his money on Garbage Pail Kids, collectors' Pez dispensers, and Halloween-themed LPs. My point being, Fake Dad No. 3's condo's gas heater is broken, so he's been staying here. He owns more purple things—bathrobes, the velvet padding in his acoustic guitar case—than I've ever seen ever.

I go down the hall with the phone and into the living room to watch some HBO, which Real Dad ordered but Mom forgot to cancel. Summers, in this living room, I'd crank the box fan and move it from the doorwell, where Mom always kept it, to right next to his recliner, and his fallen-out ponytail hair snared on the fan grates. And when I was younger—Pants-and-Nintendo Phase—and needed to look out our sliding door at night because I was scared someone was out there, he'd let me look until I was sure. *Nobody is out there Nate!* Mom said.

As in, here's Mom now—fully pantsuited, the curls in her bird's nest of hair sharpened with sweat—and Fake Dad No. 3, with his Thor-blond pageboy cut, trimmed beard, and silk R&B pajamas, coming into the kitchen for some Post-Oakland-Tire-Fire lunch. Leif Thundertrident is what I call him, for obvious reasons.

Fake Dad No. 3 leans against the living room's entrance, chest and face still pencil-eraser pink. He dangles one foot from the single step going down into the living room.

"Welcome to the day, mister," he says, voice a little woodsy and hoarse. "I trust you dreamt fulfillingly?" Which makes you want to staple his face to a moving train.

I shoulder-brush past Fake Dad No. 3 and go into the kitchen. Our fridge is puckered shut, and I nearly lose my balance opening it to get my morning Gatorade. Fake Dad No. 3 sits down at the table in what used to be my seat and crosses his legs at the thighs.

"Maybe it's because I've been touching people more, because I'm licensed now, but you've appeared in my dreams quite a bit, Nate," he says, which is creepy enough to make diapers wet themselves. "Last night I dreamt Reiki Massage hired you as my assistant. When customers would look

through our CD booklet and request music to enhance
their session, no matter what the album request, you put
in this Megadeth album you'd brought with you. A request
for Zakir Hussain: You put in Megadeth. A request for
G. N. Balasubramaniam, the Carnatic vocalist: Megadeth—
piping into the massage studio. 'It keeps deciding for me,'
you said over and over, hopelessly. But at the end of their
session, customers came out, revitalized as ever."

He pauses, like he's waiting for me to be amazed.

"Thank you," I say.

"Maybe you'd be good at it," he says. "A good worker.
A good"—and he pauses—"toucher."

Mom stabs the pan with a spatula. She doesn't scramble
eggs so much as make Nerf pancakes. "Gareth, Nate doesn't
care about work. Nate cares about . . ."

"Cares about what, Mom! Cares about what!" I say.

"Nate cares about Applebee's. And Necro. And helping
Toby pick up prosti-tots at the mall."

"Funny, Mom! Ha Ha Ha Ha Ha! Necro's got a job at
Kodak! And Toby's twenty-two now. He's got his own place."

"Well I doubt that will last very long—not on his budget." She laughs. When Mom actually does laugh, it's one
word: Ha!

The plate Mom sets in front of me wobbles flat—like
when a quarter runs out of spin.

"But what does a dream like that tell you, Nate?"

"That you still have to work at Kinko's on weekdays?"

He nods and twists his goatee with his thumb and index
finger. "That's fair, that's fair," he says. "My only point, Nate, is

the bad decisions are just as good as the good decisions. After several bad decisions amid a time of deep personal turbulence and cafard, I came to understand that I was touring the Yemeni city of Taiz, and as I became more consumed with the turbulence, I woke up in my hotel room one morning to find myself blind in my right eye. My vision would later return, but right then, I threw out my maps and wandered east, for days, among the qat fields. A group of teenagers driving an El Camino with a Howitzer mounted to the back pulled up next to me. A boy in a Walter Payton jersey approached me, drew a glass shard or perhaps a jambiya, and screamed at me in maybe a form of Zabidi . . ."

"Gareth!" Mom says, laughing one Ha! "You didn't have an itinerary?"

"I was a journeyman!" Fake Dad No. 3 says. "I was taking in the stars! When life gives you lemons, you *live*."

When the phone rings, I forget it's been in my lap, and I scoop it before it hits the floor and run into the hallway. The background noise on Necro's end sounds like rows of shopping carts crashing over and over.

"We're going to take and go to W—p—ns of Ma— at 7!" he yells, in his Section-8 Murman Riot voice, like he's giving orders, not even saying "Hey," or "Sorry I didn't call back."

"What?" I yell back. "Where were you? I was worried! Textbook Colonel Hellstache!"

"Take and—b—move—out now!" he yells again. "We're all going to take and go to Weapons— nk. Meet— T–by, L— Ch—se and Wicked College John! Take and go to Kodak Park!"

Which is already Bad Sign No. 1: Two out of every five Colonel Hellstache nights, historically, have begun with Necro calling and yelling at me in his Section-8 Murman Riot voice. And I wonder if I should bring him the scrap of paper that only had the word FUCK written on it, which Mom found in my closet when she was stuffing my old clothes into garbage bags and hanging up her blouses, so I could tell Necro: Remember when we found this Certificate of Fuck downtown, at the Pontillo's Where the Telephones Were Answered by Cats? Which maybe he'd like, and it would distract him from being Section-8 Murman. Then I say, almost by accident: Maybe I am too old for this. Or maybe what I really want is to be old, so I could stay in without worrying.

But, as with most other points in my life, I'm opening the sliding door of my bedroom closet to get my Bills jacket, and leaving.

"Going out with *Necro?*" Mom says when I walk back out into the kitchen.

"Necco, what?" Fake Dad No. 3 says.

"His name is Andrea. We call him Necro," I say.

"He moved from Louisiana," Mom says. "The Fanto family. An army family. Nate dropped his MCC classes"—she slows her voice down and lowers it to impersonate Necro—"so they could *take* and run away and get married."

"Ha Ha Ha Ha Mom! Real original! Ha Ha Ha Ha!"

"Well," Fake Dad No. 3 says, almost lispily. "Does he stick around at night?"

Which you could even ask thirteen nights ago, on New

Year's Eve, the second-to-last time Necro, me, Toby, and Lip Cheese would all stick around in the same place together. The ball dropped and, hours later, the channels went to carpet deodorant commercials. Miles of not talking between us in my basement, sitting on the crusted-over couch, when Necro leaned forward, head between his knees, and then flung himself back into the couch, violently, body bouncing forward slightly, squeaking the couch hinges, ponytail hairband flying off somewhere. Nobody spoke. The TV lit the basement's gray-painted concrete floor like the light of a fish tank. Toby leaned into the armrest on one end of the couch. Lip Cheese, on the other, tucked his knees into his T-shirt, greasing up a pillowcase. We threw our jackets over ourselves, and on the floor, I slid my hands between my knees and we fell asleep.

On New Year's Day evening, with hangover filth shrink-wrapped to our tongues, we woke up. The sun was almost down, like a nectarine cooling on ice. It felt like every Sunday evening ever condensed, drifting in thicker than dishwasher steam, and there was no way I would even say thirty words that day. We high stepped through the snow in my front yard to go to Toby's car and drove to maybe Jay's or the Highland for an omelet, and outside, it was 1999.

JOKE ROYALTY

Kodak's Eastman Avenue parking lot is broad enough to see the earth curving, empty except for Necro's Vomit Cruiser at the opposite end. Necro sits Indian-style on the hood, and when I pull in with Mom's car, I jam my foot into my gas pedal and assassin-rifle toward him. Wind slices off the windshield; ice patches crunch beneath the tires—total Nate Memorial Satan-Way.

I'm already cracking up, already way too excited. Necro's cardboard-colored parka, which we agreed would be inducted into the Necro Hall of Fame, is zipped to his nose. He waves, arm like a windmill blade, and I slide my hands around the steering wheel, as if I'm losing control, and yell, like I'm going to hit him: "no, No, No! NO! *NO!*"

I choke down on the brake pedal—smoke rises into the seat wells; an earthquake under me as the car swings out from behind. Necro slips on a mini-ice-continent on the hood of the Vomit Cruiser and falls hands-first to the ground.

"Colonel *Hellstache!*" he yells, wiping snow scum off his jeans when I get out.

"It's Nate Memorial Satan-Way. I always stop. I stopped a parking space away."

"Colonel Sandbags Ladyface Hellstache, Nate!" he says.

"Colonel Sitz-Bath Wolfhound Hellstache, Necro."

He squints at me, his triangle Dracula eyebrows narrowed in, acne scars extra pink in the cold.

"Are you actually mad?" I say.

He sits on the Vomit Cruiser's hood. The wind blows a single corkscrew of hair out from his ponytail and freezes the leftover shower-water in my slicked-back hockey hair.

"Okay, okay, okay," I say.

He clenches and unclenches his hand, where a pebble is lodged in his palm. Except now we're not saying anything. And I'm picking apart the pocket lining of my Bills jacket, because I can't tell if we're not talking because we're best friends and we don't need to talk sometimes, or if it's because I truly crossed the border into The Uncomebackable Realm of Colonel Hellstache, and maybe I should have only done Nate Happy Meal Satan-Way and not Memorial-level Satan-Way.

Because now, all Necro's doing is rolling his hand, moping at it. Like a total Hashbrown Gargoyle.

Silver pipes—some thin like bendy straws, others large enough to crawl through—run along the brick buildings of the Kodak Park production plant across the street. Men walk slowly in and out of the factory, the beep and a click, way off, from the turnstile door when they hold up their scan passes. Some of the thinner staff, managers maybe, are still wearing their protective glasses over their regular glasses. Others have purple around their eyes and thick stubble, like they had their faces professionally tinted; undershirts under open jackets, work boots in grocery bags.

So I say, just to say something: "Kodak Park Hair-Vest Cavalry, on a Friday night. Men who filter their coffee with their underwear."

Necro breathes deeply and drops his shoulders, like he has to reach down and lift his mouth from a well to even talk to me: "Off to take and treat themselves to the new upscale Subway, in Pittsford."

My brain is sweating, looking for any addition.

"What if they took and had new, like, palatial food there," Necro goes on. "Like a condor wrap?"

I'm tearing through the Joke Rolodex—a mummified sandwich found in the Pyramids; a sandwich prechewed by a cast member of *Party of Five*—and when I settle on one, it feels like I have to hurry it out of a burning building.

"A condor wrap with diamond sauce?"

"A sub made from the thigh meat of one of Winston Churchill's generals?" he says.

"Maybe, like, a sandwich that's so upscale they won't let you see it."

"When you order the sandwich they take and blindfold you and drive you into the mountains and make you eat it at gunpoint."

"You eat it and a forty-five-year-old man turns into a swan."

"You eat it and it frees all the hostages, you know, from Lebanon," he says.

"What?"

"I don't know."

And with that we've made, maybe, our last joke. Our first joke, and still the funniest word in the history of language? "Pants." "Satan" is close seconds, but Pants is Joke Royalty. Pants became Pants the night I slept over at Necro's utility-shed-sized house in the woods in Spencerport. Before we put on *Dream On*, we snuck upstairs from the basement to make sure Necro's dad was asleep. But among the stacks of yellowing mail, next to the empty gasoline tanks on the floor, Necro's dad sat upright on the sofa, asleep, tattoos up to his neck, naked except for a condom, every light in the house still on, but his pants were folded, neatly, on the cigarette-burned carpet. And then Necro yelled, wailing like he was in pain: "Oh God my *pants*!" and we rumbled back down the steps, sputtering laughter, palms skimming the stair railings.

Necro could have said anything then—even some vocab word he'll use when he can't think of a simpler one—and it still would've been the funniest thing. We became friends. And Pants became Jetpants when Necro crashed his ATV into a dirt bank in the woods, and his body flew over the handlebars, legs still bent into sitting position. And Jetpants gave us Necro's prescription Percocets, which gave me any night we stood on the trestles, my thinking cool and cube-like. And Jetpants became Maverick Jetpants when me and Necro Maverick Jetpantsed out of high school forever.

But that was two years ago, and now Necro works in Chemical Recycling in Building 38, and tonight the sky is the color of sheep wool, getting bluer with evening. Above us, a plane flies across the lot where, at the opposite end, there's a tower that looks like a milk crate. Steam exhales from it at all hours. Necro stiffens his left arm, raises it upward, draws his right arm back like he's aiming a bow and arrow, and opens his fist, fingers spread straight, and, quietly, we look up. The imaginary arrow makes a perfect curve through the air toward the plane. When the plane flies just over the tower, Necro makes a saliva-y explosion noise, and I realize we were thinking the same thing.

This won't last all day. Soon Toby and Lip Cheese and Wicked College John, who's back home for January break, will be here. So I go: "Man, what are we going to do?"

"You mean, tonight?" Necro says.

"Like, overall," I say. "Like, a Plan. Like, I gotta start making that money."

Necro scratches the back of his head, the way he does whenever he's about to say something serious and maybe nice. "I think, with you, Nate, it's a matter of finding—"

Then I hear from behind: *BWOAAAA!*

Which I expect to be Toby. But instead, it's some different shaved-headed guy I don't even know. He's wearing a wifebeater and a leather vest, and these army pants tucked into Nazi-type boots tied tight around his legs. His arms are as muscleless as the vanilla flats of an ice-cream sandwich. He has this sneery look on his face, with wire-rimmed glasses—not exactly a Rambo's Rambo. Necro doesn't even introduce me, so I'm immediately calling the guy Rambocream.

And—like this isn't Textbook Colonel Hellstache at all—Necro proceeds to actually give Rambocream a man-hug!

"And a splendid greeting to you, Sir Pocketwatch-pants Von Moneycolon!" Rambocream bellows, like banquets and chimneys.

"And a good evening to you, Sir Spectacles Von Snifter-pants!" Necro foghorns back.

I breathe down a heart tornado. Because, Necro! You use Pants with someone not named me? He's even laughing differently—this throat-cackle, when I'd counted so many nights as Nights of Quickness whenever I could get Necro to push some air through his nose.

So when Toby's car makes a wide turn across the lot's empty lanes and parks next to the Vomit Cruiser, it's clear that this is going to be the World's Most Colonel Hellstache Evening. "What is this Voltron of Retargery?" Toby says, looking over at Rambocream. "Who's Poached Death?"

"Brandon," Rambocream says, extending his hand to Toby.

And this, at least, makes me crack up. Because it would take easily 3.5 Rambocreams to out-huge Toby—and Rambocream's hand is just out there, getting pinker. And Toby just leans back, clapping his Bills mittens together, smiling with his little baby gremlin teeth. Rambocream's glasses frost up into silver dollars. Toby flares his chinfat, shaved head steaming. Then he shakes Rambocream's hand anyway.

When Wicked College John—or as I should call him, Recently-Issued-Restraining-Order John—shakes my own hand, he does this finger-hook move that you know he clearly does with his Mook-Platter friends at Bonaventure. He's tall as a male model, pores leaking cologne, permanent hangover swell under his eyes. What looks like white deodorant streak on his pea coat.

"Telling you man, it's good to be back," Wicked College John says to me and Toby.

I nod, Toby nods, but half of my face is looking at Rambocream and Necro, who are walking away toward what is, I guess, Rambocream's car—this red econo-Nissan parked along the curb on Eastman.

". . . but this whole business with the girlfriend, really been messing with my grades," Wicked College John is saying, looking around and shifting his feet. "I got two B's; I got a C. All I was doing was calling, trying to tell her I was studying, I was in deep concentration, and that I threw that coffee mug at the *wall*, out of a *general* anger. But she made, like, eighty copies—she gave the form to her work, her friends' apartments? But she's eighteen. She doesn't have an outside-world . . ."

Wicked College John's voice fades. Necro and Rambocream open Rambocream's hatchback and lean their heads in.

"So, I've had a lot of adversity, really," Wicked College John is saying, "a lot of abrasive personalities to deal with. But it's good to come back, see you guys. Really helps someone see what they have going for them away from here."

"Wait, what are you talking about?" Lip Cheese, who we've forgotten about, says from behind us. His jacket is caution-sign yellow, with bungee pull-tabs everywhere. He's wearing a pull-down mask-hat, and his lips push out beak-like through the hat's mouth hole. Just standing there.

Toby and Wicked College John laugh so hard they have to brace their hands on their thighs. Lip Cheese wipes his mouth with his sleeve, and his lips start to twitch, so you know he's shutting down a little.

Don't even bring it up, guys!" he says. "I haven't cried since the Ten-Ten-Ten Girls hit me with the pillow!"

Wicked College John claps Lip Cheese on the back and jolts him into Toby. I would laugh too. But I hear Rambocream's car trunk slam, and see Necro clearly smile at something Rambocream says as they walk back and rejoin us. Necro unfolds some yellow looseleaf sheets of paper from his pocket and hands them to Rambocream. Then, though, from the creators of *Oh Shit: The Movie*, I notice the papers in Rambocream's hand are drawings!

I try to tell myself: Maybe Rambocream just lent Necro the drawings and Necro was returning them? But one drawing is of a vampire with bear paws, a walking cane, and a collar on his cape that's as tall as a lampshade. VAMPAW, the name reads at the bottom of the paper, in Necro's square-shaped handwriting. Another of what appears to be a whale, with human hands for fins, and metal armor covering six breasts on its underside.

But Lip Cheese is in the middle of saying, ". . . I dumped it back into the wine box and taped it back up! Sorry I have respect for my parents, Toby!"

So I chime in—because Necro never not-laughs at this: "More like dumped it back into the Sock Hospital, Lip Cheese!"

I look at Necro hard to see if he's watching. But he's busy

using his hand as a clipboard, clickable pencil wobbling on its axis, shading something in on a drawing of a snake whose tongue is a hatchet.

So I jam my Bills winter hat down my jacket and into my armpit and make my voice higher and whisperier to impersonate Lip Cheese: "It's dishydrosis, guys! It's a *sweat condition*! Wait: What are you talking about?"

"Wait, what are you talking . . ." Lip Cheese begins to say.

Toby and Wicked College John crack up, but it's a total waste of an Uncomebackable Insult. Because Necro isn't paying attention, and Rambocream dangles his keys from his finger and goes: "Well, we should probably, you know."

Necro pulls down his parka zipper to his neck, and I notice he's wearing this white dress shirt and a red tie. "We have Weapons of Mankind tonight," he says.

His jaw muscle flexes. Toby and I are already looking at each other.

"We sell various rare weaponry—novelties and collectibles on a limited signal public broadcast," Rambocream says, in Upstate New York's flat-voweled nasal accent. "Factory-sharp inventory unavailable in some states. World War II-era emphasis, historical Germany. Heritage weaponry, really," he says, and, taking a deep breath, "Heritage."

Except right when Rambocream says that, I notice a patch on the left half of his vest with a sewn illustration of a large-lipped monkey dragging a pail of water in each hand. His vest has a shiny metal pin, too—not of a swastika, but the other one that looks like a plus sign, with the ends curved slightly out like trumpets. Gold border, red in the middle—tiny like a Polo emblem. That's when entire cities in my head lose their gravity. Because what Hitler did, back then? Textbook Colonel Hellstache. But I remember that I can never remember if the plus sign stood for Nazi Germany, or just World War II, or Germany's air force, or just Europe. Then I remember, I think, that the pin stands for Europe, which means I don't know anymore what the monkey stands for, and I don't know what this says about Necro.

So I ask: "Well, Necro? Are we invited to this shit show?"

Necro looks at Rambocream. Neither of them says no.

So, as with howevermany stupid years that have passed between us all, we cram into the Vomit Cruiser and follow Rambocream's car into downtown Rochester, a place big enough to be a city but small enough to have an Inner City.

On 104, grains of road salt spray through the Vomit Cruiser's undercarriage.

"I visited their weapons booth last Christmas, and mankind *is* his weapons, guys," Necro says. "Weapons are preparedness. State and local governments? They can seize your property anytime to build a highway. Look at 490. Eminent domain. Waco. Our police-state postal service? With postmaster general Nicolae Ceaușescu who can just take and control our very means of transmitting lingual expression?"

"So no Century Club tonight? Not even Jaeger Cowpunch?" Wicked College John says. "Will there at least be some Irondequoit girls there?"

Necro chuckles through his nose. Wicked College John hacks at Necro's arm from the back seat, which yanks the car one lane over. A few crumpled papers shake loose from under the passenger seat into my seat well.

As in: More drawings! On a napkin, a building that looks like a courthouse exploding, with a silhouette of a kitten with bat wings hovering in front of it. On a flattened McDonald's bag, a wizard, standing biblical and stiff, arm extended at a right angle, a stalactite of beard hanging from his chin. Behind the wizard, a castle is on fire.

Which, me and Necro: Our whole junior high, we would stay up and draw at sleepovers—a drawing of Slayer onstage maybe, or that time we made up Man-Serum Bagelheart, who had a shovel for one arm and whose digestive system can convert rocks into orange juice. But to draw now, post Trestles Phase?

Wicked College John picks up one of the drawings. "Necro, what is this Faggot-Lane Walkery?" he says, which I sort of agree with.

"Take and don't either of you even ask the subject!" Necro says, with out-of-nowhere teeth-grindingness, voice like if charcoal could bark. "Don't you dare even broach it!"

"But I want to know your feelings, bro," Wicked College John says. "A lot of expressives tend to have bad childhoods: pervy uncles, Kangaroos for Kids . . ."

"You'll be in big trouble if you keep talking, John!" Necro says.

"Don't let his eleven German Shepherds know about Kangaroo for a Kid, John," I go (because: Vampaw? the other ones?). "They're very possessive."

But I immediately feel horrible bringing up the one

Uncomebackable Insult against Necro, because Necro wasn't even at his house when Kangaroo for a Kid happened, and I never found Kangaroo for a Kid all that funny anyway. And he looks at me in the rearview mirror with this new, cold humanless look, the way some anime villains have sleek eyes with no irises. And now I know he's seen something terrible inside of me, but I have no idea what, and there's a part of me that wants to sweep every person and every sound out of the city, and follow Necro quietly through the streets for the rest of my life, and ask him, over and over: But what do you mean? But what do you mean?

Then I notice, on a sheet of yellow looseleaf: A man, whose eyes extend outward like telescopes, holding between a pair of tongs a miniature house that's on fire; he appears to be setting it in a glass case with other houses on fire. On the back of an ATM receipt, a Kodak logo with human eyes melts. But the drawing I stare at the longest, that throws a long grim-reaper hood over my brain and keeps it there forever, is on the back of what looks like a page from a school essay. In that drawing, a single, tiny sperm, tail like a fishhook, floats against the moon above a burning Applebee's. The Applebee's looks almost exactly like the sad cube of the Main Applebee's—where Necro always bought me fries—in Gates, which was always enough of a town to have an Applebee's, but not a good Applebee's with the newer menus, or with the seat leather whose color hasn't been punched out of it.

"We were kidding, Necro," I say. Which we only ever say as a last resort.

A panel of ice snaps silently off a semi ahead of us, rotates, and explodes softly on the road. We take an exit into the Mattresses in the Streets District. Houses are boarded up but with satellite dishes mounted to the roofs; others have second-floor doors on the outside but with the stairs or balconies fallen off. Necro's face is snarled up and witch-like.

"All I can say is: Life is precious, Nate," he says. "You especially, John. What I'm about to take and undertake with my life tonight, what I'm about to undertake with the world tonight, could be immense."

WEAPONS OF MANKIND

Downtown, Rambocream lifts up the guard gate to a brick building that has the words ROCHESTER PUBLIC BROAD-CASTING painted above the door. Metal clanks in a hockey bag that Necro lifts out of Rambocream's car trunk and heaves over his shoulder. Across the street, vines grow out of a mailbox at a boarded-up post office, and a place called Good Times Pizza has maybe four things on the front shelf. Houses with heavy doors have balconies that are held up with orange seat-belt-like straps from the roofs.

Right then some barrel-shaped black lady, hair pulled back tight, white-blouse-type outfit and black leather sneakers, walks toward us. With her face totally neutral, she draws back her purse—this hot maroon, rhinestone-covered thing—and whips Rambocream on the left arm with it. Necro and Wicked College John and Toby immediately get between her and Rambocream, shoes squeaking on the sidewalk. She draws her purse back again, face still neutral, and swings again.

"That patch is really not a good idea," she says, purse strap coiled around Necro's arm, voice stern in an office sort of way.

"This patch is an historical item, ma'am," Rambocream says from around Necro's head, fistfulling his vest's monkey patch and raising it at her. "By no means do any of us sympathize with any act of oppression. This is a collector's . . ."

Her purse hits him in the mouth. "We're gonna get shot," Lip Cheese mumbles to himself.

"Hitler was a product of incest, ma'am!'" Wicked College John yells, hand planted in the woman's collarbone, purse strap whipping around his torso. "A product of incest! Would I say that if we didn't hate him?"

Her body is fuming Avon. "That's a bad idea, sir. That's really not a good idea," she keeps saying, voice level as she walks away, backward, still facing us as she rounds the corner.

Rambocream sniffles and squirms away from Necro and Wicked College John. Something wet—a tear, snot—flings off of him.

"Do they know the history of these weapons?" he says, heaving. "Why don't we round up all the history books in the world and burn those? Every time a few friends want to do a show, this city, with their lawyerly word-pairings, just . . ."

Necro sets his hand on Rambocream's shoulder and says, "Take it easy buddy. We hear you." Buddy?

Even worse, I actually take it easy even less, like I've totally Been Promoted to President of the Diarrhea Fan Club, when we enter the building, into a back room with a concrete floor and a ceiling with exposed beams. Maybe thirty folding chairs face a small stage, with studio lights to its left and right. Wicked College John lights a cigarette to look less nervous. It feels, slightly, like we're not actually allowed in here, like when you visit a neighbor's house when they're on vacation.

Necro and Rambocream immediately go into military setup mode; dropping the hockey bags on the floor, gripping zippers with their fists and yanking them hard across the bags, like a samurai slashing open a stomach. Necro hangs up a large, tan curtain that extends to the floor. The lettering on the curtain reads THE WEAPONS OF MANKIND. Above the logo are fabric cuttings of two crossing knives and a large eagle head. Rambocream folds out a cafeteria table on the stage, and Necro sets three footlong lengths of tree trunk on the table, each slotted with stab marks.

Of course, there's no girls, so Wicked College John puffs teapot fumes through his cheeks, bites his lower lip and inspects the area behind the stage: a sink; a red exit sign; a child's Huffy USA bike.

Then, loud talking: Men enter the room and set their various camo or bright orange jackets on the chairs. Men with black jeans, t-shirts with the sleeves ripped off—one with a shirt that says SHUT UP AND RIDE; fat guys with devil goatees who wear shorts year-round. Necro handshakes his way through the crowd. He slaps the arm fat of a bald guy who has a Santa Claus gut and a beard big enough to smuggle a baby in.

"Loostro!" he says to Necro.

"Get my VHS tapes?" Necro says. When Necro does not lend tapes, period. And his new name is Loostro?

So me and Toby take Necro off to the side of the stage, where Rambocream lifts a hockey bag by two ends and slams it on the cafeteria table.

"Necro," I say. "You use Pants with these people?"

"You were barely up the stairs when I saw my dad's wang, Nate," Necro says. "I said Pants, therefore I own Pants. Free licensure."

"But you stole it—you stole it from you and me."

He spins around at me and says, suddenly, from the muscles in his jaw. "Like you aren't contradicting yourself at all, Nate—like you've never took and confiscated one of my original utterings and slutted it around. Look at Colonel Hellstache even."

"But who are these people?" I say.

"Right. Introduce us to these fags," Toby says.

Rambocream reaches into the hockey bag, extends his hand to Toby, and says: "Would you like a Freedom Crab to go with that handshake?"

Something black is on Rambocream's arm, something that looks alive, and Toby immediately ninja-rolls away from Rambocream—which is hard to do in an NFL-issue Bills winter jacket—and gets back to his feet.

Rambocream smirks and drops his hands to his waist. After we have a second to actually look, what me and Toby thought was a live scorpion is actually this shiny, black, scorpion-shaped metal molding held in place by three Velcro straps. Its head curves down over Rambocream's fist, and its front pincers and are sharpened into blades.

"Freedom Crab! Erection 2000!" Rambocream says, not

Bringing the Funny at all, using the scorpion weapon to hump Necro's forearm. But Necro actually cackles out loud!

A pair of studio lights poof on, cotton white, and one of the fat guys in shorts turns on the camcorder mounted to a tripod connected to a computer off to the right side of the stage.

Me, Toby, Lip Cheese, and Wicked College John take a seat in the back row. Necro takes off his jacket and puts his hair in a ponytail. Rambocream's nose bumps the microphone, setting off a deer whistle of feedback. The crowd quiets, a red light on the camera goes on, and Rambocream holds some note cards in front of his face as he reads, like a principal over a loudspeaker:

"Welcome to the Weapons of Mankind Show. And we welcome, particularly, our western New York hobbyists, whose customership we depend on when the state continues to fail to legislate an adequate appreciation of history, hobbyism, and the oldest means for land protection."

Rambocream's lips quiver. He reads from the second note card in his hand:

"We would like to thank Bambert Tolby, our distributor, who is prevented from being with us tonight due to his health. We continue to skirt the mainstream to strive toward a sovereign life, despite a contempt for free speech, and a tip from a certain disingenuous nonprofit community organization to our programming director and police that has misled the area about our views on race and weapons on the grounds that we are not proper representatives of the greater Rochester area." He flips to the next note card. "Penal Code 26501 states that one is perfectly legal to own the items in our inventory, as long as they are not cane swords, switchblades, or brass knuckles . . ."

Rambocream looks up from his note card and back down at it, like maybe some are missing or out of order.

"To that end, our first item: the Heavy Metal 24th Anniversary Sword," he says. "Upon its invention in 1975, heavy metal has captured the science fiction and fantasy communities. Sword artist Tag Rangel and fantasy artist Loro Miv have teamed up to pay tribute to a cultural icon. This sword features solid metal handle parts cast with intricate details, a 39 ¾ inch undulating stainless steel blade, and a solid wood wall plaque, so that now, you can truly remember: metal forever."

"And all the crabs you can get," I whisper to Toby.

"Seriously, there's no alcohol here?" Wicked College John whispers.

"These guys can't swing weapons," Toby says. "These guys can't fight." He waves his hand over his nose. "And it smells like the National Auto Mechanics Convention in here."

But then, Necro pulls the Heavy Metal 24th Anniversary Sword from its plastic sheath. There are cursivey-type designs along the blade. He bites down on his lip, one incisor visible. With an angry wetness in his eyes, he raises the weapon behind his head, muscles so tensed his forearms and hands shake and the sword shivers light, and he drives it, straight down, into the tree trunk. One corner of his mouth is screwed into a frown. He looks like he's just killed someone. He folds his arms to hide that he's gasping for air, and I realize I've been holding my breath this entire time.

"Call now," Necro says.

"This is weird. This is stupid," Toby whispers to me. "This is like, you have a friend, and you find out he holds an After-Hours Taint Seminar."

"What's this guys? Who has a seminar?" Lip Cheese whispers.

Rambocream flips to the next note card. "Next, we have a great historical item, a great traditional item to be cherished, um, by the whole family."

Necro sets a velvet case on the table, softly, like the case is a helicopter he's landing. The swastika on the front blazes in the lighting. He turns two tiny golden knobs on the left and right sides of the case, and two latches on the front snap upward. He dips his knees slightly, and, in this loving way, curls his fingers under the top half of the case, and hoists it open. Five knives are inside. The gleam slices through my retinas.

"Introducing the German Dress Dagger set," Rambocream says. "Includes German Air Force Dagger, Hitler Youth Knife, German SS Leader Dagger, German Dress Dagger. Constructed to replicate the actual weaponry, this set is a steal for $49.99 . . ."

No calls come in. After the hour is over, outside, some Weapons of Mankind spectators stand around a pickup, rolling cigarettes on the hood. Lip Cheese yawns. Toby breathes into his palms and places them over his ears. And Necro and Rambocream are taking forever loading up the weapons, holding mock sword fights, maneuvering like fencers.

"Necro, you know, we're not exactly in the Heated Driveway District," I say, and wave my arm toward a group of kids a block down who are in parkas, standing in front of a 7-Eleven, where one window has a spider web of cracked glass with a bullet-sized hole in the center.

Necro slings his arms around me and Wicked College John.

"Well if you two ladies have to take and get your eyes bleached at the spa, we can leave here quicker if you take and carry the two weapons bags left inside," Necro says, studying his calculator watch for a few seconds. "Get the bag with the Double-Fantasy Slayers, Nate. They're great for a fight. Provided you Shee the Fight."

Fuck him! Because, even though I'm third place in Holy Grail Points, there are five Uncomebackable Insults you don't need to know about me: Did You Shee the Fight?, Sausage Academy, Mommy?, Friend to All Animals, and especially not Taped-On Dildo. If we get into Taped-On Dildo this early, I'm through. But the Weapons of Mankind people are laughing now, when I've explained a million times that I said "see" that way because I was riding my bike home through the woods from Necro's house after we watched *The Exorcist*, and a noise startled me and I steered accidentally over a bump and bit my tongue—that scene where the girl spider-walks down the stairs is *rough*. You tell me that's not signed-by-the-Grim-Reaper shit-pants inducing.

"We need to drink *off* this place," Wicked College John says, flailing an arm to gesture over the entire street, scarf flinging out from under his coat collar. "I've been through so much this semester. I couldn't even get out of bed for the Lingerie Party this December, couldn't even dream."

I yawn. Toby looks at me. "I don't know. It's cold," I say.

Wicked College John grunts like he does after the Yankees lose.

"What," I say.

"No, I'm not mad, it just pisses me off," Wicked College John says. "I come back, and everyone's too tired to do even Jaeger Cowpunch—"

But then, I see Necro tap his calculator watch and nod to one of the fatter Weapons of Mankinders wearing jean shorts. At which point, suddenly, all the remaining Weapons of Mankinders—everyone except Necro and Rambocream—get into their cars and drive off, at once, engines echoing from blocks away.

"Two more bags, guys, and then we take and lock it down," Necro says.

He pats me and Wicked College John on the back, shoving us, kind of harder than maybe you'd expect, actually, toward the building entrance. He skips, backward, away from us, and jogs slightly up the block.

He says, raising his voice a little: "Take and give oneself over a little; everyone has to come down from the mountain, you know, the going-over . . ."

Then I don't hear the noise so much as the noise— a sharp tearing that's too loud for my ears to take in all the loudness—liquefies every bone I own. Because suddenly I'm on the ground, smelling the warm tires of a Buick, and I feel a hot, big, all-flattening breath over me. Sand-sized things— glass particles—cut my fingers when I run my hands through my hair. Swords with rubies shaped like wolf heads on their handles embed into trees, quivering metal waterfalls landing in front yards, backs of pickups.

Because, the Rochester Public Broadcasting building has exploded, and when a wooden beam spits out of the store-front and hits Wicked College John's face, his cheek ripples upward toward his eye. His head turns around almost all the way and then snaps back, shaking gel loose from his hair. His one dress shoe flies off, and when he falls to the pavement, he lands on his left forearm underneath his back. His head bounces once.

"Oh! God!" Necro yells, in that way Necro never says Oh God. Rambocream is I don't even know where. Lip Cheese runs toward the 7-Eleven to find a phone. Toby breaks into a sprint, chasing a white circular coin-sized object rolling toward a fire hydrant.

Meanwhile, I stand there. I lick the nylon sleeve of my Bills jacket to wipe the salty ashes off my tongue. The brick frame of the public access building is still there, but the front door is on the sidewalk. Something smells like burnt penny.

A softened chunk of the ceiling collapses and a refrig-erator falls from the building's second floor, orange sparks sneezing everywhere. In the road, Wicked College John's shoe says BACCO BUCCI on its sole. One of his contact lenses glows bright orange on the pavement, curling in the heat. Little things crackle. Wicked College John stares at the sky. His eyes move around. Way off and above, the sky is light purple in a way that always made me look forward to going to bed, and a single red broadcast tower light blinks at a slow-drip pace.

Because, I come out here and try to talk to Necro about a Plan. And, now? Necro knee-slides on the pavement to perform CPR on Wicked College John? Like he's trying to be Tadahito Murakami: Ninja Surgeon and save the world?

"Necro," I tell him, setting my hand on his shoulder. "Let's not get overdramatic . . ."

But he turns around, the slash of teeth—complete Roasted Face of Satan. "He's practically *dead*, man! What's the matter with you?" His eyebrows are like brush fires, and I wonder if he's mad at me.

Bits of papers spin around me. I hear, inside my head: You are a bad person. You are wrong all the time. Because, still, with me, it's the Moth-in-Sink feeling. As in: Come on Ref! *Feel the Right Thing* already!

That, and, also, about a dead body's length away from Necro, I notice a piece of paper slowly uncrumpling on the pavement. It's a drawing—his, definitely—of a shirtless, bearded, loinclothed man with rabbi curls and metallic biceps, emerging from the fiery rubble of maybe a British mansion, carrying what appears to be a younger man's body.

"Timex! A bomb! It was a Timex!" I hear Toby yell, heaving air as he runs back to us. "They used a Timex!" He holds out his palm, in which there is this bent, aluminum face of a Timex watch. He leans over, hands on knees, and spits out a yo-yo string of saliva.

Echoes sproing off the bricks of houses and into the sky. Windows of the buildings around us flicker on to bright yellow. And here Necro is, here we are, miles long from a Plan, two or three snowflakes melting on my arm, and Necro's thumb is on Wicked College John's wrist, yelling: "All right, man, you're gonna be fine, man, gonna be fine, you gotta do me a favor, man, you gotta keep your eyes open and you gotta think something for me, man, Playboy, man, give yourself a nice comfy hard-on, man, gonna have to nut up and think about something, Led Zeppelin, man; Led Zeppelin, Led Zeppelin, eyes *open*, man, Led Zeppelin, you and me we own this—right, man? right, man? right, man? right, man? right, man? right, man? Right, man?"

THE SAD ARCHIVES

One, one, one, one, one, one, I go, whispering. One, one, one, one!, like I'm pissed off, like I'm ready to punch myself in the face. I flip my bedroom pillow to the cooler side. I count sheep until the sheep melt into potatoes, and the potatoes stretch into pills, and the pills elongate into hospital stretchers.

Because when the paramedics strapped down Wicked College John, one paramedic folded up the wheels of the gurney while the other slid it into the ambulance. When I'd always thought maybe the wheels folded on their own, or always imagined how what if they separated from the gurney and coasted away, in a slow, infinite straight line that ignored gravity, the way a space shuttle peels from its tanks. And I figure out that I might be falling asleep, that tiredness has won only for now, and I'm finally no longer thinking about the zombie-mint smell of the hospital waiting area, or whether or not it's weird that Necro really wanted to sleep in his own bed and drove us back to our cars instead of waiting there longer.

But once the actual shape of my room appears through my closed eyelids—the sliding closet door with the WEASE bumper sticker on it, or, on my dresser, the Don Mattingly puppet I made from a milk carton in third grade—my brain thinks: Sleep has arrived! Then I realize I'm thinking this, and the stadium lights in my brain whoosh back on, and I jolt awake again, counting.

So when I sit up and get my night eyes, I decide to forget counting and focus, really hard, as a Sleep Portal, on this little glass particle, way off in my mind.

Hold on. It's turning into something.

I look at the light squeezing through the bottom of my bedroom door. As in, I can't remember if we always leave the hallway light on the whole night, or did Mom recently start leaving it on to make it look like we're awake when we're really asleep.

Like when I was way younger. Sometimes, I'd wake up around midnight. I could hear the dog-whistle-quiet noise from the living room's TV, and Real Dad through the air vent, watching *Mr. Show*, laughing angrily, like he was showing Mom he really got the jokes.

Or how, once, way even before that, when I decided to sneak out of my room, I could see Mom, at the kitchen table, staring at a four-pack of cigars she'd just bought—a hobby she'd taken on to one-up Real Dad's going to Bug Jar shows. But she threw up every time she smoked them.

And Real Dad would pass out in the bathroom, some Popcorn Wylie album sounding like tinsel through his Discman headphones, a large bottle of Cantillon half-full next to the sink, some issue of *Preacher* face-down in his eczema foot bath. "Woman thou hast betrayed me!" he slurred into my shirt once, when I shouldered him to the living room couch. But I'd kind of agreed with him, because why else would you take a foot bath and read *Preacher* if you weren't right?

After we helped Real Dad move into his new place in Penfield, Mom took me out for a drive. "Did you really like your father?" she said.

"I don't know," I sort of snapped at her. "I mean, didn't you?"

Her room is next to mine. I can't tell if I can hear anything in there.

There are times when I can sit in my desk chair at night, with maybe only the chalky fluorescent desk light on, and everything I've ever thought about before suddenly harmonizes into one chord. And when I stare long enough, the Fred Flintstone piggy bank on my dresser, suddenly, will look like a totem pole mask worn by whoever is going to come to me in my sleep and slit my throat.

Or, maybe this glass-particle feeling I'm feeling is that feeling when you stay awake in your room until you're sure the rest of your friends, who went out without calling you, have gone to bed.

So I start thinking that, maybe, the glass-particle feeling is like those times at night after I closed my eyes long enough and I couldn't tell if I fell asleep. I'd open my eyes, and the light at the bottom of my door would be gone. And the dishwasher would be on, sloshing water, like the inside of a dark mouth.

And the thing is, I begin to understand this glass-particle business more when I turn on CMF. Next to my bed, the red light from my radio's ON switch stretches out a few shadows in the dark. CMF has been playing the same eight songs in the exact same order between 4 and 5 a.m. for about four months. Def Leppard's "Hysteria," the fifth song in the rotation, comes on. And, during the outro, when the band coasts on the D chord, it gives me this stomach-level feeling, which made me stay in my room all night when I was fifteen, imagining girls who I liked moving out of town, until Lip Cheese or whoever called to tell me that Necro wanted to climb on the high school roof that night.

And the feeling I get, I realize: The stomach-level feeling is this same actual fifteen-year-old feeling, this basic intro-to-sad kind of thing. Not like a looking-back kind of sad—like, "Oh, I remember those sad times." The feeling I get now, while "Hysteria" ends, feels like I am actually in the present tense of being fifteen.

Like there are different levels of being sad. Fifteen-year-old sad, climbing-on-the-school-roof sad, DWI-ing-it-in-one-direction-until-gas-runs-out sad. They're still there, not gotten over, filed away. The Sad Archives, I'd probably call them. Here I am, still there.

That's what this glass-particle feeling is. The same way, when you dream, it can break your heart when someone forgets to bring a stapler to a funeral. But next scene, life is fine. But still, all the while, there's this voice in the back of everything you're dreaming. The kind of voice that, when I finally do fall asleep tonight, asks, like it's the beginning of an AM station politics debate, if freinium hens can munter themselves.

PINNING BOW TIES
ON THE DEAD

When me, Necro, Toby, and Lip Cheese actually see Wicked College John in his hospital room, that's when you say "Shit" and have it mean something.

"Jesus!" everyone—except Necro—says.

The side of Wicked College John's face is food-poisoning pale, zippered with stitches. There's a Vaseline kind of shine to his forehead, a plastic tube up his nose and another in his mouth. A length of white tape stretches across his face like a handlebar mustache, and his cheeks are blotchy. A brown, telephone-receiver-shaped saliva stain is next to his face on his bed's scratchy pillow.

And the look on Toby's face: more terrified than the rest of us, blood leaving his cheeks. Something seems to change in his eyes—pupils shrinking, irises clenching into fists. He leans down, tie dangling, and he rubs his eyes and looks at me:

"Somebody knew we were there," he says. "We just survived an assassination."

"I grant that you have a point in that this is very messed up," I say. "But maybe we should let the police . . ."

"Unacceptable. Somebody did this. This is pinning bow ties on the dead."

Toby leans back, closes his eyes, exhales, and does a double-bass-drum pattern with his boots. "Pinning, bow ties, on, the *dead*," he says, jabbing his finger into his chair's plastic armrest.

"What is that, a phrase?"

"It is a phrase, Nate. It's taking a messy situation, a death, and putting a little bow tie on it to neaten it up, to say This Didn't Happen. Pinning Bow Ties on the Dead. To cover up for the fact that this situation is much more of a nebulous, you know, *thing*. I handed that watch piece to the investigator last night, and nowhere on the news do you hear the headline: 'Watch found.' You tell me that's not the police hoping everyone forgets about this and goes back to their bread makers and their 401(k)s and their freaking dollhouse lives—*unquestioning*."

Necro stands up suddenly, twirls his keys, and relaxes his shoulders, and Toby spends a few seconds noticing this.

On a silver, pie-tin-shaped balloon tied to the armpads of a chair, a message says WELCOME BACK! Take-out containers of cold chicken wings and issues of *Maxim* have been stacked on the box heater below the window. On top of the magazines is a set of keys that has the Mercedes logo. The keychain tag reads GET BETTER!

This, when, look at any of us in formal get-better clothing—my red white and blue Bills shirt with two buttons and a collar; Lip Cheese's khakis and hair parted way off to the side; Necro's Native American braided square-dancing belt and blue jeans.

Wicked College John's Mom—whose heels you can hear stabbing the floor from down the hall—rushes back into the room from the cafeteria, comet-tail of perfume behind her because she's never not exasperated. "Can I also say you guys don't need to dress up like he's dead?" she says. "It's medically induced. People come out of comas every day. His brain is in, like, mint condition, it's just been shaken."

Her face is radioactive orange, makeup paved on, hair napalmed with bleach, figure like an aging swimsuit model. She's carrying a shot glass-sized yogurt cup in one hand, and she sits down in a chair at the bedside. When she leans over Wicked College John, I can see a tribal-type tattoo on the slice of skin on her back, between her Aerosmith T-shirt and her pre-faded, pretty-much painted-on jeans.

"I brought KFC, sweetie," she whispers into Wicked College John's ear. She waves a magazine with Carmen Electra on the cover in his face, then drops it on his thigh.

"No luck?" Toby says for no reason.

"The red freckles, those bumps on his face is a rash, it's some irritation thing from either the Compleat or the tube itself," his mom says. "I told the doctor and food services: This family can't have food with high concentrations of nickel."

"Dishydrosis," Lip Cheese says. "That's why I shouldn't have the fries at Applebee's. But I cheat all the time."

She crosses her legs habitually. "I told the cafeteria, I know your salads are pre-made," she says. "But is it rocket science to pick the almonds out? I told them: No nickel. The inside of my mouth: There are these bumps. But do these f—ing f—gners care?" she mouths the two words.

Lip Cheese's pupils spread, hypnotized by John's stomach rising and falling under a baby blue blanket. And, when the information makes its way into my brain that he is actually, one hundred percent, in a coma, I kind of say to myself: "Huh." Then I find myself thinking about how I'm starting to feel something (which is progress, maybe?), like "Huh," plus one.

"Listen, ma'am," Toby says, posture spring-tensioned. "We're here to extend our sympathies, and, in addition, to . . ."

"He's not dead yet," Wicked College John's mom says, touching Toby's arm, then jerking her hand back and squeezing some hand sanitizer into her palm. "Sorry, I'm very sensitive toward—sorry. They do jaundice phototherapy one floor down. Those babies—it's creepy."

"We understand this might be hard to take," Toby says. "But it's possible there was a domestic attack."

Wicked College John's mom brushes something off her shirt, looks into her lap, and shakes her head: "Don't tell me this, don't tell me this, don't tell me this."

Necro, this whole time, leans against the doorjamb, looking out the window at the ventilation shafts on the roof of the neighboring building. He hasn't said a word so far today. I look at him—to a) see if he'll make eye contact, and b) to therefore see whether he's mad at me about what I said to him after he went Tadahito Murakami: Ninja Surgeon on

Wicked College John, and if he's mad at me because I didn't
help him with said surgeoning.

On the walk through the cold back to the car, Necro at
least lets me bum a cigarette off him, but he just hands me
the pack, without saying, "Sure!" or "Take and be my guest."
Wind spreads Lip Cheese's hair like a helicopter hovering over
a field, and Toby removes his suit jacket, untucks his dress
shirt, and squints into the sunlight.

"Buildings don't just explode," Toby says, unlocking his
car. There's red all around his eyelids; he keeps taking deep
breaths; his lips look way fatter. "They even said they were
skirting the authorities. They even said some community
organization informed the police about them. Coincidences
don't just happen side by side."

Necro, who shrugs.

"You know who did this, I'll tell you. Ask me who it
is." Toby says, as if, suddenly, it's the end of the Clue game,
and rain is slobbering down the windows, and the lightning
is making the room only black and white. He inhales, the
camera narrows in, the violins drop your heart off a cliff.

But then he hesitates, exhales slowly, and says, like maybe
he can't think of anyone:

"Luckytown Hastings."

"Fucky-Sucky-town Hastings," Necro says.

"Luckytown Hastings?" I go.

"Wait. What are you talking about?" Lip Cheese says.

Lip Cheese has a point. Maybe it's actually very, very
weird that Toby would bring up Officer Luckytown Hastings,
once our Private Enemy No. 1, with parted hair that's so

neat it looks like it snaps on. Because, we haven't Rioted on Luckytown Hastings in at least six years. Here he was, in a picture from the *Democrat and Chronicle*, bricks of cocaine on a table, all scrubbed-clean looks, except for his right eye, which has a tiny black dot, a mini-pupil, just below his main pupil, like a moon orbiting a planet. Make a joke about the eye, you'd be carrying your legs home.

He had all those qualities and yet I've forgotten what he looks like. His real name is Tom Hander. All he did was run after us a lot. The more I think about it, the more he just seems like some *guy*.

But this is me, going to bed tonight, in my Bills Zubaz pants, moving my forehead muscles around in a caring way and caring about all this. Because, maybe Toby has a point: What about that night me and Necro paintballed Luckytown's truck, and then only a week afterward Luckytown just happened to pull Necro over for expired license plates. What about how after Necro spraypainted the phrase HULKAMANIA RIDES ALONE onto Luckytown's truck, Luckytown chased us down the street, wearing these cow-patterned slippers, and caught Lip Cheese, and pinched Lip Cheese on the tricep so hard that he had this yellow and purple sore on his arm and, from there, the flu for two weeks. And, then, as the rest of us ran away, Luckytown literally yelled into the street as we assbolted into the woods: "I will eat you alive!"

Because, when I wake up the next morning, after Mom has gone to work, the news shows that, while I was asleep, three fires occurred downtown—total Roasted Face of Satan as your downtown map. Authorities find a charred-up mattress in a boarded-up apartment building, burn patterns cursived all over the bedroom. Near the Liberty Pole, the second floor of an apartment collapses after another fire, and an old man on the second floor breaks his leg. I think at first: Maybe those two fires are simply regular fires that sort of happen and I'm just paying more attention now. But then, an explosion blows out the mirrors in the Y's weight room—and investigators find shrivelings of what might have been a soda bottle that maybe contained explosive liquid. Police detain or arrest or apprehend Rambocream, whose real name is apparently Brandon Ross, but they let him go without charges. Some radio host calls the whole thing a "race-war amalgamation."

And, while there are no suspects for the Race-War Amalgamation, people at an all-black church on Joseph Ave. hold an antiviolence vigil a few days later just in case.

Then, the next night, nothing. The phrase "race-war amalgamation" is never mentioned again, and I find my mouth hanging open in disgust when sports goes back to taking up half the news's half-hour.

Because, my mom grew up blocks away from the Liberty Pole. When I was way younger, during what I'd maybe call my Snowpants Indoors Phase if I'd known Necro then, she took me to the Pole's Christmas lightings, where they bring out the mayor and for an hour the city seems safe. Up close, the Pole looks like a junkyard harp; the tall buildings around it are quiet and the square around it empty except for maybe a lone wheelchaired person moving slowly through. Blocks away though, from East Ave? Those lights, strung along the metal wires that extend downward diagonally from the pole, look like a lit-up extension of the street, like a ramp of light, lifting suddenly into the sky.

So maybe I think the lights are nice, the way much of downtown is perfectly nice, or the way how even though I never go to House of Guitars, I still hope it stays there forever. So maybe my point here is that it sucks, is all, that nobody cares when a building in Rochester burns down.

Except, when I wake up—the next afternoon now— to get my Thurman Thomas jersey, right when I've finally worked up the most focused Pope-like Boner of Hate for Luckytown Hastings that I can, here's Mom. She appears over my shoulder with a colon full of Level 10 Bitchentery:

"Goddammit Nate! You were here this entire time? I told them you were out!"

"Told who?"

"An investigator—for an insurance adjuster!—came by this morning and wanted to ask you about that *explosion!* I told him you were out, because I just assumed, for whatever reason, that there'd be no possible way you could have been sleeping this entire time and only be getting up at 4:45 p.m."

She passes me briskly in the kitchen and heads toward her bedroom.

"Don't say it like I blew up the building!" I say.

But like all moms, if the Japanese bomb your house, she'll tell you it's your fault for living there. She turns around.

"Three hundred dollars. Rent," she says. "You will start paying at the end of April. I will *not* have a freeloading *knife collector* in this house."

"Mom!"

"Go work construction somewhere," Her Witchy Tundra-cuntedness says. "It's good for your hands." She laughs her one Ha. She hands me the investigator's card, but I'm so pissed I tear the card up and let the pieces float to the floor and walk out of there right in her face.

Because when Toby drives us to find Luckytown, you can already hear the harmonica in the wind, the Bow Tie Being Unpinned from the Dead. The gravel hisses when we pull into the lot of Goateez Sports Bar, out in the shoebox storefronts of Victor, the town where Luckytown hangs out, because we just know this, though I forget how.

On the Goateez marquee, it says: 8PM WET T-SHIRT CONTEST / 10PM CHRONIC PARADIGM. Cars are parked even on the grass across the street. Inside, it smells like peanut shells and roasted clothing. The decorations are standard Box of Atmosphere: Coors banners; dark wood lacquer that's a little greenish like old, infected chocolate; dimming softball trophies and shamrocks.

Me, Necro, Toby, and Lip Cheese shoulder-wedge through the crowd—no Genny or Labatt's or Shea's here. We stand behind Toby. I can barely see above or around his shoulders.

But when we see Luckytown Hastings—with his friends at a booth, collared shirt under a black sweater, anchorman grin perfect enough to put you to sleep after a workday—I no longer want any part of this, am suddenly so embarrassed that I'm unable to see anything in front of me, blood cells in the Pope-like Boner of Hate returning to base. The blood cells in Toby's Pope-like Boner of Hate, too, appear to be returning to base. Because when Luckytown notices us, Toby spins away to avoid eye contact.

"Actually let's just hang out," he says. "This is Colonel Hellstache. I didn't mean Luckytown when I said that."

"Wait—what are you talking about?" Lip Cheese says.

"I said I don't know why I said Luckytown Pinned Bow Ties on the Dead! I was upset! That tape over Wicked College John's face messed me up!"

"Pinned what, Toby?" Luckytown says, suddenly from behind, gnashing his whole body at us.

Toby looks down and, as if remembering to, folds his arms and says, "Nothing."

Luckytown turns to his friends, who are both wearing Dickshirts—one with the Goldschlager logo; another that says HOW DO I LIVE? on the front and FCKN' LOUD on the back. He lowers his voice, like he's maybe impersonating someone. "Does *he* have a raincoat for that?" Which his stupid friends laugh at for some reason. Like it's a joke.

"A raincoat for your *eye*, maybe!" Lip Cheese yells, pointing at Luckytown from over Toby's shoulder.

Luckytown, whose meanness alone, if you liquefied it and drank it, could kill a man, stands up from the table. He grinds his teeth down to powder. Toby's face muscles deaden with what might actually be fear. So he yells:

"Everyone! Everyone!" And when the crowd quiets, Toby appears even more scared, like he hadn't anticipated talking to a quiet room. "Um, so basically, this guy, Tom Hander, he may—or maybe not—have made a bomb out of a Timex watch to blow up the Rochester Public Broadcast building. So, you know, we were just dropping by to, you know, accuse him of that, and to make you all aware of, you know . . ." Then, Toby yells, in total Auxiliary-Level Embarrassment-Recovery Mode: "Pinning Bow Ties on the Dead! Our friend is in a coma because of this man right here!"

Except, then? Luckytown, and everyone in this Mung-Hut Dynasty of a bar, starts cracking up! The crowd noise picks up again, like they're celebrating something. Somebody pats Toby on the back, and not in a mean way.

"Pathetic, pathetic, kill yourself already, you *children*," Luckytown screams over the crowd. "The fact that some-one unconditionally loves you at all you *piece of maternally deposited . . .*"

He stops and inhales, face recomposing itself like a VCR rewinding him into calmness. "I don't feel all that sorry for anybody who associates himself with some *boy*"—and he points his finger hard at Necro—"who, when he's bored, exchanges weapons and chemicals and explosives with people who have tried to form a currency called the David!"

Something unclicks inside me. "You don't know Necro!" I say from behind Toby. "Necro's not that type of guy! Necro hasn't Unabombed anybody!"

But Necro, right now? He droops his lower lip, raises his triangle Dracula-brows, and twists a button on his Necro Hall Of Fame Parka. As the bouncer muscles Toby toward the door, Luckytown says, voice thinning into the crowd: "I don't think you know your friend here as much as you think you do." He flops his arm toward Necro. "He'll light a bomb and he'll take you by the hand; he'll lead you straight into hell, he'll lead you into . . ." and then I can't hear him anymore, because we've been nudged outside.

Riding home on 490, Toby's car's wipers whimper across the windshield.

"I was so close, so close to throwing a punch," he says. "When I think about it, I feel sorry for every person in there. Laughing like that. Who laughs at a life?"

Next to me, Necro leans against the window and smirks into the collar of his Necro Hall of Fame Parka. He mumbles something.

"What'd you say, Necro!" Toby goes, near-pulling the car over. "You laughing along with them?"

Necro leans against the window, closes his eyes, and laughs, once, into his fist.

"Kangaroo for a Kid? Kangaroo for a Kid?" Toby says. "Is that what you said? I have eleven German Shepherds, and one of them died, and the reason everyone calls me Kangaroo for a Kid is because—"

"Drop me off right here!" Necro says, pounding Toby's headrest. His eyes are bloodshot and dark, like caves where fawn fall asleep and die. "You all look at me like I'm stupid! You take and invent a conspiracy. That is animalism!" Necro says. "It's a good thing they don't have a word for you—you and your Cockdramas! Your moral masturbation! Your pleonastic intestinalism! Your hippocampal food rape!"

Toby pulls over on the side of the highway, passenger side-view mirror inches from the highway's concrete sound-blocker wall. Necro slams the door, pushing air in on us. He shrinks in the rearview mirror when Toby drives off, walking with big strides on the road shoulder.

"Well I don't know what any of that meant!" Toby says.

Minutes shift by like earth plates. The sky is light purple, and there appears to be a crane, stretched all the way up into the cold into the top floor of a skyscraper. The water spraying out of it looks like a feather.

At the exact same time, in the seat well where Necro was sitting, I find a manila folder with Necro's bootprint on it. The folder has a bunch of what appear to be printed illustrations, in color on shiny paper. One shows a knight with a single flame making a wide curl around his body and ending at his sword blade. Behind him, a silhouette of a palace, gutted bright orange with flames. The body of a young man, in a pageboy vest, lies at his feet.

"What's that?" Toby says from the front.

"Oh, just some job applications I left in here," I say. I stick the folder in my jacket.

Because, in the way old friends do, Necro always forgets to take his things with him when he leaves a place. He's left five pairs of boxers at my house, five chapsticks, one pair of swim trunks, two retainers, one bicycle, one Rygar, two Rush T-shirts, thirty-four colored pencils, one sleeping bag, two pillows, one toothbrush, and a pencil drawing of Electrus Nucleotide, a chrome bald man staring straight at you, arms muscley but straight-lined and robotic, like rock candy, each hand crunching a much smaller robot, electricity falling from their necks like confetti. The day he drew that was one of the

Big Days, years ago, a day of Crazy Stories. Beforehand, we rode our bikes, standing up on our pedals, really Maverick Jetpantsing it, one county over into the pine trees. Somehow, the gate to the Holleder Armory was open. We made up our own organization back then, the CTA, even though the letters didn't stand for anything. But we'd printed CTA bumper stickers—he's left nineteen of those at my house—and we snuck into the armory, stuck them on some army jeeps, and rode away.

I don't want to talk about this anymore. Pinning Bow Ties on the Dead? You take that phrase.

NECRONICA

The Wegmans human resources office is mocha colored, the size of a bathroom that gave up on getting a toilet. I've borrowed one of Fake Dad No. 3's purple shirts, and am wearing khakis and navy Polo socks. The tiny plastic fastener-thing that holds the socks together in the store knots up in my calf hair. I'm sitting in a plastic chair with no armrests, talking to this interviewer woman who is all shoulder pad:

"And why is it that you want to work in Meats, or in Cheese Shop?" she asks.

"I just thought it would be interesting," I say. "That cheese, you know, would be interesting."

When, actually, I checked off "Meats" and "Cheese Shop" on the application because "cheese" is a funny word. Not Pants-funny, but those were more innocent times: Cheese; Power Down!; MEOW; etc.

But after this bad job interview, and bad job interviews over the next week at Paychex, Abbott's, the Jack Astor's out near MCC, I call Necro, and I get the Robot Voice Message

that says, in its Dr. Sbaitso voice: "We cannot take your call."
I eventually go to Applebee's where, in the later afternoon,
the window booths are empty. Grown men with loosened ties
sit at the bar and eat off the workday with a buffalo chicken
salad and a radioactive-colored margarita. Rain and wet headlights are outside, a donut-glaze of ice on everything. Via the
payphone in the bathroom corridor, I manage to get ahold of
Necro—which has been like trying to get ahold of the Pope
over the last month—to meet me here.

"God I need to complain," I tell him on the phone.

So, a little consolation, I'm thinking, regarding a Job, a
Plan, etc. And also, to get a better idea of whether Necro is
mad at me, not specifically for Tadahito Murakami: Ninja
Surgeon, but maybe just mad at me in general.

I sit down at the same booth we always do, in the corner,
below the model airplanes hanging from plastic strings, in the
carpeted portion of the restaurant that's raised one step. I get
three Coke refills in before I see the Vomit Cruiser pull into a
parking space outside.

Which of course, when Necro comes in, he's shit-zero
in the way of help. With Lip Cheese behind him, he walks
in like he's just taken the best shower ever. And worse, he's
wearing his white Pink Floyd T-shirt, rust-stained from the
washer, with the picture of the guy in the suit shaking hands
with the guy on fire: Necro is always far more of an asshole
on days when he wears his Pink Floyd T-shirt.

"You tell me how I'm doing, Nate," Necro says, stuffing
the Necro Hall of Fame Parka and Lip Cheese's Bungee Cord
Drop-Zone jacket into the corner of the booth across from

me. "Two percent raises went in at work today, little currency flow, liquidity, whatnot. I got a home, I got a cash."

"Necro's got a home, he's got a cash," Lip Cheese says.

Because Necro? The same kid who gets fired like it's his job? "What does that even mean, you Maverick Shitpants?"

"I'm going to get paid to take and sell my drawings online!" Necro says.

Food climbs back up my throat. Suddenly, there's a part of my brain that says: You can always go home and have a nice Sadness Custard Montage and sell your tears at GNC. But our waiter shows up, calls us "guys" like he knows us, and instead I say: "Can I get fries and coffee?"

Necro tells me the name of the website: NecronicA. "Like Metallica," he says. "Except NecronicA." Which he laughs at harder than any joke I've ever told him.

"Necro's got a home! Necro's got a cash!" Lip Cheese says, scraping his napkin across his mouth.

"Lip Cheese: He's got a home, he's got a cash, he's got Holy Grail Points," Necro says.

"I'm doing data entry—at Paychex!" Lip Cheese, of all people, says, this same kid who once told Sandra Buckley, after he went with her to see *Ransom*: "You know something? You made a great movie even better."

"Nate's got no home, Nate's got no cash," Necro says.

"Nate, you're pathetic," Lip Cheese says. And he and Necro start cracking up! Necro, with the throat-cackle he was using around the Weapons of Mankinders, with their fat-guy shorts and their thick-lens serial-killer glasses!

"Whatever, Washcloth King," I go to Lip Cheese. "Whatever, Got Beat Up by a Girl."

But when Necro doesn't laugh at that, and Lip Cheese's ears even don't turn red from embarrassment, I feel myself getting light-headed. Because right now, Toby is leading with 1,560 Holy Grail Points, and Necro has 1,511. And I have 1,363, and Lip Cheese has 317. And I don't know how many Holy Grail Points they think Having a Home and a Cash is worth, but it starts to make me think that maybe I'll never have even 1,400 Holy Grail Points, and that maybe Lip Cheese might now finally be catching up with me Holy-Grail-Point-wise. And maybe ten years from now, I'll never have a Plan, and nobody will ever ask me what's wrong or if I need help.

Then, Necro leans over the table and tells me something I wasn't expecting.

"This NecronicA I got, this is a business opportunity venture," he says. "There's money behind this; capital—you know—expenditure or whatever. You were asking: When are we going to take and make that money? Here's where. NecronicA's receiving money from this nonprofit that I guess Bambert runs to take and revitalize the city and is going to get a metric fuck-ton of donations for. That guy, Brandon-who-you-met, told me to apply a few months ago with some work samples—it's all anonymous application-wise—and this panel of judges decided to give me a grant, to draw, like Man-Serum-Bagelheart era!"

"What, you needed his permission?" I say.

Necro sputters into his palm. "No, man! Like a grant of money. It's part of this whole thing, where I can just work on NecronicA—like an artist-in-residence studio deal. He's giving me a $17,000 stipend—what I make a year at work; he's giving me my very own Necro HQ, and the payment installments start once I move in."

"Necro's got a home, he's got a cash!" Lip Cheese says.

"After the explosion, Bambert decided he couldn't take and just sell only weapons anymore—he needed to do something positive and community-based. So, he sat in his basement, in total self-induced psychological quarantine, and had this huge revelation: The northwest quadrant of downtown Rochester is operating significantly under population capacity. And he figured, why not try to take and generate some seed money, give people monetary incentives to get back in these vacant structures—artists, culturists, futurists, and thinkers—to rebuild downtown. He said he's wrapping up paperwork on this former RG&E plant he wants to convert into lofts. Easements, whatever. So me, and a few others I think, who are getting some of this seed money, have already paid a $2,500 fee so Bambert can take care of bullshit with regards to permits and renovations. It's just because the money's all pledges right now and he doesn't actually have it monetarily in-pocket yet. But we won't not get the money. I'll totally be paid back. I'm losing money right now, but Bambert says those down payments are standard. And you have to lose money to make money, so."

I lean back to make room for the waiter when the French fries arrive. Past the waiter's arm, Necro is looking directly at me, something he never does. On his coaster, there's a drawing of an executioner, resting the handle of his axe on his shoulder, but with these deep, plush, puppy-dog eyes behind his mask.

"It'll be good, Nate," Necro says. "I reduced my work hours for this."

"So he's like a philanderer? Philanthroper? A charity?"

"He says he's got a board of directors, articles of incorporation, some bylaws," he says. "But I'm not worried about that right now. Because I was thinking: I could take and use you as sort of NecronicA's marketing guy. You'd have to learn a little HTML, but I could give you part of my revenues, in sales. You could put yourself to work, put all your talking to good use finally."

I blush. I'm flattered or totally embarrassed. I have to think only for a second.

"No, Necro!" I say. "What am I going to do? Sit at some computer, like: 'For sale? Painting of Dragoon Lance?'"

Put my talking to good use? Like I'm pathetic enough to need help?

"You say that now," Necro says. "But see if I take and ask you again. You say that now."

I say that now, but when I get home, I change into my pajama pants early, go into the den where the computer is, and type in NecronicA. Sure enough, on the computer, against a black background, the website that appears displays as the header the NecronicA logo—harpoon-points at the ends of the N and the A—with two animated gifs of lightning bolts. There's one section, T-shirts, and another, Graphics / Airbrushings, where paintings are for sale. Not just doodlings, but paintings—with shading. One is called:

"The Party Rests, In a Prelude to Hell." Paintings with sunsets reflecting off armor, castles carved into mountains. A painting of a baby with a pair of huge, purple bat wings— wide as the lava lake below.

I sit, elbows on the computer desk, in the dark, for the next three hours. Millions of NecronicA-related catch-phrases come to me: "NecronicA—Suck a Sack of Sorcerers" or "NecronicA: Not Your Grandfather's Demon-Art Apocalypse." I whisper them out loud. Bits of my saliva turn rainbow-colored on the monitor.

Then, I stand up. I bite my index finger and start to pace, the way I do only when I'm alone, and I pretend to be at a party and am really ripping on somebody. Then I spend forty good, kernel-hardening minutes hating myself, and then I take a nap. I wake up and hear the dishwasher running and Mom watching TV, and I'm so mad at Necro that when I get hungry, all I can do is drink a glass of milk and go back to sleep to kill my appetite.

I milk-glass through the next day as well, since Fake Dad No. 3 drove Mom to dinner and thus Mom has made no dinner for me. So I put on some pants, take Mom's car keys, and drive to Applebee's. I tell all of the above to Toby, at the corner airplane-model booth. He pays for my French fries, and he eats his own fries five at a time, getting grease on his wristwatch, palming the appetite-sweat off his forehead.

"Because, I saw Necro the other day," I say. "He kept on saying 'I've got a home, I've got a cash.'"

Toby massages his chinfat.

"Do you even know what that means?" I go. "Because, even worse, Necro has his own website!"

Toby pauses, mouth open, food in it. "Like what, Necro Online?"

"Exactly, Toby! Thank you!" I go. "He's selling drawings, T-shirts."

"Textbook Colonel Hellstache," Toby mumbles through the fries in his mouth.

Since it feels good to feel good, I then say to Toby, "And, hold on a second—"

I hold up one finger to let him know to wait a minute. I run out to the car and reach over the parking brake to the passenger seat, and take the folder Necro left in Toby's car, with the drawing of the knight carrying a young man with everything on fire in the background. Back at the Airplane Booth, I slap the folder on the table. "There's this."

Toby opens the folder and holds the drawing up to his face. Snot drags up his nose when he sniffles.

"And more like that on the website!" I say. "Like, when did God decide He didn't hate you, Necro? Like who died and made you talented? A home? A cash? He probably set those fires himself. Probably tried to kill all of us."

Toby's face freezes. "Holy crap, Nate. Do you think?"

"Why not? I don't know. Who knows anything?"

A corner of Toby's mouth curves into a smile. He scratches his forehead under the plastic size adjuster on the Bills hat he's got on backward.

"I mean, the way Necro bailed out of the car on 490?" Toby says. "The way he didn't have a thing to say when Luckytown

accused him of Unabombing? The way he laughed after we left
Goateez? You'd think: Your friend goes into a coma, and then
there's these fires, and he's running his online castle porn."

I laugh for the first time in weeks; I feel oxygen return to
my brow. I sip my Mountain Dew.

"And—and—and!" Toby says, face goofballing a little,
grinning a little. "Remember how Necro was the first one to
run over when Wicked College John got hit? Like he's going
out of his way to act like he cares? Or how he asked us to pick
up his weapons seconds before the building exploded? Or how
he was checking his watch? Or how after you made the joke
about Kangaroo for a Kid, he told you and Wicked College
John that life is precious?"

And I can't tell, right now, if Toby's just staging a Toby
Cockdrama—where he'll take some small comment you
mean nothing by and turn it into something that's military-
operation serious. Once, me and Necro started a joke about
how Wicked College John's SUV was so expensive it ran on
tiny butlers that lived inside the engine. Toby called Mendon
police and reported the SUV's VIN number.

"I guess I did bring up Kangaroo for a Kid," I say.

"And he brought up Did You Shee the Fight? That's one of
the Uncomebackables."

"I don't know, Toby."

"But Necro—he can assemble an explosive."

Which, okay fine. Review the Necro Archives under
"Explosion." Review the time police asked him about all those
vitamins he bought at CVS. Review the Walkman he blew up,
the GI Joes he blew up, and the fact—how did I not notice

this—that Necro never got along with Wicked College John at all.

"And what about that one time that me and Necro and Lip Cheese and Wicked College John were having Science Rock Jam in my basement that one Christmas?" I say. "And Wicked College John was on guitar, and Necro put Johnnyfangs, that inflatable bat, remember with the skull head, on keyboards?"

Toby rolls his eyes. "I absolutely hated Johnnyfangs. That bat was so stupid."

"But Wicked College John was playing 'Light My Fire' on guitar, and was complaining about how 'Light My Fire' is a keyboard-heavy song, and he suddenly screamed at Necro: 'I need a keyboardist with *fingers!*'"

"There was blood in the snow afterwards," Toby says.

I find myself running a steak knife down my forearm to scratch it. "I'm just mad, is all."

"I don't think you're mad, Nate. I think you're onto something," Toby says, dragging his voice out a little, like he may or may not be in Cockdrama Mode. "You've been defending that kid all your life. All he did was stare right back at you. He's not right, that kid."

We eat for a few minutes, me pressing my finger into the fry basket's wax paper lining to get the leftover powder-grains of salt, Toby shaking the salt from his own fry basket into his hand and licking his palm. The timed street lamps and plaza store signs turn on outside (I don't think I've ever actually caught them turning on before), and headlights turn into little dots in the rain on the restaurant windows.

Very briefly, I think: Every pebble in Rochester is a piece of Nate-itory and Necrography. And I think: But Necro's my friend. Then I naturally think: Well fuck you, Necro. Maybe you should respect the friendship before you think about going off somewhere to draw all day.

Still though, Toby: You should talk about not acting right. Because we shouldn't forget when Toby came into Applebee's, and his hands shook, and his coffee vibrated every time he picked up the cup. He'd had a dream the previous night, he said. In the dream, his father was in a public bathroom, naked, looking at himself in the mirror, playing a violin. Blood covered his father's stomach and legs; his penis was cut off, curled in the sink. But when Toby told me this, it was 2:30 p.m., the least scary time in the universe. The sky was Windex blue. And Toby was massaging his temples and cheeks.

"Is that messed up, Nate?" Toby said then. "Do other people dream this stuff?"

I should tell you he was also offered a lacrosse scholarship to Syracuse. But then I'd have to tell you he spent all semester lying in bed, spitting tobacco into a Bills game cup that he propped against his chin. Toby: home in one semester, 0.9 GPA. Tried to become a cop, but kept failing the civil service exam's five-minute memory portion.

But before all that there was that dream, that violin. And as much as everyone sometimes hates Toby, there are still subjects that are in the Realm of Pain Beyond Uncomebackability.

Because Toby's right. I'm right to be annoyed. Necro needs to learn—he needs to be fucked with at the very least—and he needs to know you can't just get up one day and decide to do certain things.

Before I get in to bed and spend the rest of the night talking to myself, I check NecronicA. I can't tell if the new illustration up there now was done in Photoshop or air-brushed or painted or both, but there's something genuinely evil in it. In the foreground is a sixteen-windowed building, real as a photograph. In each window is a different apart-ment unit, some with stereo speakers mounted to the walls; others with rust holes in the sinks. Every room, in some way, is on fire. In one, a woman scrambles around, her I LOVE NY nightshirt burning off her body.

And I don't feel the hurt in my ribs until I notice the room burning at the top right corner of the building. In that room, some kid with hair gel and thick eyebrows, in a shiny button-down date-rape shirt, is tucked under the covers in a bed. Wicked College John. But the room's furnishings—the stereo with the empty soda cans on top of the subwoofer, the way the dresser has four drawers and is positioned in the corner by the window—is that my room?!

Later that night, in my living room, the news shows roughed-up surveillance in which an explosion blows out the storefront windows of a building. It's hard to tell how recent the footage is, either from yesterday or the 1970s. The blast ex-pands jerkily, in frame-by-frame slo-mo, glass drifting across the street like a weather pattern.

MY ONE ASTERISK

Roasted Face of Satan: Part II, The Proto-Stachening: One night, two new airbrush jobs appear on NecronicA—one that shows a fire reflecting in a Terminator-like chrome skull; another of Fearjaw Spangleveins, this character I drew one time at some sleepover and haven't thought of since. His hands have molten off and his arms are burning, and you can tell it's Fearjaw because of his long banana-shaped jaw and hat-and-feather and stubby Mario Bros. legs.

I can't even tell which is worse, because the day after, on TV, two fires occur at two of the city's larger homeless shelters. Police find part of a pink Swatch watch and some burnt wire casing at a small explosion that happened near the rear, smoking-break entrance of the Frederick Douglass Shelter. At Roads Home, police find a broken window, and on the pile of clothing directly below it, traces of what they call accelerants.

So the homeless go back to the Cadillac Hotel, or under Broad Street to the old subway. Or they go to Midtown Plaza, where there's Applebee's Baghdad, where me and Lip Cheese, tonight, go too. Because the soda at this Applebee's, he says, is the most carbonated in all of Rochester.

We're sitting at one of the round high tables. At least three overhead table lamps are broken. Lip Cheese stares out at the Plaza's center court, where there's this Spirit-Bunny-type girl, standing by the court's fountain, which the managers shut off because people were washing their clothes in it.

She's wearing one of those maternal apron-y hippie dresses and corduroys with duct tape over one knee. She's standing under a tree that's completely bare except for a pair of underwear hanging from a branch.

"She smiled at me from out there earlier," Lip Cheese says. "But now, she's baking my time! What is she out there, having her pyramid?"

Watch his eyes move like squirrels. Watch him look down at his hands like they've played a trick on him by moving.

Even sadder than Lip Cheese staring at Spirit Bunny is the Plaza concourse around her: a large lane of white tile through the middle and lanes of brown tile closer to the storefronts, shiny as an evacuated banquet. The monorail track, which I rode during Christmases years ago, circles the Plaza's upper level, where all the stores are empty.

Still, Lip Cheese is the only one around tonight. And I have some things I need to learn from him.

"What is He's Got a Home, He's Got a Cash, Lip Cheese?"

"A Home? A What?" His lizard eyes widen and his lips quiver. "Oh. It was just a thing me and Necro said, for a day. It's not a thing anymore."

Lip Cheese plucks a napkin from the dispenser, runs it

through his hair, and stuffs it down his shirt and into his armpit.

"Has Necro told you anything weird lately?" I say. "About NecronicA, about Weapons of Mankind?"

"I'm so happy for him! He's really making it with Weapons of Mankind!"

So Alas, You Leave Me No Choice, said the chancellor. "Well on one of his pictures, on NecronicA?" I say. "It shows, like, this burning building with all these people on fire? And I'm worried. Because one of the people on fire is sort of short, sort of scringy, with black greasy hair parted off to the side, sort of like you?"

Which is a little messed up, maybe—that any given lie can make its way out of me so easily.

"I just hope Necro's not out there, you know, committing arson or anything," I say.

But how can you not lean back, twist your mustache and swirl your wine when you watch Lip Cheese's face, sliding downward like an egg thrown against a window.

"But I just ate Dinosaur with him and Weapons of Mankind the other day," he says.

Spirit Bunny has now wandered into the restaurant, standing near our table and staring upward, mouth open, at the TVs showing a music video of what I guess is Annie Lennox. Spirit Bunny's hair is dark and she's much tanner up close—a rough, beat-up tan. Her version of eye contact, I guess, is staring three inches above us.

"I feel so lost when I come in here!" Spirit Bunny says, apparently, to us.

"People always tell me I look lost! People called me Rain Man in high school!" Lip Cheese says, laughing where he should be breathing, unable to leave his hair alone.

"I know!" she says. "I was at the post office, where I'll go downtown, and people will hand me things, like 'Here, hold this,' because they need me to hold on to their belongings for them—like cabbage, or CD players, or just bags of things." She rubs her right eye, where capillaries have exploded into a small, red tree. "Earlier this afternoon, these guys who looked like lacrosse players pulled up to me in their van. They're like: 'You want to come to Irondequoit Bay?' Because I'm thinking I can share my things if nobody comes back to pick them up."

She runs her left index finger and thumb over a long strand of hair. "But these guys, in this van, they dropped me off outside Midtown, and they're like, 'Just wait here.' I gave one of them a back rub for the entire ride, and they never came back!"

"I don't think I've ever had a back rub," Lip Cheese says.

So I tune out at this point because Lip Cheese proceeds to tell any one of his stories about his brother: the ticket scalping; the single six-hour-long VCR tape his brother gave him that contained snippets from the green-line stir-fry of the scrambled Playboy channel. Because the only way Lip Cheese will do anything at all in life is through his brother's stories.

"And when my brother was stationed in Guam, he stopped cars at checkpoints, even if they had a headlight out, and he'd take their marijuana or, if they had it, their snacks!"

Which he says way too excitedly. And after Lip Cheese

pays for our food, Spirit Bunny says: "So, you gentlemen don't by any chance have a car to drive a lady home in?"

Lip Cheese's face scatters. He looks at me like: Life or Death: "Sure we do!"

Of course, the second I think: Oh, I'll only have to make a ten-minute drive, this girl tells us she lives seven million light-years away: in Buffalo! I can't even tell if the fog on my windows is from Lip Cheese's sweat or from outside.

The street where Spirit Bunny lives manages to hoist a loaf of frumped-up storefronts before crumbling into the rest of the city. Her apartment building has two floors, with a goopy coat of white paint on the cinder blocks. Cars are parked along the parking lot curb, engines idling, headlights on. A woman in curlers and a poofy overcoat yells something into one of their windows. We walk up a metal staircase to the second floor's concrete balcony. Fluorescent lights flinch above the doors, and immediately Spirit Bunny takes off her day voice.

"You guys are troopers, man. Troopers!" she gravels, talking a little faster, a chain-smoking and used-needle tone. She works the key into her door, whose lock and doorknob are mounted on a metal panel. "You guys like to party?"

A deadbolt thunks heavily. "They found a head in that river over there," she says, pointing somewhere to where, apparently, there is a river.

In her living room, the walls are white-out white with Sharpie drawings of tiny schools of fish. An algae'd over aquarium is positioned like it's the TV. In a birdcage, two white parakeets make Pterodactyl in a Trashcan for noise. Beer cans on the floor have holes poked in their sides, and

I smack my lips and chew on a cloud of thin, salty-tasting smoke.

Spirit Bunny brings us a few cans of Stroh's from the mini fridge next to the aquarium and sits on the floor, hugging her shins, duct tape over her right knee peeling. Lip Cheese sits on the floor too, leaning forward, plucking hair from the carpet, and begins drinking like Death's Not Wearing a Condom. He's sweating beer mist: single-tilt drinkdown, pivoting to the mini fridge. Later, he asks Spirit Bunny if she has a boyfriend.

"My last boyfriend was an irrigation tuber in California," she says.

"For what?" Lip Cheese says.

She leans forward. "Tomatoes?" Then she sputters laughter. "I gotta lie down."

And when she stands up to go to her bedroom, the whole scene slows down, and everyone's voice drags like mummies and balls and chains. Because Lip Cheese, right then, stands up too, and sets his hands on her waist, and presses his crotch against her, but in this four-year-old way, like he doesn't totally understand why he likes the feeling. His breath stutters, and his cheek twitches, and then, he shapes his lips like he's about to whistle, and he kisses Spirit Bunny. As in, on the lips.

"Um, okay," Spirit Bunny says, in the over-adult way girls do after you've kissed them on the lips and they don't want you to.

"What's wrong," Lip Cheese says, in this way that's innocent-sounding, like a child possessed by Satan. My stomach folds, grows a thumb like a boxing glove.

"You're welcome to crash on the couch if you can't drive,"

Spirit Bunny glazes, now back to her Spirit Bunny voice. "I'll leave the hall light on. I still can't believe those guys in that van today. Those Wasp, freaking Reagan-humping jocks!—that's a bit touched, man!"

Her door closes. Lip Cheese chews on his thumb and paces in front of the aquarium, whispering entire paragraphs to himself, the occasional held breath squeaking out of him.

"Shut up, Nate," he says. "Don't do another goddamn thing."

Which, I should talk. Because contrary to what you might think about me, I am not Coco Ferguson: Sex-Having Specialist. Which is the name Necro gave me when I was fifteen and told him I first became a Sex-Having Specialist with Lisa Alisi from Henrietta. And as I fall asleep in the apartment's scabies recliner, I think: Dear God please don't let anybody actually follow up with Lisa Alisi from Henrietta, because they would learn that I haven't even lost my virginity to my pillow. And then I would no longer be able to tell myself, after a bad night, "Oh well, at least people still think I lost my virginity to Lisa Alisi from Henrietta!"

Then, I'm awoken by, of all things:

"I'm Jeffrey Dahmer! I'm Arthur Shawcross! I'm Jeffrey Dahmer!"

Lip Cheese is standing in front of Spirit Bunny's bedroom door down the hall. He stares upward, no expression on his face, hands folded at his waist, waiting, neutral-like, like a Boy Scout ringing doorbells on a can drive.

Spirit Bunny opens her bedroom door, squinting at him in a tank top and orange boxers with the Coca-Cola logo.

"I ate a dude! I can do anything!" Lip Cheese says. "I've memorized this address!"

Spirit Bunny rubs her eye and drifts toward the door jamb. "Okay, that kind of abrasiveness is really not what we're about here," she whispers. "You want to sleep in the chair outside, that's tops. But you need to know that within this space, you are riding the tip. Riding—the tip."

"And you have enough hair on your head to clothe a small child!" Lip Cheese yells.

On the drive home, passenger-side windows fogging up with Lip Cheese's having to piss, probably, here comes a preview for the movie *Why Lip Cheese Will Die in a Life of Priestlike Anger: The Proto-Stachening of Lip Cheese*. Which was the joke we made up when Lip Cheese slept over once, and we noticed how movie titles were always "The [Somethening] of [Some Guy's Name]"; *The Fridgication of William Perry*, we said. Which eventually turned into the Proto-Stachening. The Proto-Stachening, right here, of why there is no way Lip Cheese will be able to live a full life:

"Hey Nate?" Lip Cheese asks, voice kernel-sized in the dark of the passenger seat.

"What."

"Will you kill me?"

"Wait. What?" I say.

"As in, just, you know, pop me in the head."

"I have to drop you off in—where am I going to get the gun?"

"Guess Necro had the right idea. Might as well light myself on fire," he says, voice getting knots in its yo-yo string.

"Lip Cheese the Maverick Jetpants. Gets *all* the women on a conveyor belt."

He's trying not to sniffle. "That girl?" I say. "How she kept rubbing her eye? That story about that van?"

But when you think the earthquake needle is about to settle, Lip Cheese shoves open the passenger door; wind rumbles in off the highway; the car jackhammers into the rumble strip.

"Lip Cheese!" I yell over the windquake.

"Gonna do it myself," he yells, seat belt stretching.

"Quit it! Quit it!" I go, slapping his shoulder, grabbing at his shirt. "I'll crash the car!"

He closes the door. I yank the car back into the lane. All quiet.

"I'm just trying to do the practical thing," he says. "I'm just trying to be practical."

So to keep him from crying until his tears form people, here's what I do. As Buffalo's early shift wakes up, me and Lip Cheese go to get Gatorades at a Wegmans in Depew or somewhere. The Wegmans building is huge, its red-lit logo turning pink in the sunrise. We walk through the heat blasters in the entrance's corridor, and inside, it's bright. Boxes and pallets are in the aisles, and men with tattoos fading under their arm hair maneuver industrial floor sweepers. Def Leppard's "Hysteria" sounds like brittle crunch through the speakers in the store's ceiling.

Me and Lip Cheese set our Gatorades on the checkout conveyor. When who is in front of us, in line, paying for coffee and a pre-rolled sandwich, but Mindy Fale?

"Nate?" she says.

She's put on weight, in a beer-and-chested-up sort of way—all tits and failure. Her chin juts like a punter's chin-guard, and under the white semi-see-through sleeve of her work shirt, there's a Tasmanian Devil tattoo on her shoulder.

"Oh. Hey. Wait—hey!" I already hate myself. I'm already back in the low-ceiling halls of high school, when Mindy Fale and me got into a mock kickboxing match once, in the hallway, shoehorning each other into pretend headlocks. I'd listen to her laugh and try to figure out how she'd sound in bed. I guess she was always okay; she was maybe my eleventh choice for a girlfriend.

"Do you live here?" I say to her.

"Nope. Still in Gates! Parents and everything!" she smiles in an angry-chipper kind of way.

"Why are you all the way in Buffalo?"

She pays for her food, sighs, plants a palm on the bagging area, and leans.

"I was at Fredonia until about November, but it's stupid, political," she says. "Professors know what they want to see, and if you don't do that, well. Now I'm making the drive to work at USNY Insurance. Buffalo office. Claims!" She makes a stiff thumbs-up sign.

The cashier scans our Gatorades. Mindy Fale looks at me, then Lip Cheese, and probably notices our reddened eyes and our pre-hangover sniffles.

"What were *you* up to last night?" she says.

And so I say—My One Asterisk: "More like, what was Lip Cheese up to?" Like I'm amazed and annoyed at him.

"Coco Ferguson, Mustache Express, this kid. A celebrity sex tape waiting to happen."

Lip Cheese pays for our Gatorades. We all three of us walk outside, where there's a lone set of tire tracks, going all the way diagonally across the parking-lot slush. Mindy Fale walks toward her car, a white Civic with no wheel covers.

"Well, if you're going to be a tape," she says, half-grinning at Lip Cheese a little. "Might as well be a—" She waves, grocery bag swinging around her arm.

After she drives off, though, look at Lip Cheese, trying not to smile. That's the asterisk, My One Asterisk, that I've tacked on to him.

"But since I'm not going to tell anyone what happened at that girl's apartment, you need to do something for me, Lip Cheese," I say.

"Sure Nate! Anything!"

"Since Necro still for whatever reason talks to you, you need to follow him around, do some Ninja Recon."

"But why?" he says, ladling it on like Sadness Molassness.

"To give him shit for NecronicA, Lip Cheese! For acting like the Colonel Hellstache Unabomber. Just, you know, to find something Uncomebackable, that's all. Maybe there's something weird in his browser history, I don't know."

Lip Cheese frowns like a toy soldier, head tilted the way dogs do when they can sense something's wrong with you.

"The kid practically set you on fire in a painting, Lip Cheese," I say. "You want to spend the rest of your life being everybody else's Washcloth Master? 'I'm Jeffrey Dahmer?' Think with your *head* once in your life."

NO!
GARRETT ALFIERI
RETURNS!

Real Dad sits on a pastel loveseat, which came with his room, resting one foot on a plastic Lego-filled storage bin that he's using as a coffee table. His Stray Cats leather jacket straddles the loveseat's right armrest, sleeves dangling, and the sun in the window turns his stray balding-ponytail hair into lightbulb filament. The rip in his jeans is big enough for his entire knee to fit through.

"Squeezebeagler, at the Bug Jar tonight," he says, rubbing his chin. "Sonic cocktail of Muler and Nod, a jigger of Hilkka, stirred with Lethargy breakdowns."

"Nice!" I say, and bounce in the pastel blue chair that also came with his room.

"It is not nice, Nate. You cannot handle that combination. You bring your Rock Condom. Because in rock and roll, you only get one condom. It's a rule."

"But it'd be awesome if there was a guy named Jigger," I say, even though I'm too jolted up to Bring the Funny. "Or a dog, or a bird you could name Jigger. I don't know."

He smirks and recrosses his legs, tasting the joke like wine. "Or name it like My Dad?" he says. "'I'd like to schedule an anal-sacs examination for My Dad at 2 p.m.? My Dad has chunks of Frisbee in his fecal samples?"

I crack up and sit on my hands. "Yeah," I say.

Real Dad leans back, ankle on knee. "Just plug it into the formula. Comedians, certainly, have tackled this: 'My Dad's been chewing on his elbow, I think he might have roundworm. I'd like to make an appointment.' Actually," he says, "speaking of appointments, did Mom take me off her insurance?"

Which, I don't know about you? But I tune the fuck out whenever I hear words like premium or HMO. Because, Real Dad is saying something about catastrophic coverage, and clobetasol propionate. And I'm more just listening to his tone when he says, sounding like he's taking a stand: "—because, if all I can get is one of these plans online with a $2,500 deductible then I am going to send photographs of myself to her every day so she can chart how I deteriorate."

So I say, just to say something: "Guess you have to let her know who's boss."

Real Dad convulses laughing suddenly, leaning over to one side, crossing his legs—this focused, aggressive-sounding cackling. When I was barely even trying to Bring the Funny, and my Joke Rolodex hasn't been stocked, technically, for days.

Which makes me feel great! Because Real Dad's joke-to-actually-laughing-at-other-people's-jokes ratio is The-Universe-to-One. Which makes me feel like I can relax, maybe even go four or five turns in conversation without having to Bring the Funny again.

"Wow. Show them who's boss," he says, still shaking off rounds of cracking up. He wipes his forehead with his palm.

Since Real Dad isn't a hug or handshake man, I open the mini fridge in his kitchenette and get the larger bottle of De Ranke Kriek. The price tag says $18.00, which he can apparently afford, and I get a tulip glass that's standing top-down and stuck to a paper towel laid on the counter next to the sink.

I pour him a glass, and he raises it, as in cheers, not looking up. "To who's boss." He raises his eyebrows and shakes his head.

So, you smell the cigarette smoke that's been left over from the practically 1700s. And you see Real Dad's Blockbuster khakis shoved into the corner; the issues of NME and Magnet in the empty fish tank, the container of pomade; the Ranger Bob WUHF lunchbox he paid eighty dollars for and the Pez dispensers—of Donald Duck, Darth Vader, etc.—arranged on his bookshelf like they're mantel ornaments. You see Real Dad's twitching eyelid, and his hands scratched red from eczema, and the picture of the guy who invented the theremin in his bedroom. But that's also kind of why I love my dad: He's forty-seven but he Brings the Funny way better than I do. He has all these VHS tapes of Robert Forster movies, and performances of Steve Gadd and Tony Levin in various bands, and some mugshot of David Bowie when he got arrested for marijuana after a War Memorial show ("The newspaper reported that also arrested was a James Osterberg, Jr., 28, of Ypsilanti, Michigan," Real Dad said, really excited about it), and he has all these weird records about Halloween and makes hilarious jokes about them, and he makes me wish I knew those things, too, so that I could rip on people as well as he does. You think I talk fast, listen to Real Dad:

"Carl, this guy who buys vinyl at the Bop Shop, used to be a record producer in the 1970s," he says. "Carl, he'll be there tonight. He and Squeezebeagler's guitar player used to be in Paul Mitchell? Before that in The Tinklemen? My previous boss at Blockhustler played lacrosse with Tam, Squeezebeagler's singer, Rocker of a Million Faces. He held cockroach-smashing parties with Tam. Take your shoe in your hand, turn off the lights, turn them back on, watch the cockroaches trickle out, and swing for the floor."

See what I mean? Real Dad and the people he knows.

"They had to give Tam a rhythm guitar to keep him from sticking his hands down his pants while he was singing."

"They're that good, he has to Touch his Puppy to it," I go.

He punches his right arm up into the sleeve of his Stray Cats jacket and slaps his pants pocket to check his keys: "A masturbation joke? No, man! That's novice! Please don't say that around anyone tonight. Please don't. Please."

He takes his tube of hand cream from his pocket and rubs the stuff over his fingers and slips it back into his pocket. He pours some De Ranke into a plastic cup for me so I can be buzzed on the ride there. Since I'm twenty, Real Dad says we need to get to the Bug Jar early, before the bouncer starts watching the door.

"There are stories about the people you'll meet tonight, stories," he says. "Sverg, one of the music writers for *City*, he'll be there—stellar guy, says some really poignant, subversive things. Sverg was telling me Squeezebeagler's guitarist, drunk one night, tried to go home and pass out in his apartment, but he woke up, and instead he was just in some lady's house!"

His forehead is getting a little sweaty, the way it does when he gets excited, like when he's talking about *Dexter's Laboratory* or Cookie Puss. So now, I'm thinking this concert is totally going to be Holy Grail Point-worthy!

Because: Necro? Really bumming me out. Really riding the tip with me. I blew through a whole tank of gas driving past Applebee's to try to find him last night, past Gitsi's, Media Play, the Wegmans parking lot, past Chad Rector's house on the off chance, the Spice Man Tower, and even the corner on Monroe where two guys, about to fight, kept yelling to each other: "This ain't no pickupsticks!"

But as soon as me and Real Dad walk into the Bug Jar, which is my first time ever to the Bug Jar, my shoulder nerves hum. Look, already, at the dim lighting and the giant papier-mâché fly, about the size of a tote bag, attached to a blade of the ceiling fan—with that alone, you and your flame-paintings can suck it, Necro. And even better, in the room next to the bar, Necro? A whole upside-down living room set, bolted to the ceiling. Recliner; books glued to the coffee table.

We take a seat in the one large booth in the corner. Real Dad's picking the label off his beer bottle, looking at the door, one-wording it whenever I ask him something. He rubs some rash cream on his hands and puts the tube back in his pocket. People trickle in. This boulder-shaped guy with a white buzz cut and maroon boots walks in.

"That's Sverg," Real Dad says. "He's crazy, that guy, crazy

like wild boars. The stories—he fell out the back of the stage door into a snow bank one time, crazy."

Real Dad gives me the One-Minute index finger and walks over to the guy.

"Sverg!" Real Dad goes. "Svergie!" squeezing Sverg's shoulder. Then he says, in this hairy, over-tanned Long Island accent: "How you doing today can I take ya aside for a drink and a hardcore mastibation session? Mastibation, mastibation, mastibation."

Which I, at least, think is funny—Real Dad's accent. But look at how Sverg looks at Real Dad, eyelids getting heavier.

"Remember? Last month?" Real Dad says, eyes open wide, doglike and gentle. "That guy, with the accent? Standing right behind you, talking through Arab on Radar? Some Twelfth Man in a Giants jacket?"

Sverg's chin drifts upward, voice reclined and half-asleep on the couch. "Standing—"

"Forget it, forget it," Real Dad says, waving his hands in front of his chest.

Sverg suddenly deadlocks eyes with Real Dad. "Are you accusing me of something?"

"Not at all, my friend," Real Dad says, jamming his hands in his pockets, rocking back and forth. "Just looking forward to some live music."

"Well, good to see you, okay?" Sverg says slowly, looking past Real Dad toward the room where the stage is.

Since I already hate this Sverg guy, I go and stand in the bathroom. It's dark but with high ceilings, overlapping band stickers of The Priests and Nerve Circus and Pengo crowding the sink mirror. When I walk out, I feel a hand on my shoulder, a hand that immediately feels like more success and heated driveways than I'll ever have.

"Nate?" the hand says.

I turn around. And, sweep the floors, change your shirt: It's Garrett Alfieri.

"Nathan Gray," he says. "Your mom took us to Chuck E. Cheese. In Gauntlet you were always the elf—Questor Nate."

Garrett Alfieri. The one friend Mom liked, the one who escaped, who stopped calling us after his mom found out he got a B. The one who volunteered at the SSJ nursing home during his lunch breaks junior year and wouldn't let us copy his homework. Look at him now—actually shaving, wearing khakis, a shiny blue shirt. His hair is bright-blond enough to almost produce a halo-like glow cloud. When here I am, flannel shirt, nylon running pants, and the world's itchiest five-day beard.

"Garrett. Wow," I say. "It has been long."

So, we stand there, nodding, praying that one of us will think of a subject. Because, when you run into someone you know but haven't seen in five years, you feel like you have to give them more than a typical Small-Talk Life Story. But if I do more than give him the Small-Talk Life Story, it will become clear I have nothing to say, have been up to nothing, and it'll end up being the Taco Bell of Conversations.

"I finished up at Alfred in six semesters," he says, shifting his weight from foot to foot when he talks. "I did this internship in Bausch & Lomb. They had an open, full-time financial analyst gig. So I took it."

"Jesus loves somebody," I say.

"There you go!" he says. "Speaking of Jesus, I run a youth group downtown—all low-income. I tell everyone at Group: four-year private universities only exist to allow time for the partiers to get their homework done. I tell them: Load up on AP credits. Know what you want to do by age eighteen. Pick something. Two years in at MCC, follow that up with a SUNY, six semesters later, it's: What's up," he points to the ceiling, "Throw down," he points downward, "Closing time." He waves his hand sideways, slamming an imaginary door.

"Holy Grail Points to you, then."

"Holy Grail Points," he holds the steadiest eye contact when he talks, which makes me realize how fidgety I've become. "Man, we said some stupid things. Uncle Frankstache!, right?"

"Colonel Hellstache," I say.

"Say again?"

"Nothing."

"Anyway, my fiancée and I just moved into an apartment in the horseshoe on Griffith Street, by the highway."

"Your own place!"

"It's pretty solid. Nice demographic mix, helps with outreach. The city shut off streetlights to save money, and we still draw our shades and remove our window-sill decorations at night, but, otherwise."

The crowd gets loud enough to have to yell over, and thick enough so I have to stand on my toes to see Real Dad gesturing wildly—like he's twirling circus streamers—to Sverg. Garrett Alfieri turns around once, and puts his hand

on my shoulder and leans toward me. His deodorant smells
like a ballroom.

"Sometimes, I peek out my window at night anyway," he
says into my ear. "Do you still keep in touch with Andrea—
or, Necro? Does he live in the city somewhere?"

Which I ignore, for obvious reasons, before the anger can
pop out of one of my back teeth. An opening band plays a
song with boogery garage-rock chords and a drum part that
sounds like a man falling down the stairs. I let a few seconds
pass to let the subject change.

"How's your mom?" Garrett Alfieri yells over the band.
"Is that your dad over there?"

Since Garrett Alfieri is someone who'll want to talk
about family and your family's history—when everyone
in Rochester is Italians—I lead him through the crowd of
sideburn kids and Fonzies to Real Dad. Who, still, is with
his Colonel Hellstache friends Sverg, and, now, Carl from
the Bop Shop, who has hockey hair and wears an untucked
T-shirt under an open, short-sleeve dress-shirt.

So, I try to ninja in a word, to say Dad! Look! Garrett
Alfieri!

But, here Real Dad is, holding open his wallet, nudging
his elbow toward the bar counter, eyebrows raised with kindness. "Pints, guys? Refills?" he says.

Sverg and Bop-Shop Carl, these two mung-huts, squint
and shrug at each other.

"What? Like I'd rape-drug your drinks?" Real Dad goes.
"Am I that much of a dog, gentlemen? Like I'm going to come
up to you and comb my mustache and ask you, 'Have our

paths intertwined previously, perhaps, in cyberspace, in the bestiality newsgroups?'"

Me, I want to crack up at that completely: Real Dad's had that joke for years. But the look on Bop-Shop Carl? Pissing his pants slowly with his face.

"Sorry my dad's not paying attention," I actually say to Garrett Alfieri.

Garrett Alfieri nods, but he smirks like he knows something.

Which makes me know something for sure: I am a terrible middleman. My neck is sweating. My back is, too: the Melting Backsickle. Garrett Alfieri: throwing me off. Necro: throwing me off. Sverg, Bop Shop Carl: throwing me off.

I'm still thrown off when we all follow Sverg and Bop-Shop Carl down into the Bug Jar basement to hang out with Squeezebeagler. Bop-Shop Carl looks at Sverg and narrows his eyebrows hard at the back of Real Dad's head. The basement walls, gangrene-colored, have stickers and logos everywhere. There are also slit-up leather recliners with upholstery pushing out, and a lamp with no lampshade. For whatever reason, on the TV sitting on a turned-over garbage can, *Dances with Wolves* is playing. My first thought is: this place? File Under Scabies. It smells sharp as gourmet trash, like Poached Death murdered a creature made of garbage.

But I stop myself from officially thinking that, because Real Dad doesn't just like things for no reason. After all, I was completely wrong about not liking that *Schizopolis* movie Real Dad took me to at the Little, and Real Dad totally called me out for dieting only on ninety-minute microwavable

Hollywood bullshit, so I thought about it, and I guess I like *Schizopolis* now.

Except Squeezebeagler isn't even down here. Just me, Real Dad, Sverg, Bop-Shop Carl, Garrett—who's keeping his hands in his pockets, dying for some hand sanitizer—and some guy sleeping in one of the chairs.

"It'll be great to see Tam again," Real Dad says. "You're lucky to be friends with him—he's a really great guy. I played lacrosse with Tam in high school, killed cockroaches with him."

When, wait. Wasn't it Real Dad's Blockhustler boss that played lacrosse with Tam?

"Didn't think I'd be learning this much about you tonight, Dale," Bop Shop Carl says.

"We've hung out, a few times," Real Dad says. "I mean, I, I, I've been down here in the basement before, before he's performed—"

"Interesting!" Sverg says, in this cocktail-party way. "We've never seen you down here. We must have missed you in this"—he bends his knees a little and makes a slow, broad, backhand gesture—"confined space."

And then, slow motion, I hear footfalls down the basement steps; the staircase cracking its knuckles. It's Squeezebeagler Tam, Rocker of a Million Faces.

Tam has dark, well-parted hair, workboots and wool socks, shorts with a belt, and a button-down short-sleeve shirt, as if he's there to deliver a package. Even though he hasn't played, there's a sweat-darkened area on his shorts above his crotch, like he wet his pants with his navel. He makes a devil sign and finds the cooler.

"Tam," Sverg says. "Listen, do you know Dale? He's an old friend of yours."

You look at Real Dad, and the room's getting dizzy with him. His lower lip moves. He makes a gun out of his fingers and presses the imaginary barrel into his chinfat.

"He knows you, Tam, knows you real well," Bop-Shop Carl says. "You guys used to play lacrosse, or kill cockroaches. This guy hung out with you all the time."

Expression flinches out of Squeezebeagler Tam's face. "Which one are you?" he says.

You can feel stadiums in Real Dad's brain collapsing, his eyes getting shinier, like there's an Oh Shit coming big enough to explode the Bible. But listen to what Real Dad says, only this once, because no way am I ever bringing this up again:

"Listen, guys, Tam, Sverg, Carl, it's. What I meant was, sometimes, your voice; you just end up saying 'I,' and what you mean is, it was your boss, or whoever it may be, in a given situation, and, and, and, but you just start saying 'I,' instead of whoever's actually—and it's just—and I'm only being honest, here, because at this point what can you even expect to—there's no point in, you know—you cut out the middleman! I believe: I am a person who believes: that the world should be entertaining, that regardless of, you know, you look at, I knew a guy at Griffiss; he's doing flyovers in Iraq—and, and, the world, the dreamscape; the alchemy—it, it's all, just—life! Storytelling!"

Sverg and Bop-Shop Carl look at each other, almost concerned now.

"I'm gonna take off," Garrett Alfieri says.

"No, wait, no!" I go.

"It was good to see you, though," Garrett Alfieri says. "Colonel Hellstache? 'Never change.' I wrote that in your yearbook, man. You kept your word. We need more of that out there in the big world. Throw-down-closing-time; that's what it's all about."

I shake his hand out of reflex.

If that weren't enough to morph you to your bed permanently and turn you into a Bed Centaur, here, still, is Real Dad:

"Dale," Bop-Shop Carl says, standing chest to chest with Real Dad now, pupils narrowing. "How about I ask you something?"

Real Dad pretends to laugh, still friends. "Okay, what's that."

"How about, we don't know you," Bop-Shop Carl says. "How about, a guy came to see a show last week at a place down the street. Nobody knew him, and he was, like you, following everybody the fuck around. That guy stabbed a friend of ours in the bathroom," he slashes his leg with his index finger. "Femoral artery. All next morning: mopping up the stall."

Real Dad raises his palms, padding the air. "Look: on a better day, friend, I swear: You and I would be toasting to live music and friendship."

"On a better day, we *wouldn't*," Bop-Shop Carl says.

"Dale," Sverg unwedges his wallet out of his jeans and hands Real Dad a twenty. "Get yourself a cab. Not your night, okay?"

Once, in kindergarten, Real Dad and I were playing Frisbee in our backyard. Several people, wearing bright orange vests, wandered onto our lawn from the woods nearby. I figured out, a few years later, they were hunters. "Get the hell out of here," I am very sure Real Dad said. I'm hoping for Part II: The Proto-Stachening of that to happen, say, right now.

But the doorman's already leading me and Real Dad out, and we're already walking out into the bar crowds on Monroe Avenue. Steam from the late-night sausage cart in front of the bank is extra visible, with a line of dudes wearing those zip-up sweater turtlenecks I could never pull off wearing. The bruise-colored light from the street lamps makes all the closed novelty shops seem foggier or grainier, like when you see dark, synthesizer-y MTV videos from 1983.

"They're just joking—they're stressed out," Real Dad tells me, hands in pockets, looking at the sidewalk. "They're musicians, journalists—deadlines."

I shoulder around a group of college women who are carrying their shoes.

"It actually looks bad on the whole club, that we're leaving first," Real Dad goes on. "We're customers. Those guys never pay a dime in there; they do nothing to support the Bug Jar economy. The irony lays claim to *them*, in actuality."

We stop at the corner of the side street where Real Dad's car is parked. His face is knotted up.

"Well what?" he says.

"What do you mean what."

"What are you thinking about, right there."

I tell him I'm not thinking about anything. But I'm really

thinking: Had God sent Garrett Alfieri from the Biblecopter tonight to make me ask if I should still be making jokes about Holy Grail Points, about Colonel Hellstache, to lock me in the Sad Archives Basement with regards to Necro Maverick Jetpantsing?

But here's what Real Dad is thinking I'm thinking: "Why are you looking at me like I'm some guy who has to retreat into my Tweed Panic Room, with my *Pet Sounds* outtakes?"

"Why would I look at you like you have a Tweed Panic Room?"

Except then, the Dam Breaking Loose. Because, out of complete nowhere, Real Dad goes: "You want to see something? You want to see Rock and Roll? Here. Watch."

"Okay, Dad, what are you going . . ."

"You don't think I can do it, do you?" he says. "You've been looking at me the whole night like I'm stand-up-comedy material, like Hi, I'm Nate, you know, The Pop Culture Essayist; the Deferential, you know, Normal-Guy Writer—let me just sit back in my flannel shirt and fold my arms and let the dramatic irony play out among the earnest. What if I told you I've thought about starting my own music magazine, sort of building on what *Suck* is doing? With raw, balls-out-of-fly commentary?" He pulls his fly zipper outward, toward me. "I talked with Carl about it tonight, talked about it with him two months ago."

He exhales toward the sky and quiets his voice: "Just— let me show you what I am going to need to do."

And suddenly I really start to really worry. As in, is he going to say: "Sometimes I think I might not make it through this life," and am I going to have to tell him: "Well, hang in there!" Because, the last time he was back at Mom's house was to do laundry, four trash bags of it. And, what if, is he going to kill himself? Is he going to hold his hand out to me, and say, padded-cell-gently: Son, watch your father, and then pull a gun from his pocket and brain-spray his head all over the storefront behind him?

So, within seconds, I have my First-Aid Rays fully charged. I care about my parents. Real Dad's not a Tweed Panic Room Hashbrown Gargoyle. We have fun together. I'm ready to Go Off the Top Ropes, ready to do a diving save if Real Dad reaches for a gun in his sock, ready to Drop an Elbow for Life.

Instead, he goes: "I'll bet you I can kick the receiver hook off that payphone at the corner."

He points to the payphone half a block down. At that point, all you can think is: Fuck.

"One clean kick, clean break. Hook: off." He smacks the heel of his right hand into his left palm. "Clean break. Twenty dollars. You're taking the bet."

He stands over me. "Can't we . . ."

"I am your father and we are not going to discuss it!"

I sit on the curb. A few blocks up, a man with longish hair—lacrosse-long—bends over and vomits into a storm drain. I'm not even looking when Real Dad takes the phone off the hook, looks both ways, gives a running start from around the corner, jumps, and jams his boot into the payphone. He does it silently, clean break, like he's been practicing all his life. The hook plinks on the ground. He drops it in my lap.

"That's great Dad, thanks," I say.

"Oh no thank *you*, Nate. Because I wouldn't be a man unless I changed your goddamn diapers. Have to let them know who's *boss*."

Back in Penfield, the house with Real Dad's room is this large, peeling, cotton-gin-era thing with a single broad, white wall as a front. The sign above the maroon front door, which is slanted in its frame, says PENFIELD MANSE.

The stairs are maroon-carpeted and squishy going up to the second floor, and the maroon changes the light to a color that, if it were a Crayola, would be called Dying Cantaloupe. Real Dad nods as he passes maybe a priest, or any one of the alone-a-thon of divorced husbands that might occasionally open their doors and lean out, in their bathrobes and flip-flops. He opens his room's sliding wooden door, where there is no lock. The showers, I remember, are communal and down the hall.

Real Dad brushes his teeth while he sits on the sofa and flips on the TV. Some old movie comes on, with Groucho Marx in it. He starts laughing, really hard, through the toothpaste, at the punchlines. Which means he's done talking for the night, and I'm leaving. "Have fun," he says, and spits into his kitchen sink.

Back home, Mom is postured like geometry on the Woolly Mammoth. Her one glass of Sam Adams, foam drying to the sides. "How was he?" she says.

"We tried to see this band Squeezebeagler and got kicked out," I say. "Then he bet me he could kick the receiver hook off a payphone."

She puts a hand to her mouth, crossing her leg, a spring

echoing through the couch's hollows. "He's funny," she says. But then she narrows her eyebrows, angering down a smile.

And then, according to the God Hates Nate Act of 1931, I change into my Bills pajama pants, go to the den, and look at NecronicA.

Mom's bedroom door closes. When I hit refresh, I flinch: The word SOLD appears in red across the thumbnail of a painting of a naked woman with a legion of army soldiers on fire behind her, faces peeling off, tongues broiling.

Which makes me think, really, the whole time so far, maybe I was lying to you about Bringing the Funny and Holy Grail Points. Maybe I'd rather not joke around with Real Dad, and maybe sometimes I'd really like to talk to Real Dad about what Garrett Alfieri told me, about how I'm still the same and I talk the same, and how I'm not good at anything, and how Necro has NecronicA and Weapons of Mankind and all this money, and Lip Cheese has a Home and a Cash and they're all happier than me.

Back when I was happier, even an hour ago, at the end of my night with Real Dad, he went to bed, and I went home. When I got in the car to drive back to Gates, from outside the Penfield Manse, Real Dad's window was the only one with a light on. Through his window, I saw him take off his shirt, posture frumped up. There was no expression on his face, no Wall of Comedy. He folded some piece of clothing, downed a glass of water in one gulp, and turned off the light.

THE NINTENDO POWER
BUCOLIC FARM

A waitress at Applebee's hovers her hand over a phone behind the hostess stand when Lip Cheese comes in and slides in across from me and next to Toby at the Airplane Booth. Static prickles his hair when he rips off his pull-down mask-hat, and he smells vaguely like hard-boiled egg. He removes a rolled-up stack of papers from the pocket of his Bungee Cord Drop-Zone jacket and places it on the table. The top page says Quitclaim Something or Other and has the word "hereby."

"Lip Cheese: What?" I say.

"I was at the County Clerk," Lip Cheese says. "I thought if you were still mad at Necro, that I could do some research to, you know."

Toby and I look at each other. I bite into a hollowed-out French fry.

"These copies cost forty-three dollars, guys!" Lip Cheese says. "It took me two hours to figure out what a deed was!"

"Lip Cheese: I just meant follow Necro around," I say. "Hang out with him until he says something Uncomebackable."

"What?" Lip Cheese says. "Llewellen the clerk was really helpful. They have a nice, quiet table there where you can sit." Toby laughs some fries out of his throat and has to store them in his left cheek. "Sorry if I suck at everything else, Toby. Sorry that I'm not good-looking and that I wasn't born with . . ."

Lip Cheese adjusts whatever paper towel or napkin he's stuffed into his armpit.

"I tried to call Necro a bunch of times," he says. "I have no idea where he is. But I checked online, and the administrative contact for the NecronicA domain name is a Mr. Bambert L. Tolby, 300-A Ridge Road. I checked that address at the County Clerk." Lip Cheese flips through some pages. A salt grain forms a bump and pinpricks through the page when he runs his index finger over a line of text. "It says on December 31st, 1998 that Kurt's Laundromat, a New York corporation having a principal place of business at 300-A Ridge Road, in the consideration paid of one and more dollars, grants to Bambert L. Tolby the land and building at this place on Ridge Road in Webster."

A lightbulb appears over my head. Because, didn't Rambocream say something during Weapons of Mankind Night? Our manager or our supplier Bambert? And didn't Necro say some guy Bambert was going to give him a grant of financial permission for NecronicA?

Lip Cheese runs a napkin through his hair and flips a page. "Does this all mean Bambert L. Tolby bought a building?" he says.

Toby plucks the page from Lip Cheese, looks at it for a second, and slams it facedown on the table. "This is all symbolage to me," he says, rolling around his car keys in his hand. "But it gives me an idea."

Which is the exact same sound the world makes when it ends. Every time Toby gets an idea, children fall asleep and never wake up.

Luckytown Hastings's house is as compact as an Easter basket. His front yard—on a green, trinkety, miniature golf course of a street—is small and hemmed tight. Toby idles his car past the mailbox, turns around at the cul-de-sac, and parks a few houses down along the curb. The sun, through the trees, is the color of wifely white wine. Two squirrels chase each other up a tree like they're running up an imaginary spiral staircase.

All of this looks strange because I'm used to seeing this street at night, like that one time me and Necro collected all the garbage bags full of leaves set out for trash collection and threw them in Luckytown's driveway.

"Necro's about to get Jungled!" Toby says.

Lip Cheese punches the back of my headrest. "You got Jungled, Necro!"

"You got *Jungled*," Toby says.

"*Jungled*," Lip Cheese says. Which isn't even their phrase; Jungled was this thing Garth Heffernan used to say!

No question: Necro has been textbook Colonel Hellstache. He still needs to be fucked with. But when Toby brings Lip Cheese's documents with him and walks toward Luckytown's house, that's when I know why we're here.

"You know, Necro is right when he says moral masturbation, Toby," I say. "Are we really being serious?"

Which is already the error. That question has never been answered once. So Toby whips around at me and says, either in Cockdrama Anger or, maybe, actual anger: "Necro doesn't like you anymore, Nate. He set your room on fire in that picture and yet you would be one to Mommy? your way out of confronting him about Pinning Bow Ties on the Dead?"

I blush like the dam breaking loose. Total Comeback Shutdown, Part II: The Proto-Stachening, when Mommy? should totally not bother me anymore. Mommy? is the oldest Uncomebackable Insult, the Training-Wheels-Level Uncomebackable. But even Lip Cheese goes: "Mommy? Mommy?" And then Toby goes, "Mommy?" right in my face, and I swallow some of his cereal breath. None of which is fair or respectful. Some things—things you said in your sleep at a sleepover that you have no control over—you only stay living just so you can forget them.

So, crossing Luckytown's buzz-cut grass, I convince myself that, since I have nothing else to do this week, maybe it would be funny to see Necro's face when police show up at his house and he has to tell them Oh hi, I'm Necro, I didn't *take* and blow up that building; I was too busy *taking* and having a Kangaroo for a Kid. And then after police leave, and there are no arrests, me and Toby and Lip Cheese could swoop in and yell: "Surprise! You got Jungled!" and we'd all be friends again, even though that's Garth Heffernan's phrase.

Toby wipes off his boots on the welcome mat and rings Luckytown's doorbell. Me and Lip Cheese stand back a bit, on the scrubbed-white sidewalk leading to the front doorstep.

The seal of the wood-grain door unsuctions. I prepare my face.

But right when you expect Luckytown to process Toby's lard into canned food, Luckytown opens the door wearing oven mitts and an apron that says M.C. GRILLER. "You are under arrest," he says.

Toby half-flinches.

"You ponyboys! I'm kidding!" Luckytown says. "Please come in."

Luckytown's dining room is clean and unused, colored like embroidered china. His kitchen has a stainless steel refrigerator where the freezer's actually the bottom drawer. A finger-shaped smear of blood, just to the right of the garbage disposal switch, looks twisted into the kitchen wallpaper.

"We come to you head in hands, believe me," Toby says. "But we wanted to let you know about some suspicious things, about our friend Andrea, and about the broadcast building explosion and several recent fires, now that we've had time to remember them more, you know, formally."

Luckytown looks away from us and raises his eyebrows quickly.

"After Necro's show ended that night, Necro was sort of shoving us toward the building, like he wanted us to be close to the building when it exploded?" Toby says.

And, I force myself to say, since This Is Going to Bring the Funny, Murman-Mango Jitney-Level: "And earlier in the evening? Before that explosion? Necro and Wicked College—John Violi—had this argument on the way to the Weapons of Mankind show?"

Luckytown removes a casserole from the oven, which throws me off a little and makes me feel like I need to explain more when I don't want to.

"Because, Necro always hates it when you say Kangaroo for a Kid, because he has all these German Shepherds in his house?" I say. "And Necro left these drawings in his car, and Wicked College John—he and Necro have never really gotten along, because once, Lip Cheese found this sweater in this abandoned home and gave it to Wicked College John as a gift. And Wicked College John didn't want it, but Necro convinced Wicked College John to wear it—you know, to be nice to Lip Cheese. But after Wicked College John put it on he got this rash—like, a whole Rash Shirt for three weeks, and he blamed Necro, so ever since then they hate each other?"

But the problem is the entire story is impossible to explain and I start to feel embarrassed, total pre-Melting Backsickle, and I forget what I was talking about.

"Have you heard of NecronicA?" Toby says.

Luckytown rips off a length of foil from the roller. "Our department tracks any number of activities."

"Because if you go to his website, NecronicA," Toby says, "you can see that he has been drawing an awful lot of fire."

Luckytown motions for us to sit in his living room, the carpeted region just to the right of his kitchen. Vine plants with red flowers hang above a small, gray TV/VCR combo. Basil-green recliners are arranged in this prim way where it feels like nobody ever sits in them. Lip Cheese sits in one, though, and sets his papers on his lap.

"So far, this year, the Rochester Fire Department has reported twenty-one arson task force investigations under way," Lip Cheese reads from some document, with Toby nodding grimly.

Lip Cheese turns to a printout he has made of all the drawings posted on NecronicA. His index finger hops over each miniaturized picture on the page. "There are twenty-one fire-related artworks on NecronicA," Lip Cheese says.

Maybe this is all still technically hilarious, but I really start to wonder: They are getting really specific with this joke.

"Hm," is all Luckytown says, folding the length of foil over the casserole before sliding the dish back into the oven.

"Do you know Bambert L. Tolby?" Toby asks.

"We know he opened a military surplus store in Webster," Luckytown says, losing his upright-barricade cop voice for a second. "On Ridge Road. Bambert's Weapons. But that's public. Something else happened with him, years back. I don't remember."

I swallow a yarnball of lightning. "Have you seen Necro there?" I say.

"Oh I don't know," Luckytown says, shredding some Parmesan on a bell-shaped shredder. "But, hey, little man, that's why we have police departments."

I won't even begin to tell you how I reacted that night to Luckytown finding out, before me, where Necro might be semi-Maverick Jetpantsing to. Taking a shower, I'm fine. But lying in bed that night, I throw an elbow into my mattress. At first, since Mom is asleep, I pick up a stereo speaker and set it down on its side, as if I've knocked it over. I roll a pen off my homework desk. After that, all I will say is that the rumors are not true and my room is normally that trashed.

The next day, there's enough leftover Off-the-Top-Ropes rage in me to drive over and pick up Toby (because Lip Cheese is working, and Toby drove yesterday, and so I'm driving today, because those are the Laws of Gas). We go to Ridge Road in Webster, if only so that you know, Necro, that no matter where you are, you will see my face.

Webster is flat, with cracked, tarred-up roads, big back-yards, and houses with storefronts. The sign on the new weapons shop, above one huge window, says *Bambert's Weapons* in italicized maroon lettering. When we enter, a tinkly "Here's a Customer" bell rings from the handle of the glass door, like the sound of Hitler making his own candy. Immediately, I'm scanning for anything that might be not just Murman-level Uncomebackable, but Pharaoh Uncomebackable, something so Pharaoh Uncomebackable that Necro will never leave his house again.

But the store is only a counter and a stack of cardboard boxes behind it. Rambocream, with a sweaty buzz cut, leans over the glass display counter, ice-cream sandwich arms spread out and palms flat on the glass top. He closes some book by H.P. Lovecraft. In the glass display are sword- and knife-shaped velvet insets but no weapons. Rambocream looks like he's not sure if he should let us know he remembers us.

"Excuse me, we're not technically open yet?" he says.

"We're looking for Andrea Fanto," I say. "And Bambert L. Tolby."

His eyebrows leap and he suddenly smiles, voice suddenly

connoisseurish: "Bambert, unfortunately, is booked solid today. I assume you're from the church?"

"Church?" Toby says.

"Are you Community Investors?" Rambocream says, apparently capitalizing those words.

Toby slants his brow, the way he does when he appears to be yelling, inside his head: I DON'T UNDERSTAND WHY I'M CONFUSED.

"All we were wondering is if you could tell us if you've seen Necro today," Toby says.

"Necro?" Rambocream says.

"Andrea," I say. "Andrea Fanto."

Rambocream folds his arms. "You mean Loostro. Are you the media?" he says.

"Necro's in here that much," Toby says.

Rambocream points to a Toyota Camry parked across the street outside, with a manila-folder-colored sparkle.

"That's Mel Reid, from the newspaper," he says. "Whenever I lock up at night and walk out, he carries this tape recorder that's the size of a Fisher-Price tape recorder. Sometimes, he'll even park outside Bambert's house, for an hour, eat a sandwich, and drive off without requesting an interview. Two weeks ago, they printed a headline titled: 'No word yet on white-supremacist explosion.' Maybe you are Loostro's friends? But I'll have to consult and see what we're comfortable with."

Rambocream closes his eyes, raises his eyebrows, and angles his head slightly away.

"Let's go, Nate," Toby says. "This guy's Colonel Hellstache.

Do you even know what that means? Colonel Hellstache? Holy Grail Points? He doesn't know. He isn't Necro's friend."

We turn around to leave, because really I should be applying for jobs right now, but then Rambocream goes: "The Nintendo Power Bucolic Farm. What about that?"

I swing myself around. I don't know if my reaction is visible.

"Because that's where he is," Rambocream says. "He goes out there to clear his head. If you know him, why don't you *take* and take a journey, with Journey, and go find him there."

When I worked so hard to stay Necro's friend, and Necro gives away even the Nintendo Power Bucolic Farm. Where the abandoned Canal Creamee had this payphone that worked without change. You and me, Necro, Off the Top Ropes, playing America's ribcage as a guitar, pranking Nintendo customer service with that phone ("Uh, are you planning on coming out with a new Nintendo game where you can, uh, make tires?"). Because, going to the Nintendo Power Bucolic Farm got me through back-to-school season. You want to give something away, Necro? Give away Shinobi Hamslicer. Give away Peanut Butter Shoulder. Give away Dorito Henderson; we never needed Dorito Henderson, Necro; you and I together were always better than Dorito Henderson. But to tell even Rambocream about the Nintendo Power Bucolic Farm? This one hurts, Necro.

"Don't be this guy's Wendy," Toby says. "This isn't worth the Cockdrama anymore."

But I lower my voice and say to Rambocream: "Oh, I

know where the Nintendo Power Bucolic Farm is. We will drive to Fishers and we will find Necro and we will bring him back here in one hour and we will *talk*."

Rambocream has this smile where his upper lip curls over his teeth, old-man style. He flips his palm upward. "All right."

"But there's motocross on! X Games Finals!" Toby says, following me outside to the car, the door handle bell dinkling again. "I didn't set the VCR!"

"Yeah, well."

On 490, after easily a whole episode of motocross passes, Toby yanks back the backrest of his seat and stares up at the ceiling. The sunset tangles into the trees. I near exit 45—the Mob Execution Exit.

"Wendy Wendy," Toby says. "Wendy Wendy Wendy, Wendy Wendy Wendy put on a Wendy Nametag."

So rather than admitting that, oh shit, I haven't been to the Nintendo Power Bucolic Farm since 1996, I totally make a tasting menu out of Toby's pissed-offedness. I slam my foot on the clutch to coast.

"Do I turn here? Exit 45? Where is Fishers again, Toby?"

"How about toward my goddamn house!"

"No, it's further this way. Past like Bloomfield and all that."

Another episode of motocross probably passes. The worst thing about getting lost in the plains is that there are no signs or landmarks. When I turn onto the country routes, there are some white, boutique-y looking buildings that I feel like I remember, and Toby rolls onto his side.

I turn onto Route 20A—a guess turn. Then another guess turn. More episodes of motocross. The street lamps run out.

I see a sign for what, I guess, is a town called Atlanta. Wheat fields drizzle by.

"If you're not their Wendy, Nate," Toby says, "then what are you? Their Mommy?"

In response—to make up for the Total Comeback Shutdown of yesterday afternoon—I turn left onto some road, and the sky opens up into a black whipped cream of cloud cover. "No, wait, I think I remember where we are now, Toby!" I say, smirking as hard as I can. "There's a church up here! Fishers is totally *this* way!"

"Fuck! This!" Toby kicks my glove compartment drawer.

I take the next left. "Oh wait! No! The Nintendo Power Bucolic Farm is totally up *this* way! I swear to God!"

A wall of cornstalks appears on our right. On Toby's second kick, the glove compartment door cracks. The light from inside it makes the crack look like a lightning bolt.

It's dark enough so that my headlights seem only to light the small bowl-shaped area of road right ahead of me. So I start to wonder, okay, seriously: Where am I.

"Let me see the map in there, Toby?"

With his pointer finger and thumb, Toby tweezes the map through the crack in the glove compartment and unfolds it.

"It's a map of Buffalo," he says, and karate chops the map to the floor.

I flip on the ceiling light and pull over. I turn off the car. I'm warm enough to unzip my Bills winter jacket. We open our doors and step out into the quiet. If there were cars coming, you'd see the headlights from a county over. Everything, my shoes on the gravel, sounds intricate, like someone whispering into your ear. Across the street from the cornfields, a hill slants upward into a patch of woods. No street lamps anywhere, no power lines.

I sit on the hood and scratch the sweat off my forehead. Toby kicks some gravel and puffs his cheeks.

"Well maybe if you'd shut up, Toby, I could've concentrated when I was on the highway and actually *found* the Nintendo Power Bucolic Farm," I say.

"Well maybe if you didn't Mommy yourself so much over Necro—"

"Fine! Fine! Fine!" I yell. The word echoes, blinking smaller into the woods.

Then, a bright, sharp, pinhole-sized red dot, from a laser pointer or a rifle, appears on the car's rear driver's side door.

A spike drives up through the middle of my brain. My muscles feel like floating ash. The dot loops around Toby's ear.

"Who's there?" Toby says, a little quiet, the way you'd speak into the dark when woken by a burglar's footsteps.

When the dot squiggles toward my crotch, I do a flailing jumping jack and land on my knees in the snow crust. Next thing, we're both in the dirt, covering our heads as the dot makes angry cursive over us, doing evasive roll moves, scrunching our heads into our shoulders.

The dot spirals wide and slow across the cornfields and, eventually, settles on my forehead.

"Get down Nate, oh God—NO! Don't shoot!" Toby says. The lettering on his Drew Bledsoe jersey is visible when he crawls back into the car and ducks into the seat well.

I crawl behind the car, gravel stabbing my knees. I look up from behind the trunk. For no reason, I say: "Necro?"

The dot pauses.

Then, the dot jerks toward my chest, then to my crotch, then back toward my chest and down again, like it's either nodding up-and-down Yes, or bludgeoning me. The dot then scribbles up and down my arms and my chest and legs, like it's trying to color me in.

I think: Coloring me in, Necro? Like coloring me in because I'm dead inside?

"Either shoot us or show yourself!" Toby yells from inside the car.

Then, slowly, the dot moves up the leg of my nylon running pants, my sweatshirt, up to my collarbone, crawling toward my eye like an insect I can't feel, and I decide, surprisingly quickly, surprisingly practically, that it's probably better to die this way rather than go on embarrassing myself the way I have. The laser point pierces my eye, and I feel some microheat on my eyebrows, and it moves to my forehead, and with the efficiency of a bank withdrawal I accept death, and I cramp my eyelids shut to brace for the bullet and, then, the point disappears.

A leftover dot-shaped, orange-sherbet-colored stain drifts in my eye. I can't see the corn or the patch of pine trees across the street. The snow crunches when I move any part of me— ice grains rolling over ice grains. No branches crack from the woods, no footsteps.

When I get back into the car, I think I hear Toby sniffle.

"You all right?" I say.

"You will never be able to win an argument with me again," he says. "If you still think you're friends with Necro. All I'm saying, if you still think you're friends."

I start the engine. I turn on the headlights. We don't hear a single thing at all.

HIGH SCHOOL
FRITO PACE-OFF

Back home, the dark from the cornfield and the tracers of the laser pointer have settled into my spine. I keep from looking at anything for too long—the spoon rest on the oven, the paint-spattered radio on top of the fridge—just in case another dot appears. Sleep never works, so I settle on an all-night High School Frito Pace-Off.

The uncrumpling of the Fritos bag is loud, like announcing it to a racetrack. I set the bag on one end of the kitchen table and a glass of milk on the other. Then I walk a lap around the table, handful some chips into my mouth, and reach the glass of milk just as I'm done chewing.

"Nate?" someone says.

Fake Dad No. 3 velvets his way into the kitchen from the living room, bare legs under his purple bathrobe, Thor-mane in a ponytail.

"I was sleeping on the couch," he says, leaning against the oven and thumb-knuckling the corner of his eye to uncrust it. "There was a great documentary on Lake Canandaigua. Canandaigua—do you know what that word means?"

Through the kitchen window, the sky milks up with pre-sunrise. He answers his own question. "It means 'the chosen place.' Isn't that interesting? That we have a body of water that was regarded as 'the chosen place?'"

I'm too busy Frito-chewing to even notice what he literally, actually says next: "You remind me of a story. One time, my friend Theebs, we called him that, he and I were camping in Nevada. He met a lady there, at the campgrounds, who had a prosthetic hand. Just two pincers to grip the phone when she talked girl-talk with her girlfriends. But Theebs, always seeking a connection, thought this lady was so ravishing, in the face, that he offered to smoke with her our hash, and she said she'd meet him later that night—with the caveat that love's arbitrary yet fluid currents might bring them closer."

I hear a coughing in the walls. The shower's turning on: Mom.

"We'd already been drinking Carlo Rossi; already were in the bag," he says. "So Theebs went out, met her, and returned to our tent nearly doubled over in pain."

I wipe the salt on my pajama pants and, before I even think about why he's telling me this, I admittedly admit that I'm sort of cracking up here. "Wait wait wait wait," I go. "A Terminator Reacharound?"

Which, obviously, reminds me of something that happened both to Necro and Lip Cheese, and they know exactly what I'm talking about.

"That's very funny," Fake Dad No. 3 says. "A lot of richness."

"That actually happened to your friend?"

"And me, too." He reaches for his robe sash. "Would you care to see the scars?"

I whip my entire body away from him. "No! Don't!"

"Kidding! You're a pushover." He crosses his ankles and his robe slides back past his right knee. "I know you think I'm the Homosexual Time Lord, or what not. But might I make you a proposition, Nate, which you are free to ignore."

I pour myself a new glass of milk and down it like a shot. Since he's already insulted much of himself for me, I say: "Okay, sure."

"I've heard you talk on the phone to your friends, and I think you might find the loam of my offer to be particularly fertile. I have my chosen place, as well. Every summer, I go to a retreat, outside Philadelphia, near King of Prussia. Have you been—to King? of Prussia?"

"It's named a king?"

"It's a series of three-day retreats—although they offer longer engagements that intersplice multiple disciplines—in a confined, but wooded, natural creative space with yeomanic clearings, stone farmhouses amid the tall grass. It's run through the Continual Center Foundation, which is world renowned, completely legitimate. The meditation technique is based on Vipassana—a twenty-five-hundred-year-old form of idea-incubation that means, loosely, truthful observation. It's a way of eliminating war, eliminating suffering." His right hand pans from his left arm outward across his body. "It

would be challenging, excruciating. You wouldn't be able to
talk at all—except for obvious emergencies—but eventually,
after multiple sessions and efforting toward an essence-forward
life, you'd come out of it not needing to prove yourself to
anyone. I donate very regularly there. And if you were interested in such a means of self-excavation, well, I could make
that happen. We draw a ragtag band: everyone from ex-
offenders to corporate executives. Yours for the low price of
tender loving care!"

When I think of Pennsylvania, it reminds me of Greta
Hollund, who I kind of liked even though I only saw her
from across the cafeteria, and who wore plaid pants and
had buttons on her book bag straps. She went to college
in Philadelphia. When the kids go back to school every
September, I'll put "Hysteria" on repeat, in her honor or
something, and I'll do a Sad Archives Transfer, and re-rig
my stomach to feel what I imagine she felt when she was
younger. And I'll imagine myself shrinking, like the thin
white rectangle after you turn off an old TV, until I think to
go do something else.

"Also—because I do walk the walk," Fake Dad No. 3
says, reaching for the Frito bag, "I remember when I was
monetarily and spiritually low. My first wife left me, so I blew
five credit cards backpacking through South America. When
I got back, I couldn't find work. I was thirty-two. I moved
into the basement of a house of grad students. All the dishes
ended up in my room, because I was too depressed to carry
them to the dishwasher when I finished eating. I tried to read
self-help books, but self-help books are all written by people

who are already successful, right? They would never need their own advice. And I couldn't reconcile that. Finally, I went to King of Prussia, in 1989, for this retreat. Could you imagine if you knew that several times a year you didn't have to talk to anybody? I almost moved there for it."

"But, so, why Mom?" I say.

He looks toward the ceiling and sighs. "That's an astute question," he says, because he says every question is a good question. "Debra commits herself. Gary: Did you take your Donnatal? Are you transferring your medical records? You have meditation on Tuesday, not Monday."

"I feel like I can never complain about anything with her," I tell him.

"I can't speak for that," he says. "But I can say, us guys, you and me,"—he nudges his elbow at me—"the other night, alone, at my apartment, I called GE to walk me through how to use the washing machine in my own complex's basement. Men won't spend their money; men will count the pasta noodles she bought before she left us."

Which, okay, is about a 4.1 on the Scale of Funny.

"The retreat would be free. It'd be in the summer. It would be an intense challenge. But a chance, for the mind."

"I would have to think about it."

Because I begin to feel something as this conversation ends. And the last time I felt it was when Real Dad drove all the way to Fairport so we could go sledding at Brooks Hill, which had the best sledding hill in Rochester. It was Super Bowl Sunday, with the Bears playing later. The other sledders packed snow together to build a jump, and poured water on it for added momentum. Skidding a glove across the snow, saliva freezing on your coat zipper, it was like the ground was punching up at us when me and Real Dad's sled plunged toward the jump, and then everything went quiet and airborne, and that, I guess, was family for three seconds.

But Mom's shower gulps to a stop. Fake Dad No. 3 sets his vitamin jars on the kitchen table, and I dive under my bed covers and pretend I've been asleep. And the next day, I totally Walk Down Faggot Lane when I meet Toby at the Airplane Booth.

"Something about a retreat sounded kind of interesting," I tell him. "Wouldn't you be almost relieved? To walk away completely?"

A French fry falls out of Toby's mouth. I blush for even bringing up the subject. Blush enough to come back home and tell Fake Dad No. 3: "I don't think so."

"But you're considering it," Fake Dad No. 3 says. "I can see it in your face; view of the lake? Simple breakfast in the morning? I'll bring pamphlets! I'm eager to help."

Eager to help. Like he, Necro, and Garrett Alfieri can walk into a room, offer help, and expect everyone to start licking themselves in strange tongues.

"Nothing against you, but a retreat sounds stupid to me," I say, a little harder.

Tell me I need some retreat, when, later, I go to bed, and I'm staring at the glow-in-the-dark stars on my ceiling and I get this tickly feeling. Like how after any party, I'd walk home, wishing the world was a quiet, empty lit town where the sun never came up and high school kids walked around outside. Cutting through store lots and peoples' backyards, I'd start to talk to myself, whispering one-liners—"Nine out of every ten sportscasters prefer Just For Men Beard Coloring!"—whispering louder and louder and louder.

THE HAPPY
ROLODEX

For spring, though, to combat the Springtime Breezes of Fear, I decide that I am Going to Be Happy. So I don't call Necro (who never calls anymore anyway), or Lip Cheese, or Toby. There's literally no Fires Gone Wild Cancun Fuckfest through all of March. So I stop checking NecronicA, and spend more time outside sitting on benches around town, where it's flu-warm, enough for the shops to prop their doors open on rubber-bottomed kickstands.

The cashier at the 7-Eleven asks me How you doing, and I tell him, "Everything's chugging along!" and I pause and look closely to see if there's any change in his face, to see if I've caused him to look deep into the sad trash that is his life.

A few times, I even visit Wicked College John, who is now at the rehabilitation section of the hospital. He can stand now; he shuffles around the bed in his room, and I nod approvingly. He turns his head and looks at me for a few seconds. "TV?" he says, and then, in another visit, he says, "This

show? Hellstache?" and then, in another, "Let's listen to that
Rusted Root bootleg now."

Back home, Mom is microwaving a cookie for dessert.
"Jobs? Anything?"

"Had some really exciting conversations!" I say, after I
interview with the managers at Zabb's and Java Joe's and
Dick's Sporting Goods. And on the back of a grocery receipt, Mom writes down numbers of some temp agencies I
haven't called.

The next morning, in the kitchen, when I handful
Product 19 from the box for breakfast, Fake Dad No. 3 stirs
up a fiber drink and asks how I am.

"Doing great, spiritually!" I say. And on my bed, he leaves
pamphlets for the retreat. There's a green background and
a picture of a mountain on the front and the address of the
retreat center. The text on the inner flap has a heading, in a
cursive font, that says: THE BUFFALO THAT ROAM THE
MIND. On a Post-it stuck to the pamphlet, Fake Dad No. 3
has written, in the teacher-like scribble I'd get on homework
papers: "Great for exploring excess & what we discussed!"

And it's like I'm creating a Happiness Rolodex. The Nate
that Necro and Garrett Alfieri and Fake Dad No. 3 think I
am, who needs help? Gone like ads in last year's newspaper.

And, by the time we get to Easter-ish, it's T-shirt weather.
And at some point, there comes a time when there comes a
time. So insert Rambo gearing up, cartridge into gun, knife
into bootleg, as I test the Happy Rolodex on Toby and Lip
Cheese at the Airplane Booth at Applebee's. I tell them, off
the top turnbuckle:

"Life's working out! Putting the 'joy' in 'enjoyment.'"

And I'm saying to myself please, please let Toby remember that time I thought I saw him sniffle when the Miami Dolphins dumped Flutie Flakes on the locker room floor and danced on them ("It's the moisture in my nose!"), or the time Lip Cheese tried to tell everyone that a laser was a solid object.

Instead, Toby heaves his mutton-pink forearms onto the tabletop. He looks at me, face heavy, like he's about to tell me he's pregnant. "Look, I don't know what you just said there," he says. "But we have some bad news."

Lip Cheese jumps in. "My friend Lewellyn? At the County Clerk? She told me there was a fire at Bambert's Weapons."

Toby closes his eyes and nods. "Retaliation burn-down."

"She said the sprinkler system was disabled," Lip Cheese says. "I drove by there. The fire was in the back room, so I couldn't see anything, but there was somebody from the fire department walking around the building with a pair of tongs and placing these little bits of burnt cloth into a paint can."

"You guys seem to have a lot of hostility," I say. "This is a bit touched, man."

"I've been thinking about this, *especially* after that laser pointer," Toby says. "Look at NecronicA: Necro draws a picture, building burns down. Necro draws a picture, building burns down. That pattern, over and over. And the buildings that have had fires set to them? Those homeless shelters? These kind of liberal places? And you remember how at Weapons of Mankind, they were complaining about their treatment within the community, and they were all, you know, *bruahrahrahrahrahrahrah*"—he makes these motions with his hands, like he's a bear clawing at a tree— "*bruah-rahrahrahrah* state laws; *bruahrahrahrahrah*, like totally anti? So maybe the first fire—the explosion—let's just say Weapons of Mankind did that one, acting out against the public access building and the neighborhood. Then, maybe, suppose the next few fires somebody set maybe out of pro-test against the Weapons of Mankind explosion—Race-War Amalgamation, etc. Then, Weapons of Mankind *in turn* sets the fires at the shelters in retaliation for those fires. Then"—and the seriousness in Toby's face breaks for a second, and he actually giggles—"someone breaks in to Bambert's Weapons, disables the sprinkler, and sets it aflame. I mean . . ."

The thing I should say here is that Toby's not mentally dis-abled. I saw him once tutoring kids at lacrosse camp. He talked about split dodges, keeping the stick head behind the shoulder for an overhand shot, building power from your hips and legs when you shoot on the run. I've seen him make sense.

"What about every other fire this year, Toby?" I say.

Toby slaps Lip Cheese on the arm, gestures toward me, and smirks. "Well I would imagine there would be some regular fires in there too, Nate."

All I can even think to do is shrug at Toby as hard as I can. Lip Cheese, though, flips through more of his docu-ments, an inch-high stack this time, stopping at a page with a lot of white space and two bold headings near the middle and bottom.

"This is a bunch of stuff from some court folder—court papers, news articles—from 1986, that says Bambert L. Tolby quote 'defrauded thirty-one investors of $571,000 which Mr.

Tolby claimed would be used to fund the development of a film, purportedly titled *Letters to God and the Third Reich* and said to be based on Mr. Tolby's historical research on World War II,'" Lip Cheese says. He slides his index finger down another page, "Mr. Tolby fabricated twenty-one messages from the IMG World agency to mislead investors about production, marketing, and expenditures for the movie." He moves his finger down the page over the paragraphs, each of them numbered. "The film budget Mr. Tolby produced was later discovered to be identical to a budget plan for an independent horror film produced in Prentiss, Mississippi." He reads again, "After six years, Tolby had produced a promotional poster for the film and a two-minute film trailer . . ." He flips to what looks like a stapled-together portion of a transcript: "Somebody here says the movie had themes of white supremacy," Lip Cheese says. "It doesn't say what kind."

Toby nods whenever Lip Cheese pauses, the fake listener's nod.

"It also says that 'from 1981 through 1985, Mr. Tolby regularly attended community functions in Brockport, as well as meetings held by the Rochester Professionals Society, to solicit investments. On April 18, 1981, he began renting an office at 92 Main Street in Brockport for a production company, Interesting Films, LLC. In or about 1982, he hired two staff to run telemarketing operations, which were carried out to seek investments.'"

I have no idea what most of more-or-less any of that means. Our waitress says, "Hi guys!" and I tell her coffee and French fries.

"And, then, the document says that he spent $26,240 of investments toward renovations on his home living room, $3,137 toward rare movie posters, $8,421 on a vacation, and $16,000 toward a German military sword said to be used during World War II." Lip Cheese looks up. "There's some other page in here that says he got some number of years in prison. He had to pay back I even forget how much."

"And, Nate," Toby takes two pieces of paper out of his Bills vest. Suddenly our booth smells tender like garbage. The papers look crumpled, and some kind of mustard appears to have crusted up on them. "I did a little dumpster diving. These are receipts from Necro's trash." He flicks one of the receipts, an 8½-by-11 sheet of paper, violently with his middle finger. "I also found a receipt from some place called Tazmanian Cash in South Carolina . . ."

"They didn't have a website that I could find," Lip Cheese says.

"Twenty-seven hundred dollars, total. Purchases of something called Quickmatch; purchases of potassium chlorate, dextrin, lactose, because he's, I don't know, lactose intolerant?" He uncrumples a receipt from Chase-Pitken. "Three hundred in fertilizer? With ammonium nitrate? All of this, on Andrea Fanto's credit card."

"Goddammit, Toby!" I say.

Whatever Happy Rolodex I had shrinks into my chest like drying palm sweat on a steering wheel, and not just because Necro apparently has a credit card. It's more that, Cockdrama In Motion or Actual Seriousness—I can't tell—maybe Toby has a point: Maybe Necro is trying to kill someone.

Toby passes the receipts across the table to me. "Talk to Necro about these, Nate. Show them to his face. It's moral to confront people."

"Should we all go together?" I say.

"You know him," Toby says. "I never hang out with Necro when you're not there—me and him have never branched off into being our own friends. But you, Nate: You have the Winston Churchill Golden Olive Branch. Let him know we can go to the police, take him down to the Zone for real this time."

Toby hands me the receipts, which I fold into the pocket of my running pants. "And think about who your friends are," he says. "Provided you're not still Friend to All Animals." Toby cracks up, mouth opening half-moon-shaped with his baby gremlin teeth.

Lip Cheese goes, "Hooo!"

"Those stuffed animals were Lip Cheese's," I try to say over them. "*Lip Cheese's!*"

But the next afternoon, at home, I'm blushing about Friend to All Animals even in private. I'm so embarrassed that I actually call Necro. I leave a message on the Robot Voice Machine saying: "We have some real Winston-Churchill-ing to do, Necro. You haven't been around recently, and I'm really worried what you're up to."

Then I think: Maybe Necro actually left town. Then I go back to Applebee's. And, as if he'd known via Doppler Natecast, Necro is sitting there, at the Airplane Booth.

I haven't seen him in a while. His face looks a little less swollen. His forearms are hairier, and there's more white in his eyes where they're usually bloodshot. He shakes my hand. "Long time, no talking points."

He hands me a bottle of Glenfiddich, aged twelve years. Because today—April 20th—I also forgot to tell you, actually is my twenty-first birthday.

Any muscle I had is chewing gum now. Any idea that Necro was the Unabomber on a Unabombing Gone Wild Cancun Fuckfest Spree falls totally out of my brain. My point all along being this: Necro's a nice guy and I just want him to be around.

"I know it probably seems like I've been, you know, self-sequestering a lot recently," Necro says. "But you've hit the big two-one."

The bottle is rich-pervert, gray-chest-hair caliber, and comes in a cardboard tube, with rounded edges and a cap you need a long thumbnail to pick off.

"Built in the Glen of Fiddich, Gaelic for 'Valley of the Deer,'" I read from the fold-out card inside the tube, "with notes of peat and spices."

"I drink it for the peat," Necro says, flipping through the cards on our table's ring-bound dessert menu. "Spices." He puffs some laughing through his cheeks. "Babies love the amped-up taste of Paul Prudhomme's habanero-banana puree," he says, in his pro-wrestler Extreme Voice.

I sputter, like laughing out car exhaust. Then I look up. "Wait. What?"

He waves one hand, batting the comment away. "I don't know."

"Gerber Cajun Selections?" I say. "Put the fire back in your baby's dietary whatever."

"Take and transcend the tongues of the earth with our Stage 3 Sweet Potatoes and Atomic Jalapeno: Buuurn your baby's face."

Necro pays for my fries, and we get in the Vomit Cruiser, and the car's smell, a caramel-and-newspaper perfume, is like a little arcade token dropping into my brain's coin slot. I brace my foot against the seat well like I always do to substitute for a seat belt. We drive past Irondequoit Bay, the way we would every night we were off to a party, and we knew Toby would've bought tobacco or a cube of Labatt's and a six of Shea's to class it up. And I'd be wondering what girl would be there that I could stare at all night.

We turn onto a dirt road where twigs flick the windshield. But near my shoe, underneath an unfinished bottle of Surge, I see a chapstick-sized metal tube, and my temples turn into absolute knuckles. Because, I wonder: There is no way that is a laser pointer. And if it is, how would Necro possibly know me and Toby were looking for the Nintendo Power Bucolic Farm, got lost, and ended up in a field? I suppose, though, Necro is sort of good at finding us—he did find us at Mighty Taco in Buffalo that time when nobody told him we were going to see WWF. Because, am I going to have to realize about Necro what everybody apparently realized, like when Missy Giordano went out with Matty De Luca, and then she found the single sentence "THIS IS NOT FAIR" written on a piece of paper somehow slipped under her bedroom pillow, and how everybody

knew that Necro did it? Or how that one time when we were
driving back through the woods from Tavis Porcelli's party out
in Macedon, and we spent the whole ride back saying nothing,
and Necro's driver's-side window was open the way it is right
now, except then, he turned to me and said: "Hey Nate?" And
I went, "What?" and he went, "What if I killed you?" And the
receipts Toby gave me feel like they're glowing in my pocket,
but then I look closer, and the metal object is only a keychain
with a pewter skeleton bone, so everything is fine again.

Necro drives us to a clearing, and, look at this: this pond-
slash-swamp with all of these boats in it: oil tankers, yachts;
ships with rust holes big enough to fit a phone booth through,
ships with chairs and trash bags piled up in their windows;
ships shouldering into the water.

"How'd you find this place?"

"Bored. It's a ship retirement yard. The navy and the
ports send old ships here to let them sort of eat themselves
in—cannibalizing. I thought you'd have fun staring at
them. Happy Birthday, Part II: The Proto-Stachening."

The dirt at the edge of the water is cold and dry. Under
a shirt in the Vomit Cruiser's backseat, Necro finds a Red
Wings plastic game cup with a yellowing logo. He pours the
scotch halfway up.

"If I could, I'd have hired a pimp on retainer to get you
a trailer full of lady people, upon which you could imple-
ment a glorious Symphony of Cock, an old-fashioned Utica
Chinstrap," Necro says.

"The old Joseph Avenue Mason's Jar," I say.

"The old Mack Avenue, Detroit, Mr. Potato Head."

"That's how they do it on Mack Avenue."

I hear a gulp in the pondwater. Even though, really, I'd rather talk about whether I'll be lonely the rest of my life.

"Cheers?" Necro says. We share the cup. I take the first sip.

"Golden chandeliers of tasteness," Necro says.

After I take the after-sip "ah," I go, "I try to call you, but you've been off Maverick Jetpantsing. I never see you!"

He shakes his head. "I'm still living with Dad, still cutting straps in Building 38, the ground-up cow bones still look like couscous."

"What about your prize money to live on your own?"

Necro breathes. "Bambert said he has money, from businesses, people from the churches, so he can take and start giving me his donated financings. I paid him this $2,500, this broker's fee type of thing, which I think I told you about" (I'm sort of flattered he remembers) "but he keeps having setbacks. He's been having more trouble acquiring various easements on some of these apartments, you know, these property structures, living quarters. So I'm waiting that out. That, coupled with immersing myself in NecronicA . . ."

Which, if Necro has no Maverick Jetpants planned yet, now is my chance to prove, once and for all, that I Am Happy: "With everything that's happened with Wicked College John—I've been trying to think more positive, thinking about doing something Huge."

Necro sips the Scotch through his teeth and hands me the cup so the side he drank from is facing away from me. "There was this toaster fire at the weapons shop," he says.

"All it did was blacken one whole wall, but nobody can work there anymore because the house's innards are basically large panels of charred bread—also known as toast, I guess. Bambert was saying how a few days earlier, a light bulb took and popped in the middle of the night once when the lights were off, so maybe the wiring was inherently flawed, and that sent an unwarranted jolt through the nerve system."

"Did somebody do it, do you think?"

Necro purses his lips, puffs his cheeks, and breathes through his nose. "If somebody did it, you'd think they would be, you know, more anthemic than a toaster. But all of Webster hated us anyway. They took and tried to ordinance us out to the Interstate with the porn stores. But that's why me and some of the Weapons of Mankind trolls are thinking about doing some of the re-lo action out near PA, where they got the Karate and Fireworks store and the Swords and Candy store," he says. "Somewhere where there's maybe more of a demographic for us."

My breath shortens to dried-up coffee nerves. "Wait. Are you leaving?"

Necro jets some air through his nostrils. "Not today. Unless I decide to invent a robotic cake."

Our shadows disappear and reappear as a cloud passes the sun. I rotate the cup with my fingers, forget what part of it Necro drank from, check to see if the sunlight shows any saliva reflection on the rim, and take a sip anyway. The scotch tastes like a well-cleaned mansion library.

"A weapons store," I say. "I could go along with that, work at a weapons store."

"Yeah, well."

"But I, you know, completely have my own opportunities, you know?" I tell him. "A Happy Rolodex."

A wrapper rolls toward us and stops, like it's startled to be in the presence of humans. I pass the cup to Necro and he chews on the edge of it when he laughs: "Nate Nate Nate."

And with that alone I feel like I have to start our friendship all over again.

"Why do you want a Plan so bad, Nate?" he says.

I think about that for a minute. "I don't have any Holy Grail Points like you. It's not so easy."

"It's not supposed to be easy! That's the paradox, Nate! On New Year's, I decided I was going to take and Not Suck. I was going to be a man in better faith, who wasn't so straight-jacketed by his own facticity. I was going to take and initiatize myself."

"But I have been feeling better! I'm putting the joy in . . ."

"Liar!" he bark-whispers. "You Plan-less, Plan-less, Plan-less liar who has lied! I see your long line of hang-ups on the answering machine!"

"What am I supposed to do?"

His eyes widen for a second. "Anything. Throw a punch out there, get on a bus."

A yacht rotates, whale-like, toward its side. On the back, its name says SEVENLY. Necro yawns, the way he does, at any time of day, before he's about to get going.

"Welp," he says, the way he ends "well" with a P, "in the name of conversational protocol, I need to say now that I should drive you back." He throws his Red Wings cup toward the boats, but the wind slings the cup back over his shoulder. "There's a thing going on tonight with the Weapons of Mankind trolls. Anyway. Happy birthday."

"Wait, Necro," I say. "No Maverick Jetpantsing just yet?"

He raises one eyebrow, investigative reporterly.

"Or, nothing," I say. "What I meant was, you're not mad at me or anything, are you?"

A Tops grocery bag skids across the dirt.

"I mean, when Wicked College John got injured, you seemed mad at me," I say. "I haven't seen you around so much since that day—it's just been me and Toby."

Necro smiles into his shoulder, which maybe means he still likes me. Because I did okay today Bringing-the-Funny-wise, right? A Day of Quickness, right? That's how they do it on Mack Avenue?

"You said on my machine we had to take and do some serious discourse about something?" he says, jamming his boot's steel-toe into the dirt, which is brownie-soft.

"Oh, no," I say. "That was it. What we just did."

Then I say: "Hey, though. What were you going to say to me that one time? Before we went to Weapons of Mankind that night? You were going to say something, like, 'I think, with you, Nate,' and you never finished the sentence, because Rambocream showed up."

"Who?"

"Your friend, with the glasses. His arms are like these flat lengths of an ice cream sandwich."

He laughs, finally, one single honk, an actual laugh. I feel like heaven struck oil.

"I'm going to take and tell him that," he says. "He will hate that."

"But what were you going to say?"

The sun is out now, baking my shoulder. Nothing makes me more nervous than April sun; the Springtime Breezes of Fear are far worse than the Hellstache January Sads. Necro shakes his head. "Maybe I'll remember. You'll have to give me time on that one. Patience comes to those who wait."

Back home, Mom stabs two candles in two chocolate cupcakes, and sings "Happy Birthday" with actual notes. She turns on the kitchen light. No other lights are on in the house, which makes me feel tired. She gets out this white box from the corner spin-drawer, removes the foam insulation from a pint glass inside, washes out the dust, and pours me a pint of Sam at the kitchen table. She cheerses with me.

"I remember, on my twenty-first birthday," Mom says, shoulders unshriveling for once. "I had finished at MCC, and the one semester I lived in the dorms at St. John's, my friends gave me a six-pack."

"Did you ever drink it?"

"I took six classes that semester!" She sets the edges of her lips to her pint glass, leaving tree-trunk-like rings of foam with each sip. "But under the bathroom sinks, there was a removable panel doohickey on the bottom, and below that panel, a hollow space. You weren't actually supposed to remove the panel, but I hid the cans there and closed the wood panel back on, so that someone else might find it who moved in after me."

And it's right here with my mom, where she hugs me Happy Birthday and my palms press into her shoulder fat, that we've maybe both said sorry. For the first time in a while, I can stay in tonight in the living room with the Fritos and milk—Inside with a capital In.

Later that night, from the kitchen, the phone rings. When Mom picks up, she peeks around the entrance to the living room, where I'm watching some VCR-Plussed Monday Night Raw. "Toby," she mouths.

I shake my head and mouth: "No."

"He's not here can I take a message?" Mom says. "Okay. Okay. Will do. Bye."

Before Mom finishes her pint of Sam Adams, she hands me an envelope containing three hundred dollars cash, for rent, which I immediately give back to her.

CUNNAHOS

The next morning, the Manpower Skills Assessment Center in Greece has gray fabric partitions to divide its six computers. The only other applicant at a computer is a large lady with a neck tattoo and a bullfrog chin.

A gray box appears at the center of the computer screen and tells me to enter the formula that adds numbers in Excel. A timer counts down in the bottom corner. On the typing test, the last sentence I type is: "Why, then, would one run in the rain, when one would get as equally wet as they would walking?"

Back in the waiting room, a rectangle with doors at both ends and a reception window, my recruiter brings out the results sheet.

"You crushed the Word functions portion, you crushed the Word typing portion." He's tall and Irish, like a college basketball player, leftover freckles in his face and these thick-framed rectangular glasses. "Your Excel?" He tilts his head at the results sheet. "Now, I can push the Word. I can go hard at that with clients. But clients are looking for Excel, at least for the positions that would be a match for your educational background. Now I'm not taking away from your C's—you passed and nobody can take that—the A in Home Ec. But, I mean, do you know Access?"

Since he's already shaking my hand, I tell him No.

"Buy a book. I mean, we'll call if we get a bite. But buy a book."

Mom has lent me the car, so I drive to Pittsford. I fill out an application at Fantastic Records. I write on the application that I would prefer not to work a register. For available hours, I write 3 p.m. to 7 p.m., Monday through Thursday. I write on my application at Richardson's: "No waiter jobs, dish-washer: yes."

Back home, I call Costello's. I call Kaufmann's. I end calls with "Hope to hear from you soon."

I check NecronicA. Two new drawings. One is this sketch of a skater kid with fat laces on his shoes and a spark coming from the tip of his shoelace. Another is of a ghost hand, spraying fire from the mouth in its palm at a pink, meat-textured car with headlight eyes who is clearly a character I drew once at a sleepover—the Hamaro, the Camaro made of ham.

So, to keep up with Necro, to keep up with NecronicA, I stack the still-hot plates from the dishwasher. I start to get hungry, so I drink a glass of milk, bring the phone down the hall to my room, and nap off a hunger headache.

Much later, in my armpit, I hear a digitized bleating noise. Which, I remember, is actually the phone, ringing me awake. I can't see anything in my room, because the blinds are closed and it's now seventy-five percent dark outside, hours past business hours.

"Nathan, how are ya this is Danielle from Kelly Services," Danielle says on the phone. I sit up and clench down a yawn. Her voice is squeaky but gentle. I've never seen her, not once.

"I'm calling because I've found a position in Henrietta that we think would be a great fit for you and they would like to set up an interview!"

"Really!" The entire inside of my body vacuums the carpets, throws the loose-elastic underwear in the hamper, scrambles to regain Happy Rolodex form.

"The job is as a cashier at a local but expanding retailer called Qualtech," she says. "The hours would be Tuesday through Sunday, 1 p.m. to 10 p.m.. Pay starts at $6.50 per hour, and increases with prolonged employment. It could be a great position—just to build some experience—before you make a bigger career move."

Immediately, the inside of my head becomes concrete-solid with what I'd be missing if I took this job. Because when Necro works a day-shift week, he gets out at 6, home at 6:30, done eating at 7, and if I don't have a chance to call him between 7 and 8, then he's out somewhere, probably sharing that "So forget about the old lady!" tagline—which me and him found funny together—with Weapons of Mankind.

"So what do you say?" Danielle says. I can almost see her smiling on the other end.

"Well—I have things going on during the weekends," I say. "I also can't use a register, so, I guess I don't think I'm interested—"

Her voice firms. "We have been inundated with applications for this position—people calling: 'What about this
cashier position?' I'm a little concerned, given our previous
attempts to place you, over what we're going to do if I can't
find another match."

"I guess I just think my strengths are in loading, unloading, stock boy."

I hear what's either phone static or a sigh on the other end.

"Well I will continue to work with you if anything comes
up!" she says, perky but annoyed. The hang-up feels like a pen
jabbed into my ear.

I call Necro. Robot Message Voice. After I go back to
bed, I hear Fake Dad No. 3's keys splash on the kitchen table.
Mom's footsteps, too. The bedroom door closes.

So I open the garage. The car's orange gas-tank Empty light
is on, but I drive out anyway. My legs feel weak and ticklish.
I feel comfy and sick, the way my body would try to convince
itself it had the flu when I wanted to stay home from school.
Light bleeds brightly everywhere in the wet road. Only a few
heads lean over tables in the Main Applebee's windows.

I drive to one of the hills we used to go to, so I can stare
at the skyline, alone, after no more Good Times are left
in locations like these. On one side of the road is a brown-
paneled apartment complex, and on the other, the hilldrop,
and far off, the skyline, where we'd look at the Hyatt and the
building with the revolving restaurant, and tell jokes about
who would win in a fight between a windmill and a water
tower, or imagine how funny it would be if women chose
boyfriends based on their Eddie Vedder impersonations

("His baritone register on 'Jeremy' was so much deeper than mine!").

But then I step out of the car and onto the slippery grass of somebody's yard. I look over the hill into the way-down-town, and a huge brain-blister explodes.

Two smoke trails converge in the sky, like a wishbone, and, below them, fires, like a pair of pumpkin eyes across the darker flats of the city. Two fires, I might add, for the two drawings on NecronicA.

So I drive around to try and find Necro—just so I know he's somewhere not near there. Because if he was around yesterday, maybe that means he's around tonight. Past the A-Plus, which is now a Hess, where Necro locked himself in the freezer; past the Harro East, where Necro bought me tickets to see Rollins; past the Penny Arcade, where there's always metal, but no Necro.

Then, back in Gates, suddenly my car won't go above three miles per hour, and I realize the car has run out of gas.

I coast to a stop on a bridge over the Erie Canal, which has fog over it and a fish-skin iridescence on the water. I walk around looking for a pay phone but don't find any. So I walk, for a while, up the longish, weeds-crowded driveway that clears into the empty park and ride.

Mosquitoes hover over pond-sized puddles surrounding the bus stop—a glass enclosure that's three phone booths long. There is no noise anywhere. After leaning against one of the bus stop's outer steel posts long enough to feel like I'm posing for a photo, headlights trickle through the plant life, and the bus hisses to a stop. I get on and nobody gets off.

Inside, the bus seats are plastic, orange like a seventies kitchen. The fluorescent lighting is stale and fluttery. Ads in Spanish line the curves where the windows meet the ceiling. Three other people sit in sweats and winter jackets, stumpy as trash bags. The bus gags into gear, wavering our shoulders, shifting our fat, putting us to sleep.

Except, it turns out the bus, actually, is heading downtown, and away from Gates. But: Are you looking at this guy sitting directly across from me?

Even if I never find Necro tonight, check off the boxes: this flat-faced, toothbrush-shaped guy, skin whiskey colored, tall enough that, when he sits, his legs are spread out spider-style; this ancient leather jacket where every crease looks stiff; shaved-headed, brow and nose angled downward. One of his scars pushes the corner of his right lip inward. And: he has this ping-pong-ball-shaped divot in his head right near his hairline. In other words, he is a Raw Dog's Raw Dog.

Because, sometimes, you have to take a bus somewhere. Right, Necro?

Raw Dog steps off the bus at One Millionth Street and Crack Avenue. When I step off the bus to follow him, I'm already a hangnail salad, given that I'm still dressed for interviews, dressed for the 2028 Khakipocalypse. A woman in a wheelchair across the street vomits into a pail. There's a cardboard panel in place of a window at a Checks Cashed.

I follow Raw Dog, around the trash bags on the sidewalk, past a porn store that smells like dish detergent. Raw Dog walks fast, in eighth gear, but he walks with a *limp*. Which would be, if I were much smarter, Bad Sign No. 1.

But I'm absolutely convinced right now, four hundred percent, that Raw Dog will out-Good-Story and out-Maverick-Jetpants anything Necro might be doing tonight.

Raw Dog double-checks behind him and goes into what looks like a building whose first floor is brick and whose second floor is blue house paneling. A sign on the window says WE RESERVE THE RIGHT TO BE SELECTIVE.

The bar's door is iron and its doorframe skims my scalp, like the frame was built in the 1600s when all men were hobbits. Inside it's as dark and bacterial as inside someone's boot. When I sit down, I'm already a tourist, a neon highlighter. Everyone else there is enormous: a grizzle-fest of only men.

"I know you from the bus," Raw Dog says, suddenly right next to me. I expect an accent, but his voice is Mr. Rogers-American. Whatever cologne he's wearing smells like sunned-up propane.

"Yeah, I ride the bus," because that's what I think people in the way-downtown say.

Raw Dog swats it off. His small-pupiled eyes are like tiny concentric rings of bluebird feathers.

"Did I see you at something down here, a while ago?" he says. Which should be Bad Sign No. 2: The Proto-Stachening, the way he phrases this, without specifying.

"Weapons of Mankind?" I say. "I went to one a while ago downtown?"

"I'm sure that's where," Raw Dog goes. "What's your name?"

"Nate," I go, trying not to stare at his head-divot. "I'm friends with Andrea. I was trying to find him."

"Andrea; right. Welcome aboard," Raw Dog goes, not introducing himself back. He shakes my hand, this soft, hairstylist-type handshake.

"Come here in this place twenty years ago?" he goes. "Guys getting thrown out of windows. The Inn upstairs, they shut it down. The phone keys were plucked off. A raccoon was living in one of the bathtubs."

"Wow!" I say, laughing girlishly.

"It's about to get way nicer now, it's already happening. I'm in real estate. We're fighting to get solid minds into apartments down here, and it's been working. See this thing?" He pulls up the left side of his button-down shirt. Clipped to his belt is this gray plastic box, the size of Lip Cheese's TI-82 calculator, with a tiny computer screen and a telephone cord that tucks into his pants.

"This cord?" he goes. "It goes into a generator, the size of a York Peppermint Patty, implanted up my butt. When I lose feeling in my legs and fingers, I press this button," he points to a green button, the size of an M&M, "and these wires send an electric shock up my spine."

"What happened?" I ask him.

"This was 1981 Old Rochester, my point being," he says. "I had to deliver papers to Philip Ayinger—the developer who liked to bet in the Canadian lottery with certain notable Italians," he goes, in this quick, casual way like this is a Stock Anecdote. "His wife was going to divorce him, and I found him in Bullwinkle's. I came in, envelope in hand, sat down next to him. He immediately takes off!"

"Oh man," I say, virginally.

"I chased him out of Bullwinkle's all the way up Lake Avenue, past the Kodak lot, past a CVS; I chased him up to near Holy Sepulchre. I chased him past three post offices. I chased him into the suburbs. And then, Ayinger swings around into the lot of a CVS, a different one, reaches into a dumpster, and pulls out a gun, like he'd taped it to the dumpster's inner wall in advance. So I run at him. I'm running—" He points his right index finger into his ribcage and his left index finger into the small of his back to mimic the bullet path. "The bullet chipped my spine. So if you want to get shot, get shot in the leg. Or, just take it through the head and get killed."

Raw Dog nods to a white guy across the room who has a beard the size of a grocery bag. "But problems like Shawcross? The Columbus Day bombings? They come in twenty-year cycles. That guts the landlord business." He gestures toward my tie. "But for a well-to-do guy like you, looking to make a move, you could get in cheap in this part of town, month to month. This building I'm talking to you about, I just rented out the second floor to a stockbroker. A day later, the city announced plans to turn some abandoned lots into parks. Gangs? You only have to worry about gangs if you're in prison."

I make a chin rest with my thumb and forefinger. A real-live Nate HQ: I'm already imagining Necro and Toby, groveling before me in designated shifts.

"We can drive down now, take a look," Raw Dog says. "I can get you in there next week. First month: Free. Hardwood floors, a billion square feet—you could turn this place into a nice little fuckpad."

We leave the bar, get into his rust-acne'd car, a Volkswagen hatchback. He revs the car until the engine sounds high-pitched, like a paper-shredder motor, then makes a right onto Lake Ave., where any walk alone is a long walk, and whose low slabs of closed businesses are broken up by grass and abandoned lots. A payphone's front panel has been ripped off. A man in a running suit is lying, facedown, on the sidewalk, arms at his sides.

And right when you think I'm going to out-Necro Necro, Raw Dog turns toward me and becomes Total Roasted Face of Satan: "Growing up here," he says, voice slower now, "there used to be a place that made white hots. I'd go in, they'd always say: Get out of here you bum! But I loved their white hots. They made the best sausage casing, Nate. I'm very specific about sausage casing."

He nudges his elbow toward the red Country Sweet restaurant, where there's a crowd outside, backlit by the light inside the place.

"All these niggers," Raw Dog goes. "They just walk around, man. Shitty apartments but everyone's got nice cars. What you doing, man? Not much, just hiding my drugs under this porch here, just hitting people in the head with a hammer. You know what these people need? They need to get somebody pregnant. Fatherhood, *that's* the real best policeman."

Get your free month, Nate, is the thought I'm clinging to. After that, find some job, and Raw Dog will be a name on a rent check.

We turn down some streets I don't recognize. Raw Dog stops the car. We get out. I don't see any apartment building, any lit-up entrances. Worse, there are no streetlights, and everything looks dark and algae-covered. Raw Dog stands over me. He leans his head-divot down toward me. "Go ahead. Stick your finger in it."

The air tightens in on me.

"You've been looking at it. Stick your finger into my head dimple."

"Oh—I can't, stick my finger—"

"Dammit, Nate, dammit!" He slaps his palm on the hood and leans his head-divot closer.

I'm stuttering for pay now: "What? I—"

"Can't, comes from the ancient word *cunnan*, which comes from Cunnahos, the ruler who burnt his children!"

"What?" I say.

"Can't, comes from *cunnan*! Which comes from Cunnahos, the ruler who burnt his children!" He is screaming this. His breath is warm like a neck against a cold hand. "Repeat it!"

"Um, can't, comes from Cunnahos, the ruler who—"

"Say it harder!" his voice echoes.

"Can't comes from cunnan which comes from Cunnahos the ruler who burnt his children!"

I press my finger into the divot and look away. It has this smoother-than-bone feeling, like skin over plastic. Technically speaking, my Holy Grail Points have punctured the heavens. But it is clear: I Have Made a Terrible Mistake Tonight.

When I look up, Raw Dog is holding a rusted crowbar.

"Hand over your wallet and don't ever come to the city again," Raw Dog says. "Hand over your wallet, with your precious, moneyed, lightened, plural hands."

Except out of nowhere, I feel something like rabies gush through my spine. Because I can't get a job, can't get a Plan, can't get a Home or a Cash and can't get a Nate HQ. Suddenly I'm whipping index fingers, closing my eyes, and yelling into the air in front of me: "You thought I was rich? You thought I could move into an apartment and make a place nicer? My food chews itself, out of fear. When I make love to the ground, trees grow! I hope you have a lot more room up there besides that prod, because—"

I don't see or feel it so much as I get this computer reaction of: I have been hit, in the forehead, with a crowbar. A sneaker scrapes the pavement near my ear, everything the color of burlesque. I feel my wallet float upward, whispering against my pocket lining's fabric, and a second later, feel it slap down between my shoulder blades.

When I wake up, I'm nowhere to be found. A van is parked nearby with missing tires. The boltwork of the overpass above me loosens when cars pass.

I stick a newspaper to my head and stand up. The top three inches of my head feel like they're draining through a water filter. The blood tonguing down my face turns everything mucus colored.

After years of sidewalks and store-window gates, I walk into what is apparently a diner—I can't tell completely because if I look straight ahead I get blood in my eyes. The brightness inside empties out my head.

"All right?" a waitress asks me in a Spanish accent. Forks tick against plates.

"Just call a cab," I say.

She sits me down at a booth. "Put this on," she says and wraps two dishrags around my head. Her face is like seeing a million pictures of moms bunched into one.

I try to scratch the back of my head, so I maybe look casual. Because, my initial reaction is, I'm actually embarrassed. As in, can I get a job looking like this? Will girls not like me because I'm bleeding? Then, I feel the first sobs being sucked out of my face. Here they come.

"I can't do anything right," I say.

The waitress yells something in Spanish. One of the cooks dials on a rotary phone.

"All anyone does is lie to me," I say.

"Cab is on the way," she says, then pats my shoulder and hands me a napkin. She does this all with one hand, because, with her other hand, she's holding a dinner plate with a hamburger on it.

After the cab comes, I'll get thrown out and walk the rest of the way when the driver finds out I have no money. But for now, sliding up the 490 onramp, I listen for the different grades of pavement—the way the cab sounds like water through pipes on a gray patch of bridge, or the way it sounds creamier over sections of newer, blacker pavement. Cars with blacklights mounted to their undercarriages blast by, and the cab feels better than a bed on wheels, with me finally knowing, my God, the city actually ends.

THE SADNESS
CUSTARD MONTAGE

A tornado-swipe later, my head is on Mom's lap in the back-seat of Fake Dad No. 3's Hyundai. Street lamps are overhead, a BlueCross BlueShield blimp in the sky. The fluids in my head shift as the car shifts lanes.

"That's not a fight," Fake Dad No. 3 says, his voice weirdly non-Thundertrident-ish. "In a sustained physical altercation, there would be a real mangled quality."

"But look at him bleed," Mom says. Her palm is sweating when she places it on my forehead.

"Please try not to Patronize the Victim, Debra," Fake Dad No. 3 says.

"I'm not Patronizing the Victim, Gareth."

"Goddammit Debra you are Patronizing the Victim, you're only using one parental tool. If you only use one parental tool, you're going to inflict trauma!" he says, yanking the car over a lane. "I'm only being transparent with you, okay; I'm only being transparent with you."

Mom leans over me, so I can only see her face and a little

bit of one of the Holy-Shit Handles above the rear passenger-side window. And Mom, whose maiden name is Portfolio Insurance, she literally whispers to me:

"If somebody hurt you, in a fight, I can call a friend who knows someone who is a trained professional, who can take care of people who do these things."

"Mom, what?" I say.

Which makes me start crying, because even if I am laughing, I'm still bleeding operas all over the car. Mom tries to squeeze my arm, but I twist toward the seat well because I don't like it when she touches me.

Later that night, two butter-colored curtains separate off my hospital bed from the other beds. When the doctor arrives, I stare at his mouth cover. Out of the corner of my left eye, I see him pull a thread, stretched tight, thin like a saliva strand, out from my forehead. The X-rays show a white, pencil-line crack running across my skull's cheek, ending at the eyehole. Otherwise, my skull looks like every skull I've seen in history, and this causes a Sadness Custard Montage within a Sadness Custard Montage.

"Do I need a skull-cast?" I ask the nurse.

"Heads generally heal on their own," she tells me.

Back home, the afternoon is beautiful, tree leaves like flashing camera bulbs in the sun. Outside, Mom runs the lawnmower underneath the living room window. On the TV, celebrities walk around with their smug, unscarred foreheads.

Before dinner, while I'm in the bathroom, I hear the phone ring. "He's not here, Toby," Mom says. I peel the bandages off. A crayon-line of scar curves across the right side of my forehead. I have a swollen werewolf brow; my right eye is maroon and puffed shut.

When I meet Real Dad at his room in Penfield Manse, I barely recognize him. His hair is buzzed short, and he's wearing a tweed jacket, plaid shirt, and black jeans. His place, for whatever reason, is bright, well swept, and smells like Windex. The hardwood floor shines, the fish tank with music magazines is gone, dishes no longer piled up to the chin of the sink faucet. The little ashtrays he made out of tinfoil, that he folded into the shapes of boats or stars, that he set on everywhere so he wouldn't have to lean forward to ash out his cigarettes—gone too.

"After the last time I saw you, I figured: Time for Change. Mötley Crüe," he says. "The way that album is all Midgets and Piss, and then impossibly, inexplicably, the last song is 'Time for Change,' with a children's choir."

I sit down on the loveseat, whose cushions and creases have been cleared of crumbs and novelty rock cards—which are like baseball cards, but with members of Saxon.

"Because," he continues, "all I've spent my money on since I've moved here is Belgian beer and these workplace training and conduct videos that I like to make fun of. What would the nightlife guides say? Saunter around the 'suppository-wrapper-littered' bedroom floor in this BoHo entry with the 'finest samplings' from the 'condiment fridge?'"

Which immediately reminds me of how Raw Dog described my non-Nate-HQ, and I get that knot in my throat, the Sniffling, Part 8: The Proto-Proto-Stachening. The tightening in the pipes, whole parts of my life pulling out of me through my eyes.

He leans forward, standing over me. "Well, your Mom is still with BCBS," he says, in his stable, un-sneery, talking-to-Mom voice, which he never uses around me. Which can only mean I've done something horrible or really acted out in some way I can't even understand.

"The stitches alone: probably a $2,000 operation," Real Dad says. "You're expensive."

My shoulders buckle. His hand hovers over my back, like he's trying to figure out whether to pat it.

"Okay, let's not," Real Dad says, looking around for a Kleenex, maybe. "Just settle down for a second."

He sits down next to me. He has a new coffee table as well—black and rectangular in a sushi-place way.

I drag a few sniffles the weight of staplers. "I have a question."

Real Dad sits forward, forearms on knees, and folds his hands and looks at me. No Wall of Comedy.

"You don't think I'm stupid, right?" I go. "You think I'm funny, right?"

Real Dad cycles through a few facial expressions. I stare at the floor, and feel his weight shift on the loveseat.

"You know, the last time I heard of anyone being down on Lake Avenue was that Foreigner song, 'Rev on the Red Line.' Only song, ever, about Rochester that went national," he says. "Completely inaccurate. This is the most difficult city in America to get laid in. You've seen me keep the two-second distance; seen my well-placed signaling. Women here are not at all after good drivers."

I laugh. The snot muscles diffuse a bit. I can breathe regularly again.

"At least there's this." He reaches down under an end table between the loveseat and the wall, and tosses a crumpled ball of birthday wrapping paper in my lap. "It's late. But Guns N' Roses never performed on time either, and you know what it got them?"

"Are you asking? Right now?"

"Pussy. The old Bensonhurst Grapevine."

"The old Manchester Pizza Hut," I sniffle residually.

"The old Klem Road North Medicine Ball."

I toss the wrapping-paper ball from hand to hand. Real Dad runs his thumb along his cheek, like he's unused to how it feels after shaving.

"How about you just open it before I start to hate myself?" he says.

I un-wad the Happy Birthday layer of the wrapping-paper ball. Then, in a way that sort of looks like finding a piece of steak spit into a napkin—and I mean that in the most neutral way possible—I see this piece of loose-leaf paper, folded into eights. Written on it are the letters G, A, D, Bm, G, A, D, Bm, all the way down the page.

"Oh wow! Thanks Dad! Wow! This is—this is great! Wow! Thanks!"

He plucks the piece of paper from my hand. "You don't know what it is yet—you don't even have the perceivability to even *intuit* what this is."

"So what is it?"

"What—it—it's a song!"

"Oh."

"The lyrics aren't all in place yet," he goes. "Still sort of in the conceptual phase."

"So, it's just chords?"

"Chords is half the song, Nate! Did Van Dyke Parks walk into the studio and shit out the Metropolitan Museum of Art? He had chords." He shapes the chords with his left hand. "But the song's about, I've decided right now, it's how you don't take crap from people when, say, you're stopped at a red light, and some guy comes up, opens your hood, and jerks off into your brake fluid."

The sun gets some cloud cover, which rounds away the sharp shadows but makes the room brighter. "I know you're on the rocks with your friends," he says. "Debra said something about this Toby guy. Calling you. And, I can sense, this Toby, he's been stressing you out, man."

"It's Necro. He's supposed to get thousands of dollars from this guy—" I begin to say, but Real Dad's pulling out his bass guitar case from under the loveseat and unlatching it, and I think the case rumbling across the wood floor drowns me out.

"That's what I'm getting at with this song," he says. "Because Toby? He's thinking, this Nate guy, he's got one up on me. He's thinking," and, then, Real Dad plucks a single note on the bass quietly, "he's thinking, 'I have nothing. So how can I jerk off into Nate's brake fluid?'"

Before this conversation gets strange, I go: "Wow. G, A, D—this sounds good."

Before I even get to the hallway to leave, I'm already squeezing out laughter to myself, joke material squiggling through my head like mosquitoes.

MOCKTANE / SNAKESHIELD

But one evening, warm with almost-June, the phone rings.

Ring! The thin wall of air between my heart and my chest. I'm thinking: Pinning Bow Ties on the Dead still, Toby? Why don't you take your dairy-quake face and—

"Nate?" a girl's voice says on the phone. "Hi! This is Mindy Fale!"

Immediately, I'm pacing in the dark in my kitchen. My face still looks like a drag-queen werewolf—my eyes are marooned and yellowed, my brow still swollen. The white in my right eye is deep red. Since water is bad for the scar, I still shower with Mom's shower cap.

"I've been looking through the phone book." Her voice is milder, less like an angry Bills fan's, on the phone. "And I thought: Nate!"

She goes on. "You remember Goody, Ertsy, Ninjacotta— those guys are back. And I was calling, well, because my friend Chad knows about a party at the Pines, and he's pretty cool, and, so, you should go."

Immediately, I'm polished by choir voices. I slick back my hockey hair and grab my black windbreaker, the nice one, and head out the door.

The party is in Fairport, a suburb on the Erie Canal with craft-showsy houses. The Pines of Perinton is Fairport's equivalent to the projects—these white, plaster-sided apartment buildings hoisted up by steel beams, with parking spaces underneath.

I walk up the steeper-than-normal stairs and hear music rubbing up against the walls. Inside the apartment, it's Pubertypalooza. Here was me at any party, thin enough to shine a flashlight through my chest; me, before I started carrying my wallet in my back pocket.

The oven light is the only light on in the place. Whoever's apartment this is is furnished like a porn set: no pictures on the walls; a single chair in the living room and one of those fold-out sofas that's all foam padding and no wooden frame—the idea of a furnished place. A sweatpantsed woman with a wide part down the middle of her hair reads the newspaper and eats microwaved fish at the kitchen table. A glass pipe is next to her coffee mug.

Through the living room, I step over a few bird-shaped girls with baggy pants and greasy hair dye who sit Indian-style on the office-gray carpet; girls with chain wallets who will either rediscover the Gap and grow into the nasal, flat-A's Rochester accent, or commit permanently to Gargoyle Trashdom. The boys have their various neck beads, skater pants, and T-shirts that go down to their thighs. One comes up to me and says, in a robot-type voice: "The only system that can function is an egalitarian system because humans by nature are non-autonomous." He marches away. All his friends laugh.

In a spare bedroom with no windows or closet, Mindy Fale is sitting on a bare mattress on the floor. She has blond highlights in her hair since I last saw her and extra cheek mass. She's touching the arm of this wolfman-looking guy who has a full head of wild gray hair and a shirt that says "Chaditude" on the front with a picture of him skydiving. She's still in what look like work clothes—black pants and those black, both-sex Reeboks, white button-down shirt untucked.

You talk to Necro, and he'll yell out: Night at the Stalls! Which was Necro's phrase to describe loud, lumbering girls. You talk to Toby, he'll tell you how she married that twenty-six-year-old guy, named Jamie Something, who went off to the military, and how they divorced after he came home and he spent all day wandering Irondequoit Mall, buying nothing. But I always thought Mindy Fale was nice. I liked having her to stare at. I got high once and told Necro I wanted to drink her face.

"Whoa Nate!" she says to my face. "You in a fight?"

"No," I say. "Accident—car."

"Did they throw all the debris in your car afterward? Did you have to draw the accident?" she says. She leans forward, up from the wall, and pinches my wrist from the mattress—"*Mmmmocktane!*"

I refuse to say Snakeshield. I always hated that joke.

"What? No Snakeshield? Chad has Snakeshield; he's curse-insulated."

"Good for both of you."

"I met Chad earlier this afternoon," she says. "He was staring at the book I was reading—Anne Rice!—when I was at Denny's." She gestures to the wolfman guy on the couch. "Chad! This is Nate, and this is Nate's face!"

Chaditude nods his head and resumes staring at Mindy Fale. He's a guy who I already know doesn't laugh or who owns a pet snake or makes his own guitars. He'll be the guy I'll pray leaves first.

That was one thing about Mindy Fale, always: She befriends the worst people. Here she was, once—back when she was much bonier and her T-shirts fitted her like nightshirts—at Countryside Billiards, which looked like a dentist's office converted to a pool hall. "Nate! This is Adrik! He speaks Russian!" she said then, and pointed to a crumpled man with a denim baseball hat standing near the vending machines.

Along those lines, I sit down in a beanbag chair—when beanbag chairs are always taken at parties—and settle in for a wait-off between me and Chaditude.

"Because Neil Peart, what Neil did was those ride patterns." Chaditude air-drums the patterns, right hand twitching epileptically. He slides his arm around her, holds both her hands up, as if to have her play air drums.

But, sometimes, you're looking through your brain's archives, and next thing, I remember stories I haven't told anyone in years. I tell Mindy Fale about that one time me and Necro were standing in the high school parking lot, doing nothing illegal, and we bolted when the school's red security van pulled into the parking lot just because we wanted to be

chased, and so we ran through the woods, and I slid across
the ice of the creek and my knee fell in, and how I could feel
my one pant-leg stiffening. "Hey Mr. Education: You can't
Riot with us!" I tell them I yelled, even though it was actually Necro. I tell them about the time I got a disorderly after
I Nazi-saluted Luckytown Hastings, and spent over twenty-
four hours in jail because Mom was on vacation in Bakersfield
and Real Dad was at a show at the Bug Jar. I get Mindy Fale
to laugh so hard she leans over and places her hand on my
knee. I tell them about The Pizzeria Uno Bag on Necro's
Car—all the best ones.

Chaditude crosses his legs, tightly, at his ankles, and begins to say: "We used to race cars sometimes—"

"We once lifted a soccer goal and set it in the road!" I go,
totally cutting him off.

I talk so much and so loud my voice gets sandpapery;
I talk so much that Chaditude doesn't even have a chance to
speak—total Conversation Box-Out. Until finally, later that
night, Chaditude braces his hands against his knees to push
himself up. "Well, shit. I'm gonna go," he says.

As in, slow motion replay: W-E-L-L, S-H-I-T, I'M,
G-O-N-N-A, G-O.

"Well nice to meet you today," Mindy Fale says, etc. etc.
etc.! We'll completely read together in the park, she tells him,
etc., etc.; of course you can play with my hair, etc., etc.!

"And then it'll be like we're married," Chaditude says,
tartening himself up into Pity-Jello.

"Of course, sweetie."

And because Chaditude apparently runs an absolute

Bakery of Long Goodbyes, of course she has to hug the guy, and he has to run his hand through her hair, and hug her again, and, then, finally! He leaves.

I've spent so much of the night looking at Mindy Fale that I don't even notice that everyone—except the goth-trash still sitting on the living-room floor—has left the apartment. There are cigarette burn marks on the mattress, an empty Tostitos bag floated against a table lamp, a yellow scrunchie on the bedroom carpet.

"Mocktane," she pinches my shoulder when she sits back down.

I still refuse to do Snakeshield.

She lights a menthol. Her purple-sparkle nail polish is chipped. "So, your face, man."

I bum a menthol off her; the smoke is like Dentyne and Novocain. I tell her about Raw Dog, about going into the Mattresses in the Streets District. I rest my head against the wall. Blood and mucus drain into my throat, and I swallow.

"What were you doing down there at all," she says, more accusing me than asking.

Which I have no answer for. "Bored."

She stares at the ceiling and shakes her head. "Only men, who do this," she says, "who think if they do that one stupid thing just once then everything will change. At least when Chad saw me today, he could talk about my shirt. He could at least notice that if I can't stay in school, I can still look good."

That's what I hate. She will never, ever say no to a man.

"He's also total Chaditude," she says, tonguing something off one of her incisors. "Speaking of downtown." She slaps her thighs and stands up. "Ertsy and Mike found this video. You will love this."

We move to the living room and sit on the foam sofa. The goth-trash sitting on the floor lean toward one another more, and the VCR makes a blender noise as the tape rewinds.

The video itself, a colorized thing made in 1963 by Jam Handy with Rochester Gas and Electric as a sponsor, is some advertisement for the city. Women, dressed up like boxed chocolate, walk through Midtown Plaza. The title flashes, in white lettering: ROCHESTER: A CITY OF QUALITY. Faces are pink and cheeks extra shaded like dolls. But actually, I'm too busy staring at Mindy Fale's rainbow socks.

"Oh! How is John Violi? Ravioli Violi," she says. "You heard what happened, right?"

"I was right there."

"So you almost died, then."

I shrug at her. "If you're going to be negative about it."

"Did you ever kind of think that maybe Necro— Conspiracy Booth Andrea—did it? Like maybe that joke was true? Like we'd all wake up one day, and the skyline would be gone, and Andrea would be walking away, kicking a rock, like, 'I took and dropped my cigarette in a bucket of paint thinner,' or whatever?"

I feel myself working into an earthquake.

"Well you don't need to look at me," she says. "It's a joke."

The video shows Midtown Plaza's Clock of Nations— a white pillar with a red clock face at the top, with spinning chandelier arms and, at their ends, silver pods, each big enough to fit a toddler into. Every hour, the video's narrator says, the doors to the pods open, and marionettes, representing different nationalities, spin on strings inside.

The video shows overhead shots of the Genesee River, crowded with trees. The narrator says that, according to Native American myth, the Finger Lakes were formed when a giant reached down and scraped his fingers through the soil.

"I'm not mad that you brought it up," I say. "Necro: talking about weapons and emanating domain. It's just—I wish people I knew had to carry around a card with them, like a driver's license, that said, 'Yes, I'm Staying,' or 'No, I'm sorry.'"

"I hear you, I hear you," she says. "Like: I'm someone who really hates fakery and hypocrisy. Those are just two things with me. Like Kelly Elmwood. If I didn't know her and love her, I'd hate her. I swear to God that bitch is so dumb."

"And Wicked College John, too," I say. "I mean, it's awful—his condition. Don't get me wrong. It's very sad. But there was this friend of his who they called Sleeps when I visited Bonaventure last fall. Sleeps had this chrome skull mounted above the license plate of his SUV, and the skull's eyes lit up—red—when he hit the brakes. Sleeps had some friend up from New Haven that weekend, too, this kid who had a teardrop tattooed under his eye, so everyone in the dorm was whispering, "He killed somebody." We spent the whole weekend driving this kid, who was in the Solids, to campus movie night, or to the coffee shop, or across the countryside foliage in this skull SUV. And Wicked College John was trying not to look scared around this kid, trying to talk up the one time he drove past—not down, past—Cuba

Place looking for drugs? And nobody calls Colonel Hellstache on this? About Wicked College John? About the skull?"

Mindy Fale nudges her elbow toward the screen.

"Have you ever heard of Genesee Fever?" the narrator says. "Historically, it was probably some kind of rash encountered by Colonel Nathaniel Rochester when he decided to utilize the water power of the Genesee Falls and build a settlement here."

"But yeah, Wicked College John is doing better," I say. "They have him on exercises."

The sunrise is like the top of a can being pulled off the sky. The narrator talks about how Rochester planned for future communities with "self-liquidating municipal parking units." A shot of the Kodak building, a shot of Bausch & Lomb and Xerox and the SC Electronics Store. "The stability of the work-force in Rochester makes for the stability of investments in Rochester," the narrator says. Eventually, the credits roll.

"Ken Nordine narrated this?" I say. "My dad has one of his albums."

"Midtown Plaza? Kind of a nice place then."

"Where was this city a few weeks ago?"

"Oh it's all right here," she says. "You can work hard if you want, but you don't have to work hard to survive, don't need money to be sophisticated. It's sort of recession-proof. Skull License Plate SUV Boy, at Bonaventure, could do very well here."

"He has a white wine and cocaine gland in his brain," I say.

"His stomach produces its own duck meat so he can digest it, crap it out, and donate it to charity."

"He's so sophisticated, he paid a doctor to perform plastic surgery on his colon," I go.

"He paid to have his nipples pinkened," she says.

"His shins gelatinized."

"He's so sophisticated, his cock is bilingual."

The laughing builds until we run out of room in our chests, until our lungs stutter their way up to our shoulders and can't go any further, until our ribs strain, until our necks hurt and there's sweat in the crease between my eyelids and my forehead. When we look up, the smoke in the middle of the room looks like a gorilla's face. Then, more laughing.

"He's so sophisticated," I say, "his balls bring their own glassware to wine-tasting parties."

The laughing whiffles out, and we come up for air.

"He's so sophisticated," she says, sputtering, "his taint's *agent*"—more sputtering—"his taint's *agent* regularly attends the Vienna ballet with him."

Which I'm not sure makes any sense, but we're sore now. I think at least the fabric of both our shirts is touching, but I can't tell if the feeling in my arm nerves is her, or me trying to make my brain squint hard enough to move her an inch closer.

"Nate!" Mindy Fale says before I leave, holding her arms out to hug me. Bilingual Cock? If I could marry a joke, I would.

The goth-trash rub their eyes and pull the cushions off the couch for pillows, in a routine-seeming way that implies they've dropped out of school and have gone to bed at this time on weeknights for the last year or two. I'm in such a good mood I drive through Irondequoit, and I drive past Kodak Park to stare at the Milk Crate Tower, its steam pinkened and sun-frothed. The parking lot is stretched out like elastic, and the cars look violent when the sun whites out their windshields.

Somewhere in there, beyond the right angles of pipes, Necro is working. Or sleeping. Like that one time he told me that napping spots were hidden across the factory, with pillows and blankets tucked away between machinery.

Maybe that's where he is, while I'm out here getting hugged: in a utility room or a crawl space of the factory where someone—thirty-five years ago, when Rochester was a City of Quality—brought in some old sheets, set them on the floor, and, in a legend-like way of their own, or maybe a reverse-legend, told nobody.

THE SIXTY-SIXTH LETTER

Except, Toby! I cross my front lawn in my socks to leave out the Monday trash, and his Taurus, all its windows rolled down, dust-bowls up my gravel driveway. "Come on get in, get in," he yells over the engine, the ends of his baby-gremlin-teeth smile tucked into his face-fat. "We found Necro. He's in Brockport. He's at that Weapons of Mankind Guy— Bambert L. Tolby? His house. I looked up the address! We're going Rioting on him."

Lip Cheese is in the rear passenger seat, because Lip Cheese knows I ride shotgun and never to call Shotgun No-Blitz No-Combat on me. He leans out his window and wipes the corners of his lips, spraying saliva. "I was bored the other night, so I drove past Necro's house?" he says. "So I park, and I sneak up to the driveway, and there's a manila folder in the front seat of Necro's car. And I try the door handle? And it's unlocked! So of course I go into Necro's car, and in the folder, I find this paper that says Bill of Lading? And it's from Dubai, in the United Arab Emir—you know, for potassium nitrate? Copper benzoate?"

Toby narrows his brow and bounces once or twice in his seat, either from amusement or adrenaline. "Go on, go on—get to the next part."

"I noticed: The bill was addressed to—you'll just love this, Nate, love it!—somebody by the name of James Mason."

Lip Cheese wipes his mouth again. "Mason? *Mister* Mason?" he says.

Bugs bounce off Toby's headlights.

Lip Cheese smacks the heel of his hand into his forehead. "The last name Mason? A reference to Mr. Mason? In *Red Dawn*?" he says. "It's a fake name, Nate. Timothy McVeigh did almost the exact same thing. One of McVeigh's favorite movies was *Brazil*, and he sometimes used the name 'Tuttle' as, like, a handle? They say him and his friend used fake names to rent storage space. These kinds of people that Necro hangs out with? They love *Red Dawn*."

And I realize that I have done something awful: I have created a Runaway Cockdrama. Because, we've never had a Cockdrama last longer than three months, which is the criteria for a Runaway Cockdrama. The average length of a Cockdrama? Nine days. Previous longest: the Great 1996 Cockdrama of TJ's Big Boy, which lasted one month. I don't even know if Toby and Lip Cheese even know if they're joking anymore, or if they've been joking for so long they've become serious.

I wonder if maybe I've actually been serious this whole time, too. Because, as much as a Runaway Cockdrama is more Textbook Colonel Hellstache than Gunpowder Gym Shorts (which, ask Toby about that), I've tried calling Necro, to tell him about Mindy Fale. Because, that hug from Mindy Fale? I turn that hug into gasoline. I ride that hug into the ground for all it's worth. So you'd think his Necro Doppler Natecast Sense would be blowing fuses right now, the way how, whenever something good is happening to one of us, whenever Holy Grail Points are being earned, we can detect it from across the city. So there's a part of me that still wonders: What has he been doing?

So I put on my flip-flops and get into Toby's car. We drive to the stiff grass and Camaros that make up Brockport. Because now that I think about it, I could stand to see Toby try to walk into whatever White Power Dungeon Bambert L. Tolby's presiding over, get into a few fights, see him and some Weapons of Mankind trolls swing their stomachs at each other. Combine that with Frank Sinatra songs, and you pretty much have the mood I've been in.

Except, when we get to the house in question, all these cars are parked on the sides of the streets. The house is this one-floor, sweat-stain-yellow thing with white window shut-ters on a block with basketball hoops and driveways that are long and flat enough to serve as makeshift half-courts. Three floodlights make a dome in the house's front yard. Meat hisses on a grill. Two lines of teenagers face each other and take turns doing running-man dance moves, in that way church kids love to dance. Adults in the lit, open garage gesture calmly and eat hamburgers and hot dogs held in napkins.

Toby and Lip Cheese get out and stare. Their faces? Round and mopey, like planets that were too dumb to get into the solar system.

"This was the address it said it was," Toby says to somebody.

A man with a sunken chest under a pink plaid dress shirt, backlit in the floodlight, walks up to us. He's shorter than me, shorter than most women, thin and muscley as a lead guitarist. There's no chinfat on him. His eyes and forehead are huge, with a gray buzz cut and skin as tan as pottery.

"Are you gentlemen from church?" the man says. His voice is like a mousse, like Casey's Top 40 putting me to bed on Sunday nights when I still listened to PXY.

And Toby suddenly, like a kid who just rang somebody's doorbell, says: "Is Andrea here?"

The man claps his hands together. "I am afraid he just left. There is, I'd venture, a forty percent chance of his return. But if you know Andrea, you know me. I'm Bambert Tolby, and I'm an *honest* boring buy on New Year's."

He doesn't so much smile as show us his upper and lower gums.

"It's a twist on a news quote, from a childhood friend, describing a very famous investor. We'll get you caught up. Shake my hand already! I'm hosting a fundraiser."

"Nate," I say. His handshake is strong but unintimidating in this dadlike way, like he's capable of giving really sheltering hugs, if things ever came to that.

"*The* Nate?" he pauses, like he's narrating *War of the Worlds*. "Could it be that I am beholding the legendary?

Pants-and-Nintendo, the Condor Wrap? I feel like I *know*. I feel like I was *there* for those conversations. What was that? 'Are you an adult? I—' The punch line escapes me."

"I've been tried as one." Which, I totally stole that joke from *Get a Life*, or *The Simpsons* maybe, and have just been carrying it around with me.

"Bah!" Bambert snaps his fingers. "That's it! I was close. Anyway, that's a welcome addition to the community quotables repertoire—we're all about community here."

But if I can Bring the Funny to Bambert, and Bambert can Bring the Funny to Necro, there is no way I'm giving away where I got that joke from.

"And I take it this is Toby?" Bambert says. "Hambone Toby Winter? Breaker of a Thousand Quarterbacks' Necks."

And since Hambone is the only nice nickname Toby's ever had, Toby shivers, like kindness just shot up his spine.

"And a knuckle-cruncher of a handshake," Bambert says, flexing his fingers after shaking Toby's hand. "You know, I should have you talk. I just had a conversation with the Gates-Chili district athletic director, and he told me they are hoping to fill an assistant coaching position for the fall. And how about you, Nate? What's new on your job front?"

I scan my brain for a grown-up way to respond: "It's slow going."

He raises his eyebrows and sighs. "I am surprised and not surprised. We've been a Kodak and Xerox town for so long that Rochesterians have forgotten how to network. We've forgotten how to engage—or, let me amend that—entrepreneurialize. I'll pull the ear of my contact at Ascentek. They're a recruiter on

East Ave. Very cool companies they're working with. Start-ups, entry-level sales."

So it goes on like this: me, fine dining on compliments and overall really polite conversation. Bambert turns to Lip Cheese, who's wiping his mouth, scratching his scalp. "Everyone pretty much calls me Lip Cheese," Lip Cheese says.

"The *smart* one," Bambert says.

"Wait—what?"

Inside Bambert's house, soda bottles and bowls and casserole pans crowd the space on the kitchen table, plastic wrap peeled off the tops of pasta bowls and bunched up. Each room is painted a different color—a deep red or a wet-concrete gray. In the living room, there's a single leather recliner and bulky, refrigerator-sized plasma-screen TV. On the floor, dust bunnies glide across a large, unoccupied space, where maybe a couch or coffee table was recently removed.

Which Lip Cheese squints at for a second, and Bambert pivots over quickly and tugs on his sleeve: "How about let me show you the basement?"

The basement is brightly lit, with bare sheetrock and carpets thrown over the floor. There are empty weapons racks and hook-like holders bolted to the walls. Propped up in the corner, on the floor, is a single hatchet with some Japanese logo on the blade. There are two metal-framed futons.

"I used to keep weapons," Bambert says. "We were just off-loading some inventory. Sit, sit."

He keeps looking at Lip Cheese. "How's your friend? Andrea visited him and said he's thinking sharp."

"He beat me at Connect Four," Toby says.

"What wonderful news, wonderful." Bambert leans back and folds his hands. "Maybe Andrea told you: I tried to open a weapons store in Webster, and there was this fire there. I do many things—a real multihyphenate. But after my insurance claim was denied"—Bambert looks upward—"that, right there, was a sign that maybe I should devote my full attention to what I've always wanted to do: generate community and housing reinvestment strategies and promote ideal-exchange thereof—like a local Habitat for Humanity with an addendum that we also promote artistic and futurist thinking. These people here tonight—churchgoers, real estate developers, donors, the local elites. There's some real pull, in that front yard. You are among the giving."

Bambert keeps looking at Lip Cheese, who squats down and touches the flat of the hatchet blade. "So!" Bambert's chin flicks upward. "You taking a helicopter to Paychex yet? Company car?"

I totally get ready for Lip Cheese to rain stutters and saliva. But instead he goes: "Well? My supervisor finally ended the relationship with my staffing agency and brought me on as a full-time employee—I'm sure they don't miss the fees. Generally they've got me reviewing payroll forms, following up with clients if they forget to give us somebody's Social; putting out fires when we process a check for 350 hours in the week as opposed to 35, things like that."

I look at Toby, because how is Lip Cheese's office talk not directly in Toby's wheelhouse? Except Toby, too, is leaning forward this whole time, forearms on his thighs, holding eye contact with Bambert and settling his face into a frown like he's talking business.

"And Hambone Toby Winter, you're bred right here in Rochester?" Bambert says.

Toby wipes some flattery sweat off the side of his nose. "Actually, England, man, England," he says, in this corporate-casual tone that I'm totally sure he uses all the time at American Canning Co. "Born in England, but only for a second."

England!!?! I clench my chest to keep from cracking up. "My grandparents had my dad in Bury, England," Toby says. "And my grandmother raised my dad in England, while Grumpiss went to America for a few years after the Lever brothers worked out this deal to build their office in—what, Nate."

I throw up my hands and look at Bambert, who recrosses his legs. As a last resort, I look at Lip Cheese, but he also crosses his legs at me.

"Come on," I say. "England?"

"Grumpiss worked for the contractor that constructed Lever House in Manhattan in the 1950s, Nate," Toby says. "It's a city landmark. And years later, my dad, back in England, met my mom, and they had me. I was hardly even born yet when Grumpiss helped my dad get a job in the Lever soap factory in Philadelphia, unloading the copra."

I literally slap my knee. "I'm sorry. It's the soap. I mean—"

Bambert folds his arms, makes a chinrest with his thumb and index finger. So if Toby and Lip Cheese are going to ball-hog the compliments, then Perhaps a Decree is in Order, to

Turn This Titanic of Conversation Back Into the Darkness, said Cunnahos, the ruler who burned his children.

"So Toby and Lip Cheese wanted to figure out what Necro does when he comes here," I say.

Bambert chuckles in this hazelnut, Christmas-special way. "He does lots of things. He's drawn up a few flyers, done a few mass mailers, he worked on producing an introductory video explaining what we do. I met him and his dad at a parks department meeting, of all places, earlier last year. He cares about the area. But mostly, all me and Andrea are, are two renegade lunatics who played Magic before you got here."

"Because it's funny," I say. "Lip Cheese was thinking Andrea was buying chemicals under fake names. Like Timothy McVeigh's storage."

But before Toby and Lip Cheese can schedule a primetime begging contest for me to unsay that, something pinkens in the tanness of Bambert's forehead.

"Right now, gentlemen, Andrea and myself want to get interesting ideas and sustainable housing innovations on the table. I'm not interested in spinning yarns, or the implication inherent in denial. We're interested in the study by the Boston Fed that found rampant discrimination in housing lending practices. We're interested in neighborhoods that need these initiatives. Neighborhoods want residencies for people like Andrea, and neighborhoods get angry when city paperwork holds them back. That's why Interesting Ideas is this organization's name."

"Is that part of Interesting Films?" Lip Cheese says.

Bambert's Adam's apple turns over. His pupils retreat into his eyes. His lower lip forms two or three words before he says, hoarsely, like he swallowed an ice cube: "E-excuse me, what was that?"

"Your film company," Lip Cheese says. "You made some movie, and some Retargers of Retargery charged you with stealing their money and said you made some racist movie?"

Bambert narrows his brow at Lip Cheese, looking for secret codes. He appears to find what he's looking for and resets his face.

"Right. Transparency. Didn't remember the name of my own company for a second!" He shakes his head and laughs through his nose. "The smart one! Now, look. At the most, in my life, I merely dipped my toes into White Power. I had friends, who I'd long ago lost touch with, who put commas between their first and last names as a linguistic maneuver to ward off the IRS. I had friends who would listen only to vocal recordings by a eunuch in Switzerland because that was the only music they could listen to that was cleansed of non-white influence. But my movie was not hateful. My movie was supposed to be a futuristic send-up of the German propaganda during the war. The problem is, when someone gives you money, for anything, it becomes work. I got as far as the poster."

He pulls a cardboard tube out from under the basement stairwell and unrolls a poster inside. The title says LETTERS TO GOD AND THE THIRD REICH. In the foreground, the poster shows a younger, military-uniformed Bambert Tolby, with blacker hair, standing on a beach, sneering angrily into the distance, and carrying a laser rifle in one hand and, in the other a dead soldier wrapped in the German flag. The slightly faded faces of different characters float in a Mount Rushmore-like cluster in the background: a fresh-faced soldier with a cigarette in his ear and a smirk; a Native American with a feather head-dress; and, then, this gremlin-like creature with butterfly wings.

"And," he continues, "when it becomes work, you ask yourself, do you really want to continue this project? Do you even like this project anymore? When I asked myself that last question, suddenly I could no longer create—" He puts a pause around that word to let it get fatter. "I would go home at night after shooting a chase scene in the parking lot of Wegmans, pace around my house, and say 'I need to kill myself!' over and over again. 'God it's so bad!' That's when I knew I had to quit White Power. I was so embarrassed about that movie I used the money that all those generous and stupid people gave me to travel to Africa. I have two million Zimbabwean dollars left from that trip. And when I returned, when the court sentenced me, I needed to let myself be punished—to end that part of my life. Relationships end. I've grown, Andrea's grown, even since I met him. Sometimes the only way to accomplish a goodbye is through violent expul-sion. It's interesting you bring up McVeigh, an Upstate New Yorker himself, who, after all, said goodbye to whoever he had left as friends by destroying a federal building."

A finger stabs up into my brain: "Wait. What do you mean?"

Toby and Lip Cheese have no reaction. Bambert leans back and recrosses his legs.

"After McVeigh left this area, left town forever, he journeyed, some said shiftlessly, into the small towns of the country and desert. In transition, he sent back some sixty-six letters to a childhood friend of his. The sixty-sixth was sent the summer before the Oklahoma City bombing. In its twenty-three pages, McVeigh, already very lonely or at least isolated, explained that he was ending their friendship, which had been poisoned irreparably by their political differences. 'Blood will flow in the streets,' he wrote at one point. 'Good versus evil. I pray it is not your blood, my friend.' Just like this," Bambert snaps his fingers. "Farewell old friend. I'm off to blow up a building."

Bambert stands up and dusts off his thighs. Conversations from upstairs turn hearable again. "Well on that upbeat note, gentlemen, we should get back. I am sure my guests are awaiting you and they don't even know it yet."

We follow him up the white-painted staircase, wooden with no support beams between the floor and the top. Light re-enters my head. I realize I've been picking at the corner of my pinky nail until it's frayed into three or four mini layers.

Bambert leads us past the people in the kitchen and living room, who stand around holding small plastic wine cups and paper snack plates.

"I don't know if Andrea'll be back, but you guys stay as long as you like," Bambert says, and he wanders into the front yard under the floodlights.

In the front yard, more people are here than when we showed up: collared shirts, khaki shorts, Docksiders and no socks, shadows in the floodlight stretching to the road. More people have joined whatever dancing game the church kids are playing, and it becomes clear that Necro's not coming.

So Toby shrugs, opens the cooler next to the front door, and scoops a can of Surge floating in the ice water. And so we spend the evening wandering around a total stranger's front yard. Some lady with tiny shoulders, a paisley vest over a short-sleeve shirt and gray, mushroom-shaped hair introduces herself to Lip Cheese. As tax law changes, we're always adapting, I overhear Lip Cheese say. Toby drifts toward the grill, positioned at the garage-end of the driveway, and shakes hands with a man who is dressed like a golfer. People walk by me. Toby assumes grill duty, pressing hamburgers with the flat of the spatula; checking blood color; opening up hamburger buns and setting them on the warming rack, serving them on paper plates.

"But the screw threads were all English standards," Toby maybe tells the man. And it annoys me that I can't get talked to even among the nicest people, and that Toby and Lip Cheese, maybe, haven't so much been pretending to be grown-up as: This is how they act when we aren't around one another.

And my brain, for a second, darts in a direction I don't mean it to, and I think about the Evening with Raw Dog, and then I wonder if, maybe, Bambert L. Tolby this whole time has been lying to us.

Someone grabs my forearm. "Quick! Will you be the new person?" a bulky girl in a Brockport High soccer uniform says.

Have I ever danced before? Maybe probably not. But the girl leads me into the two lines of church kids dancing. In the yard, on a wooden chair, there's a radio, and she presses Play, and the disco-y Jamiroquai song that plays sounds extra loud and tinny, like it might give the radio a nosebleed.

The teenagers around me do the Charleston and assorted chicken-wing dances, throwing themselves hard into the moves, like they've been practicing, during homework nights, for this exact situation. I bend my knees a little. I feel the weight of the fat in my arms. And, just in case Toby and Lip Cheese see me, I grab my ankle and swing my knee back and forth so I can look like I'm actually totally ripping on all these people. But I figure out very quickly that the knee-swing is funny only once, and I can never use it again.

The girl presses Stop. I stand on my left foot, holding my right foot behind me. Some of the younger kids look at each other and giggle. I squint one last time at all of these people and relax my arms, cram all my energy into my left leg, and settle in. The last one of us not to fall wins.

PARIS GREEN

But then, the Saturday before the Fourth of July, I drink some of Mom's Sam Adamses and type in NecronicA. The white screen scalds my eyes: "VivaWeb cannot find page," the screen says. I refresh. Same message.

A gyroscope turns in my stomach. Because, as much as NecronicA made me feel like I would never earn more than 1,500 Holy Grail Points and that Necro didn't want to be my friend anymore, I could at least imagine him, in his basement, alone, drawing something.

So I lie on the bed and stare at the receipts Toby gave me. That's what I'll settle for: reading the explosives—quickmatch, dextrin, etc. The dot-matrix-y print on the receipts has been thumbed away from the receipts' being in various pockets of mine, and the paper has been crumpled and recrumpled to have the texture of Kleenex. One receipt is dated 4/02/99 at 3:21 p.m. The last four digits of Necro's credit card are 9214.

Except the next day, on July 4th, the news reports a small fire that took place the previous night at the Monroe County

Democratic Committee Headquarters. A broken front window in the office; a roll of paper towels doused in lighter fluid. The burns, shown on TV, look like somebody emptied a can of black spray paint on an office corner near the window. Police say witnesses saw a "tall man" in a hooded sweatshirt—maybe a gray one like the one Necro used to wear to tag football, when we did that sort of thing in certain Septembers. I call Necro: Robot Voice Machine. Because I think: Maybe when Necro lit my room on fire in that one painting, this is all his way of saying goodbye to me.

"Sticking around tonight Nate?" Fake Dad No. 3 says from the living room. "We have cheesecake."

"Oh no thanks!" I try to say as cheerfully as possible.

Nonetheless, though: Fake Dad No. 3, despite his black Dungeons and Dragons jeans, Tevas, and parachute-y white button-down shirt, on a scale of 1 to 10, he's okay. He drives me to Wegmans every Friday to pick up dinner for NBA Food Jam Weekends.

Nonetheless, I'm tying my shoes to take the car out, to find Necro—maybe just to have one last nice time with him, or maybe just to say goodbye before he goes to prison.

"Stay in," Fake Dad No. 3 whispers, maintaining eye contact even when he sucks his wine through the space in his front teeth. "Fuck people. It's cheesecake. It's devilishly, devilishly good," which he says in this handlebar-mustache, exquisite-cuisine kind of way. "There's a *Seinfeld* on before the Macy's show."

It used to be the *Simpsons* for me at 6 p.m., then I'd go out. But Fox has begun airing back-to-back *Simpsonses* from 6 to 7, and I've been gliding, with age maybe, into *Seinfeld*, which is on at 7, and waiting until *Seinfeld* ends to go find my friends. But I, tonight, apparently, have a best-friendship to ruin.

Fake Dad No. 3 follows me through the kitchen, watching me check my pockets. "Did you read the literature I provided?" he says. "Have you given any thought to it?"

"What thought?"

"King! Of! Prussia!" he pounds the table, rattling a stray spoon, to the rhythm of a crowd saying, "Wheel, of, Fortune!"

"King of—Fortune?"

"The BLT, Nate! Bacon, lettuce, and Truth!" he says. "You should really make the leap, today, if you'd like to join us for our August retreat. People might accuse you of seeming above them afterward, but that's only because you *are*."

"I haven't had time to—"

"One would be dismayed if our last openings were commandeered by another stressed out MBA from National City looking not to expand the space between his inner constellations, as in pure astronomy, but only to alter his economic and testicular luck, a testiculoeconomic fortitude." He gives two or three quick, microscopic shakes of his head. "Forgive me, I'm just doing a little free association."

When right now, I would love nothing more than to drive far away and shut the fuck up. But my shoes are tied, and my pockets are checked. So after driving to Applebee's, and then to the bagel place, and to the Necro Flammable Chair in Greece and out to the Pylon of Awfulness in the canal, I find Necro's Vomit Cruiser parked in the grass that Veterans Park has made into a parking lot for the Fourth.

People in khaki shorts and fluorescent hats set down coolers and blankets and lawn chairs on the grass. It's dark enough to see a kid's floating face staring at a lit sparkler. I look across the park. Necro's at the opposite end, head sticking out over everybody else's, standing where the grass meets some pine trees.

I make my way through the bug spray smell and the four-year-olds trying to do somersaults. Up closer, the sleeves of Necro's Section-8 Dad's Air Force jacket are rolled up. His triangle brows look thinner. He's wearing a pair of those shoes that look like bowling shoes that people wear in the bigger cities. He waves when he sees me, arm still like a windmill blade. Lip Cheese is there with him, holding a large plastic bottle of green Pucker by its neck.

"Get something in the fifty-thousand PPS range," Lip Cheese is telling Necro, "you could really have something robust, get those rakes of light going, like what they have with Pink Floyd at the Planetarium."

I pretend like I'm really interested in the ice-cream truck at the park's edge, and the manila-colored light coming from the truck's server window. Really interested in that.

"They use lasers in more and more things—give spectators that jolt," Lip Cheese says. "Throw that in there, that would be a fireworks show."

So I tell Lip Cheese, just so I can have a turn in this conversation: "I'm sure that'll work real well, Washcloth Master."

Which Necro ignores. Lip Cheese, though, smirks, and backwashes into the Pucker bottle. "It seemed to work on you just fine, Nate," he says.

I begin to ask What does that mean, Washcloth Master? But right then, Lip Cheese pulls a laser pointer from the pocket of his jean shorts. He squiggles the dot of laser up my pant leg. Two large objects, made of deep gravitational space metal, slam together in my chest. Because, my God: Was that Lip Cheese, in the cornfields, on Night of Nintendo Power Bucolic Farm?

"You got Jungled, Nate!" Lip Cheese says, so excited that he jumps, keeping his legs together and his arms braced against his body while in the air.

When, Lip Cheese? This is the kid who, the last time he tried stalking anybody was when he tried following Deandra Esposito when his car was stopped in *front* of hers at a stoplight, and he essentially reverse-followed her into Spencerport, watching her turn signals through his rearview mirror and squeezing in his turns accordingly, until he ripped his front tire open on a curb. This is the kid who, on one dance night, when we were on the roof of Gates Chili High School looking through the gymnasium windows so he could spy on Karen Lombardi, walked off angrily when he spotted some kid with her in the gymnasium corner, just hugging. But he forgot to stop walking when he neared the roof ledge, and he walked straight off, bounced off some tree branches, and landed in a bush. "What? I'm tired!" he said from below.

And now he's going to stand here, like he's Detective Emil Von Schaufenhausen, in this new world, pointing a laser straight into my mouth because he can do that now.

"Why did—how did you even—" I start saying.

"Skills," Lip Cheese says. He points the laser pointer

upward. The red laser line goes on and on into the sky, stopping seemingly at the atmosphere's ceiling. "Man!" he jumps again. "'Don't shoot; don't shoot!' You got Time-Bomb Jungled."

"That's Garth Heffernan's phrase," I manage to say.

He slaps me on the shoulder. "What—? I thought that's what we were doing that one week. I got Jungled when you and Toby ripped on me when I looked up all those files; Necro got Jungled when we showed them to Luckytown, and—"

Necro's body revolves, slowly, toward us. His jaw muscles are clenched, spine arched. Lip Cheese's chin retreats into his neckfat.

"It was Nate's idea!" Lip Cheese says, and he immediately runs away, Igor-like, back hunched, darting around blankets, jumping over coolers, and then I never see him again. I heard he's a payroll specialist, still at Paychex, downtown.

Necro folds his arms. Everything in my body is moving fast and thinning out. "I never had any ideas," I say into my shoulder.

Because, I can't look at him. Look at him! He's just staring at me, some feeling or another damming up behind his cheeks.

"Two months ago," he says, "the police took and walked right into my house. Like they were dinner guests, completely eschewing whatever stipulations various legal echelons have against doing such initiatives. It took me forever to get my computer back from them. The police department said they wanted to see a receipt." He slams his fist downward, hitting an imaginary table. "Who has a receipt for a computer just filed away for their documentation purposes?"

"Clearly they didn't arrest you," I say. "Sometimes police just investigate stuff. We barely even—"

Then I stop myself. Necro sniffles, angrily, once, either for no reason or for every reason ever. And so of course, now I've learned officially, Pope's Decree, that having the police Riot on Necro's house was an awful thing to do, was never funny and probably illegal, and didn't even need to be done, because I haven't been in nearly as horrible a mood about myself recently, I don't think, and it's never good to try to stop people from moving on. But since I know this, now I have to sit through this entire conversation while Necro Goes Off the Top Ropes on me.

"At least you bother to take and self-own it," Necro says. "Owned something, you Friend to All Animals."

Which for obvious reasons is completely uncalled for. Necro knows I threw out that pair of underwear, and all my stuffed animals—even the yellow bear we named Shut Up and the leather E.T. doll we named Grandpa—so that nobody would bring up Friend to All Animals ever again. And so if Necro's going to start Cooking with Gas on me, I widen my eyes and turn my head, slowly, right back at him. Because, I find myself in that position where, because Necro is being so Colonel Hellstache, I end up arguing for everything Toby has been saying, which I totally don't agree with, just so I can defend myself.

"Let's look at how every time a picture appeared on NecronicA, a building burned down," I say.

Necro juts his chin toward somewhere behind me, maybe a third of the park away.

"What about those homeless shelters?" I say. "What about how, just before Wicked College John got hit, you were shoving us toward that building?" And, I swallow some TV static in my chest here: "And why'd you burn down my room in that one painting?"

And rather than answer an easy question, Necro apparently has to say:

"That's a new thing we're doing, Nate. Me and the Unabomber decided that along with our assorted manifestos, we're only going to communicate in explosions. One firebomb means Yes; two means No. For even our casual socializations, we just aim explosions at each other. Boy, that was one coy explosion!"

"But we've seen your drawings," I go. And then Bambert Tolby? Comparing you to Timothy McVeigh?"

"He has no money. He sold his weapons and furniture to pay house bills. He tried to burn down his own store."

"Timothy McVeigh?"

"*Bambert!*" He spears his face forward at me. "There's no nonprofit! No altruistic machinations! He took and gave back all his various accrued funds. He told the clerk at some church, 'You're too kind for me to do this to you,' pleading, like terrified."

"Was he a con man?"

"That, or pipe dreams and incompetence. He doesn't answer his door now. He's sitting in there waiting to be arrested."

But before I can ask further, Necro, though, turns into a Complete Bowl of Skittles! He begins walking, stiff-legged, in a circle. "What is up, college dude, do you like 311?" he says, in his happy-robot voice.

Campus-Tron 4000, Necro. I get it. But he goes on like this for practically six more years: "Interact with me!" he pivots on his right heel and walks away from me.

"Interact with your Kangaroo for a Kid," I stand on my toes and say at the back of his neck. "Your Kangaroo for a *Kid!*" I say again, in case he didn't hear me.

But he keeps walking that way, opening and closing his mouth Pac-Man style, holding his arms forward, leaving his wrists limp.

So, I reach into my pocket. I show him the receipts Toby gave me. Necro's brow muscles and the flab under his chin loosen like a noose dropping.

"Where did you get those," he says.

There's some polite applause from the people sitting on the park grass, and the PA begins playing some trilly marching-band music, which I have to yell over. "We're just wondering where you've been, man! You never call us! I miss you!"

He flails around, away from me, arms trailing like tetherballs. "I can't even believe you would go through my—"

A firework goes off, like a popped balloon held to a megaphone. People go "ooh" like they've seen expensive jewelry.

"Necro!" I yell. "Simple question! What's this bill for copper benzoate for James Mason? Because if you've gone off to spill blood in the streets, if you were trying to tell me something, in that painting, when my room was on fire, if this is all your way of saying that you've Maverick Jetpantsed beyond me, and our friendship is over, well, I would just be unhappy, is all."

Some chandeliers and tinsel pop in the sky and leave tracers when I blink. Necro rips the receipts from my hand.

"Do you even know what dextrin and lactose are?" Necro yells. "Do you know what they take and use copper benzoate even for?"

"I can barely hear you!" I yell over some smiley faces spreading across the sky.

"Blue!" Necro yells. He points to the sky. "Blue color! You can't get Paris Green anymore so you have to use the copper. Look up!"

"What?"

"Look *up*!"

Right then, blue-colored fireworks explode—blue fingers and willow trees.

We can see the shadows of trees and of ourselves, flickering, while the fireworks pop, sometimes four shadows at once, like an "x." It's too loud for me to hear myself saying, "You have got to be kidding me."

Necro lunges forward and yells down into the space between my eyes: "The town took and helped my dad and me run fireworks this year!" he yells. "Hunan province had a huge factory explosion, so we had to change up where we order from. James Mason's company imports the fireworks!"

Explosion imprints, like banana peels made of smoke, drift to the left.

"You bag of asshole," Necro says. "There's a muzzle on your brain, and Toby has the leash. And that muzzle has been taped on. Like a dildo."

No! Even if Necro didn't Pin Bow Ties on the Dead, you ask him a simple question, and he Taped-On Dildos you!

"I explained Taped-On Dildo to you years ago," I say. "You *know* the Toys 'R Us is miles away from Lyell Video and News!"

Necro sets his hand, coach-like, on my shoulder. His fingernails are full, unbitten unlike mine, like he might actually clip them now. Then he says, in this practical way, like he's announcing layoffs: "Your dad was a gelding and your mother was a whale, and they gave birth to a suitcase with a flesh mask inside."

Which, I have no idea what that means, but I have to squeeze my bladder shut when he says it.

"Toby is not going to like what I tell him about you," I say.

The next day, I meet Toby at the Airplane Booth. It's 4 p.m. Nobody's there. A waitress at a corner booth rolls silverware into napkins and the hose water from the dish room drumrolls off a pan.

"Necro Pinned Bow Ties on the Dead," I tell Toby. "He said it to my face. Even this most recent one at that Democratic building."

Toby freezes for a second, like he's surprised to be told he's right. He picks up a French fry and holds it midway between the basket and his face. "What should we do?"

I bite down on my plastic straw and drag it through my front teeth.

"Should we call 911?" Toby says.

Which I don't have an answer for. So we both, instead,

manage to look angry enough, sorting through our fries after we've finished speaking and people start to come in for dinner and someone slightly dims the lighting.

Because, like I don't have any comebacks against you, Necro. Kangaroo for a Kid? No end, Necro, no end. Necro: trying to stare me down during fireworks, calling me Taped-On Dildo. Taped-On Dildo! He's lucky I didn't kick his ass right then.

HOME OF TRISCUIT

When I say Mindy Fale makes friends with the worst people, what I mean is she makes me drive to Greece so I can meet her at Conor Ricketts's parents' house, where he's having people over. Which Conor Ricketts deserves completely—living with his parents I mean—because without Conor Ricketts, there would be no Sausage Academy. And with no Sausage Academy, I would not be this person who one day, if people don't get better about asking Are You Alright, might just walk, fully clothed, down into a swimming pool and float there, facedown, until I finally stop thinking.

And I hope for the drive to be long, but I get to Conor Ricketts's house way too fast. He wastes no time at all, still with his Colonel Hellstache Phish T-shirt and his Colonel Hellstache hair that parts in the middle and flops just above his ears. He immediately shoehorns me into a headlock when I walk in.

"Look at that forehead! Look at this headwound!" he says, voice still squinty as his face. "That scar is *ripe*. Where were you the last three years, Sausage Gray?"

He's a medium like me, but he squeezes my head into his ribcage, and I feel some head-cartilage pop, and some blood-juice sling around my head, and I wonder if I'm going to faint, soil myself in front of everyone, and therefore have to change my name and move to another country.

"Just gonna grab some of this chorizo," he says, mellowly, like a doctor doing a physical, before twisting a handful of my stomach fat. "Just gonna mix that with some peppercorns and beef. Then we can spawn an infant Sausage Academy."

I squirm away and try to laugh it off. But my face is already scalding red. Even worse, my response: "Or spawn an infant Bags Gigolo."

Right then? Back to Sad Archives. Back to age sixteen, when Bags Gigolo was everyone's nickname for Conor Ricketts and not, somehow, Rickets.

His house is like a worn-out college rental—walls thin enough to vibrate the whole place if you punched them, stairs to the second floor right there when you get in. There are nicer, parentish things: gold picture frames, a wall unit, carpets and furniture colored like different degrees of creamed coffee. I sidestep my way past the red party cups on the glass end table. Around Kim Stanton, Kim Piscarelli, Kim Opec, all still here; around Mike Falconi; around the other Mike Falconi who did track and jazz band. I set the cube of Labatt's I brought on the sticky kitchen floor, and, in a Clinic of Hellstachery, Mindy Fale has not arrived yet, and there is nobody to talk to.

Nobody, except for Conor Ricketts, who, I decide: Why not go stand around while he talks to Eric Ashner and some kid who is maybe Jeremy Near.

And if you've ever just had a standaround with someone who has ripped on you your whole life, the conversation
always feels four jokes ahead of you. But since Conor Ricketts
is one of these people I always think I'll never see again (until
I always see him again), I get this post-headlock, really-terrific
chipper hate in me:

"So, Conor! Are you in school?" I go, slapping him on
the arm.

And the only good part of the night is right here, when
his face unsquints, for a second, like I'm maybe finally seeing
the face that got nervous on the bus to school, or the face that
told his mom he felt like he had no friends. But he collapses
halfway and goes: "Can't do it, man. Can't do it!" He looks
to Ashner and the other kid who, actually, might be Kevin
Keaveny if Kevin Keaveny burned his neck really bad. "He's
just Sausage Academy. Slim Jims as pencils, books with pages
made of sliced turkey."

And because she is already a Life Mistake, Mindy Fale
chooses to arrive right now, with her work shirt and stretch
pants and perfume of raspberry-scented paint thinner. She
kisses Conor Ricketts on the cheek. Which why tell me I
should come here if she's going to be that way.

"Academy what?" she says.

I flex my head muscles with anger at her. "Oh it was just
this time," I say, "when Conor stuck a sausage—"

He gets me in another headlock before I can finish, and
it feels like I'm underwater, and people start to laugh, and
he wrestles me to the floor, pressing my cheek into his parents' carpet. And suddenly, I relax. And I begin to think:

Of the Top Five Uncomebackables You Don't Need to Know About Me, if Taped-On Dildo is the final boss, then Sausage Academy is the bonus quest after you beat the game. Not even Necro, Toby, or Lip Cheese know what Sausage Academy means. But rather than simply reseal Sausage Academy into the Nate Expanding Zoo of Lies, something happens that can only be described as the entire history of vitamins typhooning upward into every nerve-hole that Sausage Academy has dug me into since I was fifteen. And what I decide is, if Necro is going to Joke-Hostage me with Taped-On Dildo, and Conor Ricketts is going to Joke-Hostage me with Sausage Academy, maybe I can Un-Joke-Hostage myself by making a habit of telling the truth.

So I put my hand on Conor Ricketts's waist, gently, in a way that I guess he understands means Enough, No Really, and he un-headlocks me. People have gathered around us in the living room, like they're not sure whether to expect a fight. I stand straight, let some headlock-fizz drain into my cheeks, and hold my breath, like I'm about to make an Olympic dive.

"Basically, Mindy, what Sausage Academy was—*is*—" and I can feel my mind, like a digestive tract, trying to pull back down everything I'm about to say. "What it was, was, basically—I was in a study group with Conor here, and Jessica Stanfeld. We were in Jessica's bedroom, and we all ate several tablespoons of nutmeg. We sat around licking our lips, and then, I forget what we were talking about, but Jessica asks, out of nowhere, 'Nate: Are you circumcised?'"

And the biggest Bowl of Skittles about this is that I start

to get Crazy Stories Wheels, and I'm leaning forward, making big spidery gestures, like I'm doing stand-up, like maybe I can make Sausage Academy sound like something Holy Grail Point worthy.

"Now, obviously I know what circumcised means now—I mean who doesn't? It's so obvious—but back then, I was like: 'Circumcised? Like circumscribed?'" I smack my right temple. "So I said, 'Circumcised? No.' And Conor and Jess start cracking up. And Jessica asks, 'So do you just have, like, a hood?' And I tell her, totally on autopilot, 'No, no way. It's pretty standard-issue down there: See?' And next thing, Conor here"—I put my arm around him—"lets out this *BWOAAAGH* and dives for the corner. Jessica begins to cry, because my hands, without mentally documenting it, have undone my fly and just completely taken it out. Like I could just do this, no editing box."

Mindy Fale is the only one laughing. Conor Ricketts has this frown that looks like, I would say, the *Vice President* of the Diarrhea Fan Club. Which makes me feel like I've steered the crowd away from him. Soon, someone will begin to clap, slowly, and they will love His Natorade for his honesty, because we're all just walking bags of pain who have one or two chances ever to speak truthfully. Because the next part of Sausage Academy—the Sausage Academy Tapes—Conor has been nice enough this entire time not to tell anybody.

"And the craziest part," I go on, "is that I look down, standing over Conor and Jessica, and not only have I taken it out, but there's some actual crotchular *movement*, like maybe the horror of this sort of turns me on. And when I realize this,

I'm double horrified, and I start going 'AHHH! AHHH!' and I stumble into the bathroom. And I can't calm down, and the only thing I can think to do to relax is pleasure myself, pleasure the horror out of me. And Conor here doesn't know this, but the fear—the total creepiness of it right then in Jessica Stanfeld's bathroom—feels awesome, awesome like hollowed-out-my-pelvis. So *that* turns me on! So back home that night, I think, Well the rest of the school year's already ruined, so why not just see where the demons take you. So I work out another round in my bedroom. But now I'm horrified that I have let this horror be enjoyable, and now I have a headache, and my brain is so fogged up from demon boner gas that I don't sleep, and so I pleasure the horror out of me again to tire myself out. I tell my mom to make a sick call to the nurse's office. And when she goes to work, I wait forty-five minutes to download this porn clip—just some man-on-woman to normal a bro out. But in the clip, the woman yells 'Oh Jesus!' and the guy yells, 'Jesus never fucked you like this!' Which is awful! So I throw my hands over my eyes, and I run into the bathroom and yell into the mirror: 'Cultaneous! Cultaneous! Cultaneous!' yelling this made-up word, slapping my face. 'Cultaneous! Cultaneous!' So that's Sausage Academy."

Even Conor Ricketts has a loosened look on his face. This respectful look, like he's at the funeral of someone he hates.

"I was high on nutmeg you squares!" I say. "It was instinct. Curiosity. You think Christopher Columbus would have gone very far without curiosity? You could all learn something from this, all of you, still living at home. And Conor: *His last name is Ricketts!*"

People walk into other rooms, start other conversations. Conor Ricketts puts his hand on my shoulder. "I am glad I am not you," he says.

Minutes or hours later, I'm sitting on the living room couch. It feels too much like I've lit my face on fire to know if I'm relieved or if I've done irreversible harm to myself. Since I'll take any reason to get out of here, I hear Mindy Fale ask her friends if they want to go to the Millcreek Pool Club to light up a spliff. So, I do the thing where, if you want to invite yourself someplace, you quietly follow the people headed to that place for a while, and then I become the Cloaked Man and slip into the backseat of Mindy Fale's car when they go: the Classic Nate Slip-In.

We follow her friends' car to Millcreek, and then her friends wander into the trees out behind the diving board. And here's me and Mindy Fale, sitting on top of the monkey bars, legs hanging down over the weeds, me trying to taste her saliva on the joint. The pool is drained, but at night its bright blue paint job looks like moonlight.

After eight or nine long, angry inhales, the area behind my eyes knots up. I look at Mindy Fale's chest, and somewhere, deep in the nerve vortex of my cock, a telephone rings. But I can feel a Sad High fighting its way up to my head.

"I'm finally at that point where I can kill myself," I say, but accidentally like it's an accomplishment.

"Right. Right," she says. Then, after an extra second: "Sometimes I get so tired when I smoke. It made my old jobs a disaster. My dad was co-owner of Salty's when I was a junior, and I'd hang banners and place ads when he'd do boxing events there. One time when he was talking to the promoter, I fell asleep in the change room on Cisco Arriaga's lap, the boxer. He was so sweet about it. He didn't try to get up or anything."

"I can't believe I spilled the beans on Sausage Academy," I say, slowly. But I'm way too conscious how serious my face looks to give what I say sufficient Sad-backing.

"I can't believe they believed it," she says.

And the closest I get to a realization of what this means is hearing a voice from my brain's echo-filled sewers—a black saxophone player's baritone voice that says: WHOA. Some puppet strings attached to the corners of my mouth pull upward, which must mean I'm smiling.

"You talk a mean game of bullshit, Nathan Gray," she says. "After you told that whole story, Josh DuGoff asked me: Is Nate dying?"

I start to nod and to laugh, seemingly uncontrollably, like my head's trying to pull my body upward. "I'd run into the woods and, you know, *pleasure it through again*," my voice gets squealy, "But I'd be so scared!"

Mindy Fale sprays spit. Each bubble of cracking-up hardens into a laughter kidney stone in my cranium.

"But I'm totally meeting you where you're at!" she says.

I take another hefty inhale, a coast-inhale.

"Like, Eddie Izzard," she says. "At work I just go out and talk with these old ladies at lunch, and I'll make references to Eddie Izzard jokes when they're talking about their husband's government health insurance. And when nobody gets them I drive home like: Yes."

I start to say something, but I can apparently tell Mindy Fale has wanted to talk about what she's about to tell me, and has been waiting for a way to segue into it, which I feel very respectful of.

"But I love driving around high, or after mushroom tea," she says. "Driving past the malls at night, past Marketplace or out to Eastview. I had 'Second Toughest in the Infants' in the tape player—Underworld?—which Chadvertisement said helps him concentrate. And one night, I'm driving around, past the farms, past the schools. Everything is closed, like this deep mind-techno rattling the speakers; that 'Pearl's Girl' song: I remember thinking it sounded like when they show cities in fast motion. I drive past this stretch of field past Victor, where there are no street lamps. And I swear, I'm driving, and right then, my headlights catch this white baby's shoe on the side of the road—absolutely glowing."

"That is amazing!" I say. "That is, like, a child—"

"I got teary," she says. "It was the funnest fear I'd ever had."

And even though Real Dad's line about Eddie Izzard— he's this transvestite and he just *stands there!*—pulls my head softly to the right like a news ticker, hearing Mindy talk about baby shoes tastes like Snapple in my heart.

"We should do that," she says. "Hey, hey, hey."

"Yeah, hey."

"Do you want to drive to Niagara Falls?" she asks.

"We pretty much have to now!"

To even be in someone's car that isn't mine or Toby's, to have to move my feet around a different pile of junk; coffee cups with a Hess logo as opposed to McDonald's; this tote bag with an old Videk logo—letters fat, square, and digital-looking; to even have to adjust the seat because it hasn't been adjusted, yet, by me—all of that is pretty neat.

On I-90, the after-sweat of almost-August whips through the windows. Into the America side of Niagara Falls, we pass a factory, which looks like an expansive white six-pack. A yellow banner across its top says: NABISCO: HOME OF TRISCUIT. Which we both laugh at. The roads are empty, street lamps like huge lowercase r's. A lone booth is open at the Rainbow Bridge.

"We're just here to see the falls," Mindy Fale says to the booth guy, who waves us through with his index finger.

I remember Mom, sitting in the passenger seat, looking back at me when we went over the Peace Bridge, saying, "This bridge represents friendship between our country and Canada," when Real Dad wanted to drag Mom to the Ripley's Believe It or Not Museum. The lights are off in the clown-colored storefronts and the tower that says CASINO on it. We pass the Burger King, over which rises a giant sculpture of Frankenstein's head, his hand holding a hamburger.

But instead of going straight to the falls, Mindy Fale, totally out of nowhere, turns hard into the parking lot of Plaza, a liquidy executive-class tower hotel with a lightbulb-studded gold ceiling over the pull-up loop.

"I feel really sick," she says. "What time is it?"

Mindy Fale hurries into the hotel's airport-terminal-sized lobby, check-in desks on opposing sides, polished granite I'm still high enough to want to lick. Palm trees surround the glass elevator shafts, inner balconies of each floor shrinking upward like we're inside a gold accordion. The attendant charges $200 to Mindy Fale's credit card. She yanks her tote bag off the desk counter and walks, heels like hammers, toward the elevators.

"Shut up, shut up, do not talk, do not ask me a thing," she says.

"Did I do something?" I say to the back of her head.

She jabs the elevator button a bunch of times. "I have to get to a bed. I can't drive."

Our room is on the eighteenth floor, light the color of cowhide, microwave on top of a mini bar; a circular table with a spread of information pamphlets. Mindy Fale sits next to me on the bed. I lean my right shoulder into her. My right armpit is soaked with sweat. I take her hand, and I am sure now this time, as before all other future interruptions, that we finally love each other. Her knuckles are chapped. She stands up: "I have to take my—" she says, and yanks her tote bag across her arm and strides into the bathroom.

I hear a fan go on and what sounds like Tic Tacs rattling. When she comes out, she takes off her shoes, lays down, still in her work clothes, and falls immediately asleep.

Her hands are folded on her stomach, in that way where I never fold my hands when I sleep on my back, because when I was younger I worried someone might think I was dead and bury me in my sleep. Every three or four seconds, her throat cracks open and releases a pencil-thick tube of air. Which is annoying, so to be annoying back at her, I look through her tote bag. There's a ball of tinfoil, a pair of sunglasses, a rolled-up copy of the *Rochester Real Estate Journal,* and an earwax-colored pill jar with a yellow sticker wrapped around it showing an icon of a half-opened eye.

Rolled into the corner of her pack of cigarettes are a one-hitter that looks like a cigarette and a plastic bag, the size that spare coat buttons come in. The one chunk of pot left in the bag looks like a tiny, freeze-dried Christmas tree. So out of revenge against her—and the way she hugged Conor Ricketts, or how she said Don't Ask Me Anything and fell asleep so now I'm stuck here and bitch-bored—I tap the one-hitter against the bathroom sink and crumble in a few pinches of weed. Then—just to have at least some Crazy Stories—I spark it, exhaling into the ceiling fan, coughing grains of solidified electricity until the plastic bag is empty, and my heart rate speeds up and floats, moth-like, out of my body.

When I leave the bathroom, my face glows with a calm, very discerning expression, like Harrison Ford. I assess the room. Curtains cover one wall. No sound anywhere, except my socks on the carpet. A cozy, echoless sound, like dialogue on late-night anime.

I lie down next to her and slip my hand under hers, which feels dry and slender, a Victorian hand. I place my palm on her right breast. I make a few rotations, scientifically. Her chest expands and contracts, like we've always been falling asleep in a bed that's too small for us.

When I sit up, I notice on the *Rochester Real Estate Journal* cover the phrase SAVE TOUCH AND DIE written in large, hip-looking type that's apparently supposed to resemble handwriting. Since that phrase seems like some life comment I don't understand, I open the magazine. Some listings are pre-circled, like an edgier way to highlight notable properties. Some of the articles display photos of homes, with messages

in the margins like "use this" next to a picture of a granite
fireplace; and "!!!!" Which I realize, then, is all just Mindy
Fale's handwriting, balloony in a murdery kind of way. But
then I see this article about code enforcement, with pictures
of rusted pipes.

I eye-stroke the article's first four words over and over, but
a paragraph near the center of the page reads: "After a gas leak
explosion at the Rochester Public Access Building that injured
a St. Bonaventure student, the city condemned 21 properties
in the two w——."

I make a Bible-sized gulp. A picture, light harsh from the
flash, shows a buffalo-sized gas tank—a cylinder on four legs,
covered with rust and white and green infections. The caption
says: "The gasoline tank had corroded due to excessive water
at the . . ." I blink over a few sentences. "Tests had not been
conducted since 1987."

But then, Bible-Sized Gulp No. 2: "—a department
research coordinator, said that outliers had created mislead-
ing statistics. This month, a juvenile, 14, pled guilty to arson
charges in connection with fire incidents at two homeless
shelters, the Monroe County Democ . . ."

I set the magazine down because my lips feel heavy. My
head feels like it's about to fall off. Did I seriously not see this
in the news? Did I miss all of this only because 11 p.m. runs
directly into Rochester Drivearound hour? Was the Fires Gone
Wild Runaway Cockdrama, this whole time, just some kid,
a juvenile, who the magazine doesn't identify, along with a
bunch of oven burners left on? For an answer, all I can hear
is a low-pitched, synthesizery noise, tunneling in on me, low

like monks' blow horns. Then, in a wallpapery pattern, 8-bit images of Necro flash, in time with my heart rate, on the inner side of my cornea. My lungs close when I swallow. My mind free falls. My thoughts very quickly reason their way to hell.

I imagine I'm giving a toast in front of an audience, and Necro runs up to me and yells "You fraud!" I hear myself say that if Toby finds Necro, he'll kill him. He'll kill him and go to the police, and I need to show him this article, right now, need to watch him read it over to uproot the Runaway Cockdrama. I try to breathe deep—to get my brain to tread some water—but the best I can do is stand up. Then I think: You can never lie again. And I maybe, right here, get myself to fully form the thought of: if I can tell the truth about Sausage Academy, I can tell Toby the truth about Necro. But then I hear a girl yell in what is the opposite of a voice: *You are going to die this way.*

"Hey. Wake up," I say to Mindy Fale, at conversation volume.

Some saliva at the back of her throat pops when she breathes.

I tap her shoulder. "We have to get out of here," I say. Her hands, folded, rise and fall on her stomach. "My friend's in trouble. I have to apologize to him."

She smacks her lips and rolls over. Since I'm relieved to at least be annoyed by this, I rip open the curtains, and behind them the entire time was a sliding door, which opens to a balcony, which overlooks the Horseshoe Falls.

The falls are so loud, curving like a broad, raging fingernail, that I'm amazed the balcony's concrete floor is still there when

I step out. The mist is thick enough to comb your face. I kick
some cobwebs off the chair and tip it forward to dump the
puddle from the cushions.

After two or three pairs of headlights slide by—however
long that is—Mindy Fale comes out to the balcony. The tim-
ing of which, for obvious reasons, is total Colonel Shortchange
Moonteeth Hellstache.

"These new pills must have reacted—" she yells, before the
loudness of the falls makes her impossible to hear, "—of my
stalkers there."

"Yeah!" I say, because I can't get my head around asking
her to repeat herself.

And I would think to tell her we need to leave, but I'm in
Weird Politeness Recoil now that she's out here with me. She
hugs herself against the balcony railing and mouths something I can't hear. So I stand up next to her.

"Sometimes, the falls freeze all the way across!" she yells.
"Tourists used to go out and party on the ice! There were
liquor stores!"

"Yeah!" I yell. Mindy Fale's been destined for temp jobs.
But in class once, the teacher was talking about Einstein's
brain being preserved in a tank. Her hand darted up: "You
mean like Napoleon's penis?!"

A strand of her hair is stuck to my shirt sleeve. I can't tell
if her arm is touching mine. And, how sad is it that, right now,
I'm thinking about Frankenstein, eating a hamburger, and
how me and Necro, long ago, could have totally joked about
a horror-themed restaurant with intentionally-poorly-named
menu items like the Horror Burger, or the Chicken Salad

with Werewolf Fingers, or the Really-Scary, Awful-Tasting Spaghetti with Vampire Meatballs. How sad that I have to go to Niagara Falls to figure out that I've chosen Toby's Cockdramas and women over Necro? Because what do you say, with some girl who is kind of a Level 3 Frumptruck, some woman you'll only use to think of someone else, and in my head, Necro is yelling to me "That was my life!" and another voice yells "Take him to court, Necro!" before something in my body tells my brain That's Enough. And only now am I able to punch a hand, mentally, through my brain's cemetery dirt and tell myself: I Am Absolutely Blazing.

"Well, there they are!" she yells over the falls.

"There they are," I say.

THE AURORIST

The Genesee Falls downtown, however, are green. When me and Toby cross the bridge, the air from the water feels me up through my shirt in that way where you can't tell whether you smell the deodorant of every person living here, or every person being murdered here, or whether it's just back-to-school season. But you saw me—even though I went to bed first, and when I woke up the next day the Brain-Chafing Fraud High was done and I only felt urgentless—you saw me show Toby that article today. You saw his eyes moving over the words. So I tell him one more time, just to make sure: "Turned out, after all this, it wasn't Necro. It was a gas leak. It was some kid, a juvenile." I force a laugh out. "We're retards!"

"Retards. Huh."

"I already called Necro to apologize," I say. "I left a message from us."

Toby's facial expression doesn't change, still stuck on Will Put Body Parts in Suitcases.

But, have you seen what Toby does all day? I've been

with him since before noon just to keep him from generating Havoc Rays over Going Off the Top Ropes on Necro. I got in his car and we dumped some trash bags behind the post office. I stood in line with him while he talked to the girl at MotoPhoto ("Make extra duplicates; you know the ones I like," he told her).

"So, find a place? Watch preseason?" I say, because Necro would never end up at a Bills bar.

But Toby's brow suddenly crumples. His pupils harden, like there's an apocalypse of fear only he can see on the horizon. I wonder if he's heard a police siren, which is what we came into the city for, because Toby loves to listen for sirens.

"He's right up there," he mumbles into his shirt collar.

"Up there who?"

"I was downtown yesterday and I knew it was him."

We get to the end of the bridge and pass some club with a chrome façade and black windows. A tall kid with a Euro soccer jacket zipped up to the collar says to a group of kids with side bags: "You gays like techno?" in this California-therapist voice. "House? Deep house? Chicago? Oakenfold? Berlin? I'm spinning at Freakazoids: Tuesdays and Fridays. The Aurorist. Come check it out—"

Then, the kid, who's handing out laminated, postcard-sized fliers—right when he sees us, he takes off!

And Toby follows him! Chain wallet swinging with his fat, his sprint-form somehow really professional looking.

Except, right then—I put back together what I just saw: That kid—despite the dyed-gray jeans and short white hair—had a swollen face and triangle Draculabrows. That kid was Necro! Necro, but dressed totally different and with a personality-changing haircut!

Toby chases him over the fence behind Dinosaur BBQ, down a short hill into a grassed-over trench the width of two car lanes. At the entrance of Rochester's abandoned subway system—an entrance the size of a garage door, black as an eye socket of a large skull—they disappear. I swallow hard, and go in after them.

The Rochester subway. I've heard there's still paperwork on the desk inside the dispatch office, dispatching Ghost Trains, or Trains of the Dead, or the C.H.U.D.way—jokes I tried out once on Necro years ago but were forgotten after ten minutes.

Faint light reflects off the puddles, and what looks vaguely like chubby graffiti floats over the walls. I pass a raised platform, maybe where passengers waited, where a stairwell leads straight into a concrete ceiling. Just past that, I walk into an area with long rows of pillars to my left and right, black like underwater chess pieces on a board that won't end.

"Toby?" I say. "Necro?"

Echoing burbles from somewhere.

I press my thumb into the button that turns on my watch light—one of the bright blue kinds. I point my wrist forward. My shoe-echoes shriek when I jog through the large pillary area, and I arrive at a series of narrow metal walkways right-angling in labyrinth-type directions. Way off at one end, some archways overlooking the Genesee let in some half-moons of city light, the color of candle flame. Water pours out of a pipe somewhere.

I hear some footsteps, then some clanging metal, and then a splash.

"Toby?" I say.

Palms and legs slap in the water. "Brhghghhggg!" the body in the water says.

There's enough light that I can see a long, straight path on one of the walkways. Far off, under one archway, where the light is at its whitest, I see a silhouette turn, delicately, ninja-like, and run. I run, too—on my toes, like I've got winged sneakers, wind slicking my hair back, metal of the walkway bending a little under me, until I end up at the portion of the subway tracks that run underneath the Aqueduct.

I've actually heard about the Aqueduct, which I think the Erie Canal passed through a million years ago. The curves of its brick archways recede like skipping rocks. The graffiti on the pillars overlaps, brightly colored as stuffed animals inside a drop-claw prize machine.

The shadow stands at the opposite end of the Aqueduct, collar turned up, one shoulder turned toward me, like it should be holding a katana, like it's waiting for me. I make another ass-bolt toward the shadow, the soles of my shoes soft, like there should be a ledge up ahead and, after it, deep space and the broad blue curve of the Earth below.

The shadow stands there and, as I get closer, the shadow becomes a person. Necro. With a face. "What!" Necro screams.

That Necro knows his way around an abandoned subway in the dark? A little hurtful.

"The Aurorist, Necro?"

"That's what they call me now, as of current. That's what

I'm trying to do, something positive with my life. Trance, deep house. Got a new URL, got some photography on there and shit. Stuff of the future: 'Curio Goldwing dirges: It'll be an integument of clean destitude.' Or at least that's how, I imagine, sarcasm will sound like, two hundred years from now, in music reviews," he says, somehow, still with anger.

I pucker my lips, to suck on a pretend pacifier, and hold out my arm: "Touch my arm, Necro! Touch it! Please!"

Instead, Necro reaches into his pants pocket and wings his keys at my face. Some of the teeth of one key nick my left eye. The feeling is more annoying than it is painful, the kind of annoyance you can only get rid of by one way.

"You threw your keys at me," I say.

"Yeah, well."

"*You threw your keys at me!*"

My tear ducts swell like boiling fruit juice. Because, I've never for-real fought Necro before. And even though fighting won't at all be like when we were younger—when you could throw a log at Toby's head one day and call him up the next—I lower my shoulders and charge.

Necro is ready. I close my eyes. My arm hooks his stomach and the rest of me whiplashes forward. My right thumb jams into some muscle between his ribs. My left hand crumples his ear. I punch him in the thigh. My forehead rubs against his collarbone. He smells like wood and hair. I sniffle violently. My left eye waters. I open my mouth, and one of us yelps quietly. My midsection collapses—Necro has just cock-kneed me. His breath is like horseradish on the back of my neck. I punch him in his left buttock. He sniffles and inhales through his teeth. I try to head-ram him in the stomach, but he reverse-pelvic-thrusts away and I miss. Both sides of his Euro jacket hang down around my ears. He bites my shoulder. I think about reaching down his pants and grabbing his wang, not to inflict pain, but just to confuse him, but decide against it. I clamp my arms around him. We pull ourselves toward each other for a few seconds longer, and I realize that, probably, we look pretty much like two dudes who are trying to hug and rob each other at the same time.

I fall and manage to backward-somersault away. I look up at him. My lungs taste like penny-flavored mucus.

"I fucked up, Necro," I say.

I spit out a grain of something. And, then, I start laughing. I look up at Necro, who is leaning over, one hand on his knee, right arm dangling. The corner of his mouth—I *think*; in hindsight I have to—curves upward, like he's about to laugh, too.

He opens his mouth, and if he responds, we can at least begin the process of un-fucking-this-up. But from behind me, Toby, shoes quacking with water, juggernauts through and shoulders into Necro. Necro's body flies in the air for about a second, his back bounces up off the dirt, and he rolls over on his side. His head sounds like a rock dropped in the mud when Toby punches him.

"Wait wait wait wait wait!" I yell.

I try to grab Toby by the shoulders, but he flings me to the side. Some dirt scrapes up my calf. I see Necro's cheek break open when Toby hits him again—a large, parenthesis-shaped opening.

"I told you Necro was buying fireworks, Toby!"

Necro's brow is snarled up. His digital calculator watch is broken. Blood is smeared on his sleeve. Toby wipes the gravel scruff off his jacket, picks up Necro's hand, and shakes it.

"You got Jungled, Necro!" Toby says into his face.

On the bridge pavement above us, a semi truck hits a seam in the concrete, and bass vibrates through my scalp. The wind rolls an aluminum can from one side of the Aqueduct to the other.

"What!" Toby shrieks. "*Laugh already!*"

A TORTURABLE PLACE

So, all of that happens. Weeks after, Mom sets the red pepper jar in front of my egg plate, where my morning Gatorade should be. She snaps a dry spaghetti noodle into small pieces, unscrews the salt jar, and sticks the pieces into the salt.

"I ran into Cheryl Violi outside Kaufmann's," she said. "She said John's doing well in speech therapy."

The thought that shoots through my head is: I must be some asshole. Because, this whole time, when was the last time I even visited Wicked College John?

"Cheryl hasn't told many people," Mom says. "John doesn't really want to see anyone."

But I go anyway. Have you seen the Heated Driveway District in Mendon, where Wicked College John lives? Hilly new developments with long, noodly roads. Houses with pillars on front doorsteps; dirt covered with this Christmas-colored green spray. Wicked College John's house is mocha colored with an uphill driveway and a lipstick-red front door, two skylights on one long slant of roof. His mom's Dodge

Viper is parked outside the garage. Her keys jangle when she shuts the front screen door. She's wearing pointy white high heels, tank top, and leather pants, and carrying this bright turquoise purse. Freckles are everywhere on her tan. She walks down to the end of the driveway and lights a menthol.

"Oh Nate, sweetie, his speech isn't all there," she says before I can say hello.

I ask if I can go in.

She does a short inhale. "You can try. But he's really being a little shit right now. He's not eating. I try to breathe slowly around him. I try to touch his arm. I say my name all the time." She nods her head toward the screen door. "But he's in a torturable place. And I need a break." She pauses. "I need, need, need a break."

"What happened?"

"I tried to tell him, sweetie, you're alive. You're making amazing progress. I tried to tell him again what he'd been through, and"—she whispers this part—"he yells at me: 'I don't care what happened! Look at my face!'"

Through the screen door, I can see MLB 2000 on PlayStation on the living room's TV. Wicked College John himself: sitting on the leather living room sofa. His body looks milked and thin under his T-shirt, hemp necklace and cargo pants. His hair is un-gelled, combed down over his forehead. One crayon-line of scar makes a giant comma across his cheek.

"Sit," he says, slowly but sharply, like there are weights mounted to his lips.

Crowd noise ensues from the video game. Around him

are sheets of yellow loose leaf paper, each with tiny sketches of baseball diamonds, some with the bases filled in black. That's when I feel like I'd better cram at least fifty missed visits into this one.

"I used to be—" He pauses like it's the end of a sentence. "Good at this game." I see him write "Nate" in the top margin of a yellow sheet of paper. He drops the controller, either on accident or on purpose.

"You'll get better," I say.

"No I won't," he says, voice NyQuil paced. "That won't happen."

"Do you want to go outside? It's warmer out there."

"I can enjoy more than nature, Nate. I can still think."

An infielder on Wicked College John's team positions himself under a pop up, but dives out of the way at the last second, and Wicked College John punches himself in the thigh.

"I have this walker," his voice jerks a little.

"So there goes your what—modeling career?" I take off my Bills hat and show him the dent I have in my forehead from Raw Dog. "Man, we're just a bunch of ugly—"

"Yeah, but that's you," he bites his thumb. "The doctor says some people don't fully recover from these kinds of injuries. Which means," he says, swallowing more now, "I might always be this stupid."

"But you *know* you're stupid!" I say. "That's the smarter part of your brain working. You build off of that!"

"So you're saying I'm stupid," he says.

"John! Look on the bright side!" When as friends, we've

never had terms for "bright side." "Have you seen what's her face? That girlfriend?"

His head bounces slightly when he collapses against the headrest of the couch. I remember his head hitting the pavement in front of the Weapons of Mankind building, and I half-stand up to see if he's okay.

"Word of advice, bro," he says. "Do not talk to a girl if you cannot actually talk."

"What did you do to her?" I ask.

"I was just happy my dick worked again," he says. "She came to the hospital. I tried to tell her 'Sorry.' I thought I could handle the word 'sorry' in my brain, but when I tried to say it, I kept saying 'Tongue.' And the more I tried to say 'Sorry' the more I kept saying 'Tongue.' I had this really mad, red look on my face: tongue, tongue, tongue. So no, she hasn't called. No Welcome-Back Chinese Tape Deck."

"Chinese Tape Deck! A little Tokyo Rocking Horse! Those are jokes, from your memory!"

"Whatever," he says. "Taco Island Pepper Grinder."

"*Whatever* whatever. You're very lucky." I'm on the edge of the recliner, almost setting my hand on his knee. "You could be, I don't know, eating applesauce through an IV, you could be—"

He smiles for a second. Even though I'm not making a joke, he begins to crack up.

"Applesauce," he says, eyebrows hoisted. "I'll give you that. I'm the boss, applesauce!"

Then he chokes the laughing back.

"I think you have to go," he says.

So, forgive me, when I whip a trash bag from the trash bag roll at home, go to my room, and spend an entire day throwing out the pictures we took of the pizza delivery woman for no reason that one time me and Lip Cheese ordered Domino's; the sheet of paper me and Necro found downtown that said: "freedom for len freedom for len Freedom for Len Freedom For Len FREEDOM FOR LEN FREEDOM FOR LEN *FREEDOM FOR LEN.*" I throw out the first picture of Man-Serum Bagelheart, on loose leaf paper, his beard a bunch of squiggles in pencil, and I throw out the last drawing, I think, me and Necro ever made, where Man-Serum Bagelheart's limbs grow weak from ague (which Necro pronounced "agoo"), which Man-Serum had come down with from watching a seventy-hour broadcast that just showed a pair of testicles, and worrying, deeply, over whether they were his. Then I think: We were weird kids.

CRYSTAL-LYNN MAUER

Because we're at Mindy Fale's house and her parents are away, all we've done through the evening is feel each other up on the two-cushion couch in her living room. We're in the dark, lit only by the computer that's set up against the stairwell's half-wall, and after a good hour of General Makeout Fest, well after Conan, I'm feeling sort of fluish, one shoe suddenly off, staring into the fruit-punch vortex on her monitor's screen-saver. Which makes General Makeout Fests way sadder and way more annoying than you would imagine.

"It's just Necro," I say. Her forehead is pressed into my cheek. "The Aurorist?"

She rolls over. "Bitter, Nate."

Her living room is cramped as the inside of a music box, porcelain trinkets on heavy wooden shelves built into the walls.

My lips feel raw from kissing. She's crushing my chest a little, so I squirm, and she props herself up on one elbow. "You need to get involved in something. Maybe church. It'd be good for you."

"What does everybody always mean, good for me?"

I know I'm starting to depend on her more, because she has the kind of pity where it makes me want to shoot down her advice so I can get more pity. The screensaver changes to blue, to red, to yellow, and makes flickery shadows of the porcelain figurines on the shelves—a lumberjack, a swan, a newsboy, an archer. Each figurine stands next to a sign displaying a suit of a playing card.

"Something good has to come from your situation," she goes.

"Well, it won't," I say.

She stands up and puts her hands on her hips.

"Whatever. You don't care," I say.

"If I didn't care would I be—" she gestures broadly to the couch. "Never mind."

Mindy Fale leads me up the stairs, which ascend more at the angle of a ladder than a staircase. Her bed is waist-high, bedspread woolly as cotton candy, dolls and teddy bears piled two or three deep on the bed and her dresser. She reaches forearm-deep into the pile of dolls, pulling out the smallest, most mangled one.

The doll has a green Girl Scouts-type dress, a picnic-table-cloth Raggedy Ann face, and loose hemming where its right arm meets her body.

"This is Patty," she says. "I thought you should meet her."

I lie down. She lies down. The sheets are clean and stiff, like they were broiled dry. Some cartilage pops in my chest when she lays on top of me. She turns off the reading light attached to the bed's headboard.

"Could be worse," she pauses, thinking, which is also annoying. "You could be in Ethiopia."

"Don't be stupid."

She shakes her head. Her shoulders collapse and her brow crumples. "Well it seems like you're trying to sad your way into bed with me," she says, voice coming from some future where nothing is ever a joke. She's taken her hand out of my hair, like how some girls can move themselves away from me without me noticing, in that way where they're always smarter than me in all the ways that count.

So I say, with the last shreds of Happy Rolodex I can gather, Happy Rolodex's Last Stand: "I don't know. It's different with every girl."

"Different, like, with who, specifically?"

From her window, I see some light move. She knows I'm lying. "I—um, I, I—" Make something up. Give her a name she can't track. "Crystal-Lynn Mauer."

Who I hope doesn't actually exist. Then I remember that Crystal-Lynn Mauer does, in fact, exist, because she worked at the Science Store in Eastview, where me and Necro asked if we could buy gravity.

"Don't get freaked out," Mindy Fale says. "I just feel bad for you. You just seem like the unhappiest person I've ever met."

Which: unhappiest person? Tell that to my pants, when she rolls on top of me, pressing me halfway deep into the mattress, and sticks her hand through my fly, and it feels like she's rummaging for a stray tissue in her purse, but it's good enough, and I get into pushup position over her, and I don't even think to say to myself, with no friends left to even say it to: Well this is it! Flight Deck of the Enterprise!

After that, the whole thing feels pretty much like I imagined. The pillowcase is halfway off my pillow. A steam bubble cools in my head. Some enormous part of my personality feels as if it's been pulled out of me, like a bunch of tied-together handkerchiefs from a magician's mouth. The sheets feel less papery. The bedspread covers my left thigh. My underwear is rolled up into the fold where the bed sheets tuck under the mattress. My brain feels like the Snoopy nightlight in her bedroom, hovering in the dark, tracers batting across my eyes when I blink.

"Playing anything good on finger drums?" she says.

Because I've, on total autopilot, been tapping out a drumbeat on her waist. "Oh, it was nothing."

She rolls over and digs her chin into my chest. "Tell Mindy."

My stomach catches some shine from the nightlight when I inhale. "Well, it started out as Phil Collins's 'Take Me Home.'" She rolls away and laughs into the headboard. "But only for a second, I swear! And then it redeemed itself, sort of, by turning into 'Rikki Don't Lose That Number!'"

She bolts out of bed and claps her hands to her face, standing now, brow tense with important things. Her paunch line and vagina just out there.

"I was just thinking—*just thinking*—that was the song you were playing," she says, serious like she's dug up a lost Bible chapter. "Like I was half-thinking it, and then you said it. My dad used to sing that song to me in the car and change Rikki to Mindy. I was literally raised on that song."

I sit up and pull the covers over my crotch. She points to her eyes with her index and middle finger and then points to mine. "I'm very passionate about connections. We are buying that album first thing when we get an apartment!"

Even I wonder about this. Even I try to raise some doubt in her. "But what am I going to do for money?" I say.

"Dude. I make $26,000 a year."

I fall back down with my arms spread out. She throws herself on the bed and I bounce upward slightly. She is this awesome naked linebacker of a woman; her whole body is marshmallowy, made for breastfeeding, this girl, who can whoop my ass in bed, who I can get weird and desperate with. I had no idea we were together.

A THING TO INVEST

When I wake up one afternoon, Mom isn't home yet. In our kitchen, a light blinks on the message machine. I shake off the sleep and press it:

"Nathan this is Todd Vick from Kodak Park your friend Andrea told us to give you a call for a possible job at our industrial park downtown, uh, please give me a call back if you'd like to set up an interview, uh, Andrea gave you a very positive recommendation, and we'd like to get to know you a bit more and uh, if you'd like to give me a call back you can do so. oooOkaybye."

Just like this! Todd Vick, speaking with every stretched-thin, flat-A vowel available in the Rochester accent. Necro doesn't answer when I call him to see what any of this means. But, I figure, this means we're still friends. I figure that means me and Necro will have forklift races on the job the way he always promised if he could find me one, or smoke cigarettes in the factory alleys on our midnight lunch break and listen to the city's faint gunshots, or take naps in our own sleep corners. The Kodak Park Winjas—part wizard, part ninja—we'd call ourselves.

When I actually drive to Kodak Park for the interview, I park in the visitor's lot, across from this wedge-shaped brick building with no windows that extends forever down Ridge Road. Inside, Todd Vick is wearing a white, nylon-pajama-looking suit, a hairnet, and plastic goggles. He and everybody else who works at Kodak Park has a mustache. He goes for the handshake:

"Nathan Gray! Todd Vick nice to meet you how are ya welcome to Kodak Park. Just gonna have you fill out some paperwork."

We tour rooms with whiteboards that have numbers and diagrams. All Todd Vick asks me is: Can you lift fifty pounds? Can you follow specific directions? Work independently and with a team environment? All of which, as it finally hits me, I need to say yes to. He hands me a clean-suit, a nylon onesie packaged in shrink-wrapped plastic, and I tear open the packaging, unzip the suit, and step into it. He leads me deeper into the plant, through long, white, well-sanitized hallways into longer, darker hallways with only the dimmest striplighting on the floors. Todd Vick yells, "Yope!" and, from someone at the far opposite end of the hallway, I hear a whistle echo like an ocean bottom. Then he turns, suddenly, through a few sets of doors and we're back into the light, in a large, concrete room with maybe six vats, doors that look like garage doors, and metal carts holding jugs of chemicals.

There's some sort of cherry-rubber smell in the room. "This is the Building 38 Cart Loader," he says. Then he shows me Chemical Recycling, a room with a broad, gray floor, with a straight conveyor belt that runs along one wall, and, in the center of the room, a Humvee-sized metal box with a short, horseshoe-shaped conveyor belt curving into and out of it. On a desk near the wall, there's a booklet titled "Let's Build a Film," open to a page describing a step called Knurling. Then, with no specific reaction or another, I walk out with a job.

Which, honestly, feels better than Holy Grail Points, better than even the Pope's Scratch-Off Magic: It feels really pretty good. Because: Kodak: it's been here forever. Some guy— maybe sportscaster Rich Funke but without the mustache— narrates one of the workplace intro videos during my orientation the next day. It's cameras; I've used cameras.

So, dinner then.

When I call Necro so I can take him out for a Plate, a low pasty female voice answers the phone: Necro's in the woods behind his house.

In the woods, apparently, kicking at a sogged mat of dead leaves. The trees are knuckly and veiny, and Necro's hands are in his jacket pockets.

"I wanted to tell you thanks," I say, "for whatever recommendation you put in for me for Kodak."

He doesn't look up.

"Celebrations tonight? Get a Plate?"

"Come this way," he says.

I follow him, ducking under pine branches and stepping over rotted tree trunks, down a hill that's just steep enough to make my shoes skid.

At the bottom of the hill there's a crater, the size maybe of a cul-de-sac. There are beer cans, some rusted barrels, and what appears to be an airplane propeller, easily taller than me, mounted to a metal disc. Half of it is buried in the ground.

"Hawker Tempest prototype. Propeller, drive shaft, radiator—all intact," Necro says.

"Jesus, Necro."

"Give me a hand."

When we pull, the propeller-thing heaves up, vomiting chunks of dirt, dangling with roots. The propeller blades wobble when Necro drops it to the ground. "Before World War II, the government used to test planes over this area," he says. "One of them crashed, but it never made the papers. Then, an Italian immigrant and deer hunter, Cosimus Belvende, found some of the precious engine metals, in this very location, from this very plane's Napier Sabre. He discovered that when he took and welded down those metals to liquid form, he could make tantalum oxide, which he would use to make the first camera lens. The public name everyone knew this man by? George Eastman. This is the last part from that test plane. So, hold on to it. Let that thing accumulate some value-add. It's worth some stuff when you get it to the right collector or museum. Rochester and the Eastman House would probably pay, I don't know, $40,000? Italy maybe more? Give you a chance to take and implement some arbitrage. Give you a thing to invest in."

Which for the record: $40,000, converted, is 45 billion Holy Grail Points. "Then why don't you take it?" I say.

He starts to laugh, and not in his sniffly I'm-with-Nate way. "Didn't have room," he says. "Just didn't have room to pack it before I left tonight."

"Left? As in, what?"

"As in, town."

A balloon of nerve-syrup pops in my chest. I feel some aerosol behind my eyes, which makes it hard to stare straight ahead.

"My uncle. He took and found me a cashier job at the Swords and Candy store off I-90, in Pennsylvania," he says. "That, and I took and bought some stock in Howard Stern. Allow me to get away from *that*." He jabs his thumb behind him, toward his house and the whole city maybe.

"Now you have it all, victor and the spoils," he says. "You got my job. You got this patch of dirt in the woods. You got my propeller. You're me."

"Wait wait wait wait wait, Necro," I go. "What do you mean 'get away from that?'"

"I wouldn't wish that job on my most hated enemy."

"But—why?"

He laugh-coughs into his fist. Only the Great Walls of China dividing me and the division of labor in there. I don't even know where those canisters go after I send them down the conveyor. Every day we just take and shuffle chemical scrambled eggs from one room to another."

"But I thought we were going to do Kodak Park Winjas," I say. "They're giving me my own ESL account. I mean, it's cameras."

Necro lets his eyes get lazy at me. "There's no cameras,

Nate. They're a repurposer of equipment. I heard Kodak wants to research fuel cells in Tel Aviv."

I have no idea what that means. "So, you think you'll have enough money to cover expenses in PA? What if you get fired?"

He adjusts the shoulders on his jacket and steps toward me, chest first. He says, like he's been waiting sage prophecies of time to say this: "Goddamn Nate Rochefoucauld. Goddamn Nate Rochefoucauld, with his good night's sleep. You can't even take and support the people you *like*. The more altruistic people are to you, the more malice you apply to them and then, in turn, the more altruistic they'll be to you because they're thinking: 'Did I do something wrong? Did I offend him?' Until they epiphanize that you're like this-niceness-to-meanness-currency exchange, and people give you altruism dollars and you take and shit out drachmas at them. And this is how you go through people."

A leaf falls, sticks in my hair, hangs over my face for a second, and tumbles down my shirt. "So do you, just, not like me anymore?" I say.

I sit on a rock. The woods smell like really old fire. Necro shakes his head.

"If you don't want to talk to me ever again, I understand," I say. "But know that I'm sorry."

"The scope here is bigger than you," he says. "Over the last few months, I've been dedicating myself to the absorption of various, you know, tomes, about the relationship between linguistics and general man-to-man harsh treatment. As I try to take and synthesize these various texts—Lecercle, Pinker, et al—I've begun to suggest, in my thinking, that violence occurs within a cultural subset as that subset's phraseology gets too stale. Like: Colonel Hellstache, Colonel Hellstache—that's all we ever say. No new modes of expression. When the existing modes of expression are made stale or co-opted into oblivion by government agencies, man becomes incarcerated by his own linguistic detritus, and the result, eventually, is always violence. They say the government should be over-thrown every sixty years. And I would argue that, you know, that maybe language should be overthrown every sixty years. Change the name of things. Change the mindset."

"But we do change the mindset, Necro!" I say. "It's not just Colonel Hellstache. Sometimes it's Colonel Maritime Jason Hellstache. What about Condor Wrap with Diamond Sauce?"

Necro shakes his head. "But even Condor Wrap with Diamond Sauce, Nate. If you recall, I fed you the premise to Condor Wrap with Diamond Sauce. And Condor Wrap with Diamond Sauce was just a re-amalgamation of that Chilled Leopard Jaw with Braised Keith joke you made two years ago."

And now I know for certain that I can't convince him, at the last second, to let me Maverick Jetpants out of here with him off to Pennsylvania and overthrow language together. It's a thought that hits me in this practical way, like an accoun-tant passing along paperwork.

The next thought hits me slightly harder: At some point in our friendship, I started making Necro dumber. When I said Condor Wrap with Diamond Sauce, I was actually restricting both of our Joke Rolodexes, giving him less to say, pushing him to a life of Weapons of Mankind.

Necro smoothes out his jacket and exhales. "Welp. That said, I *could* use some sustenance. Get a Plate somewhere? Beans?" Necro gets his Plates with beans. I never understood people who get their Plates with beans.

"I'm going to stay here, actually," I say. "Think for a while."

Necro walks back up the crater's incline, European shoes crunching in the leaves, quieter and quieter, until he walks away forever.

I stand and let things get dark. My heart feels dumb. I think, for a while, that I am actually not thinking any thoughts. I am not even thinking about how people can live without one real friend; how all I have left are all my problems. I thumb at the propeller. It's wooden. Splinters dig into my hand when I pull one of the blades. I stretch my sweatshirt sleeve around my fingers and pull the propeller harder. The propeller moves, leaves catching on the radiator disk. It's maybe only as heavy as a canoe, but my hand muscles almost immediately cramp, and my shoes dig into the fudge layer of dirt under the leaves. I walk backward, pulling the propeller through the smooth rises and dips of the woods, the blade leaving a long trail through the leaves. The air freezes my front teeth when I inhale. My nostril hairs stiffen. Eventually, I find a nice stretch of woods that have nothing the propeller can catch on, and I start to build momentum.

At Necro's house, the lights are off except in the rectangular window in the basement that used to be Necro's room. I kneel down and look in. There's concrete floor where the carpet used to be; leftover hardcover Native American history books, a road sign, a leash, a three-ring binder, maybe one of the ones where he kept printouts of Encarta entries on things like Utilitarianism, the Greenhouse Effect, Niels Bohr.

I take out a receipt that's been in my wallet since I was sixteen—$2.59 worth of Gummi Bears from the Wegmans bulk section, on September 26, 1994. School had just started, I'd just gotten my license, and that night me and Necro stood outside the Ames and did breakdance moves and told shoppers we were the East Side Breakers and needed money to get to London. I pull up the grass with my fists, and dig into the ground with my index and middle fingers until they're swollen and there's a basketball-sized hole in the ground. I drop the receipt in the hole and armful the dirt back in.

The moonlight is chalk colored, shadows of branches visible. It's cold now, the season of cross-country and toilet-papered trees and amazing-tasting cigarettes. Good is not how I feel at all. But I do feel like I could walk past the sliding doors of apartment complexes and wander into parties by myself, give myself a new name for every day if I wanted: Colson McNeil, Kent Rigg, Brian Robinson, Jack Stelson, Mason Devereaux, Blake Chilton, Grant Jackson, John Puma, Ricky Esposito, Scott Grant, Dax Maysinger, Matt Helkinfauer, Jed Carlyle, Jake Mustang, Auggie MacIntyre, Griff Batmanson, Jason Grange. Any one of those.

TWO BALLERINAS,
FALLING

I wake up another day with the sun bleaching the edges off
everything in Mindy Fale's room. She and her parents have
gone to work, and it's always quieter when you're alone in a
house that's not yours, like you could stand in their kitchen
and scream and hear a tiny ringing in the metal of a frying
pan. Those are my keys, almost falling off her nightstand.
There is the car, leftover heat from the summer fattening its
insides. Nearly a month of this. For our two-month anniversary, she glued me together an ashtray with glitter-hearts, so
I can smoke menthols in bed. She makes me dinner and uses
real garlic. Big cloves, the kind you have to hit with a hammer
to get the peelings off.

After her work, Mindy Fale brings me along to Meigs
Street to look at an apartment, closer to the Bug Jar. The
place echoes like a church: the sunlight inside it is tan as a
WANTED poster in a Western; brick walls like a fire station;
hardwood floors like a basketball court.

The real estate agent, a college-age girl with a tank top

243

and a long skirt, taps her clipboard and says, "It's a very young, hip area."

Mindy Fale tugs my finger. "This place is so mine," she says. Her hair is pulled back; highlights in the brown, the way hairdying and bleaching gradually age into hair-highlighting. She giggles and bites the side of my cheek, which really irritates me for a second, like I could have broken up with her right there.

"We'll take it," I say.

Mindy Fale lets out a long "eeeee" in my ear, and now, I guess, I'm finally Platinum-Murman-Card Gold Membership Nate. No more High School Frito Pace-Offs. No more Rochester Classic Drivearounds.

Neither of us read the lease. On move-in day I listen to my bedroom get more echo-y as I move a few boxes and take my fifth last look at the four punctures in the carpet where the bedposts used to be. I take the tape of the techno song Necro and I made in my basement after Necro got that keyboard and we sampled me saying "My name is Owlie Fatburger" over Techno-Pyramid Beats. I take the Cosimus Belvende Propeller from the basement and wedge it diagonally into the U-Haul.

Mom buys me cubes of toilet paper rolls and paper towels; a silverware set; a placemat set with sketches of maple trees on them; a water-powered vacuum cleaner with the bubbles moving up the plastic tube on the body; boxes of dish detergent, with the metal pour tab that you need a Thumbnail of Iron to pick open. She also buys herself a new car and transfers ownership of her old one over to me.

The new apartment? I sweat through two T-shirts moving

boxes in. Me and Mindy Fale sit on the floor and use a turned-over plastic bin as a table for a few days. The bathroom is small and humid and has a way of retaining shaving cream scent but not soap scent. I buy aerators for the faucets; I buy caulking tape; I set up a lawn chair by the window and make a point to sit during afternoons and imagine cozy-sounding piano playing as all the different lives and whatnot walk through this city; I buy a broom.

I also put on my pre-faded going-out jeans that Mindy Fale bought me and walk with her to the East End Festival, where they tent off parts of East Avenue, set up white plastic chairs for the crowds, and serve wine in plastic cups. The bands playing are the Skycoasters, who say they're New York's No. 1 Party Band, and Nik and The Nice Guys, who say they're America's No. 1 Party Band.

The sky is the color of Pinot Grigio. Under the tents are women with bright white visors and tanned fifty-year-old men in pastel yellow shirts and Dockers. When me and Mindy Fale go up to the counter in the beer tent, I smell a combination of locker-room sex and rotting toothpaste that can only mean one thing.

Toby. Standing over us, yellow on the edges of his white dress-shirt collar. He hasn't shaven. His hair, and receding hairlines, have grown out, liquor sweat all over him. Which only makes me realize how much, now, I actually do shave. His lower lip is puffed downward.

"Oh Nate, you're here," he says. He looks at Mindy Fale and rubs the corners of his lips.

"Toby, you know Mindy," I say.

"Mindy?" he says. "You look, uh, healthy! You've really—I mean, it's good to see you."

Mindy Fale—even though she's fully aware that Toby's practically made a plaque that says National Night at the Stalls Award for her—she looks at him, smiles out of the corner of her mouth, and waves with her fingers!

The sunset snots up in Toby's forehead sweat. He looks like he has pink eye. "I've got a girl too, Nate. We're getting married. She's almost eighteen."

He crushes a plastic wine cup on the ground when he takes one step backward.

"What's wrong?" Mindy Fale asks.

"It's just that we can't exactly get married now," he says. He slings his arm around Mindy Fale, which immediately has me planning for a way to Warp Whistle out of here. He sucks in his gut. "Can't get married for like, two or three years, maybe," he says. "At least."

"Why?" I say.

"Parents," he says. "Her parents." He smears his palm across his right eye. "They want us to break up."

"Aww," Mindy Fale says, like she's spotted a one-eyed stray.

"She's very school-oriented," Toby says. "She said she had homework until eight, very grade-oriented. Whereas I'm more relationship-oriented. So until she can move out, we'll just have to wait for each other."

"She will," Mindy Fale says, side-hugging him. "I dated a guy who beat up a Wegmans cashier who said he was too drunk to buy beer for football. He was in jail for a little while. We weathered it."

"I've just, I've been really kind of down, lately, on my-self," he says, face drooped, like a sad pie. "Between this girl, and ever since I Went Off the Top Ropes on Necro. I gotta get some control, you know. I've been on these prescriptions. But I take them and I'll think, for real, that out of the corner of my eye, that I see somebody—the mailman!—in my basement!"

And with that, after one last play in my head of the Toby and Nate Great Plays Highlight Reel of any time I tried to tackle him on the way home from some party in the woods, or anytime he played that VCR tape of "Bum Olympics" on *Life Without Shame*, I look to Mindy Fale, fake yawn, and I am no longer friends with Toby.

Except, I fake-yawn again. How long is she going to let Toby's arm stay around her? I raise my eyebrows and shift my eyes toward the street—all of which are Classic Warp Whistle Gestures to let someone know you want to get out of here. But instead she mouths, angrily, "What?"

"That's why, very soon, Nate, I need to bang her," Toby says, and, voice getting hoarse, suddenly, like he breathes an aerosol form of sausage: "The parental decree could come any day where they just tell her 'no more.' After which my dick is fucked. My dick is a can of worms."

Because, what Mindy Fale doesn't know is the last time Toby's dick was a can of worms? There were teeth marks on his neck, and not in a good way.

"That's why, Nate, I need a favor. I had to sell my car, I'm trying to take classes at MCC, take this downness I'm feeling and squash it. I need a ride, to go find her tonight."

"I'd give you a ride," I tell Toby, "but Mindy has to work tomorrow, and we walked—"

"We live three blocks away, Nate," she says. "I'm a big girl, I can walk myself."

I look at Mindy Fale, Warp-Whistle Gesturing until my face evaporates.

"Go on, go! Help your friends!" she says, shoving my arm.

"This deed will not go unrewarded, Nate," Toby says. "This deed is, like, the Sacred Gold Coin, buried in the Secret Cave of Zargon or Whatever, worth 8 billion points. Let me just go tell my mom."

Toby sits down at a white plastic table under one of the tents, and touches the arm of some arthritis-faced lady with a pink sweater tied around her neck and whose hair is thin like blond cotton candy. Which, I guess, is his mom, who I've never seen ever, in all the years I've pulled into his driveway.

"Why are you being weird?" Mindy Fale says.

"I'm not being weird! I'm trying to get out of here."

"You can't be tired. You're off tomorrow."

Toby slings his arm around my neck and we walk off to my car. The street lamps are turning on, mansions on East Ave, some converted to dentist's offices, others still mansions for whoever here has money, with goldshine in the windows. I think to myself: I wish I were bored more often. Your nerves shrink when you're bored. That's why time moves slower.

But, nerve shrinkage. Just reciting the things Mindy Fale knows calms me down: Nobody knows why or how cats purr. Or how the red in your eyes in photographs isn't from the film quality, or the lighting in the room, or even from the camera at all. It's from the blood in your pupils, reflecting back at you like violent coins.

On 490, Toby has the passenger window down, forearm on the windowsill, turning the radio to the Nerve. We head into Pittsford, an electric-awning bread maker of a town. We turn into a neighborhood whose name involves an animal trail—Fox Gulch Something—where there are pastel-colored houses and timed sprinklers still rotating in some front yards.

"This is her house!" Toby says. "Turn off your headlights! Turn off your headlights!"

Toby's girlfriend sits Indian-style on her front lawn, shin bones shiny. Her hair is dark and short in the back but reaches down to her chin in the front. Her shirt, a tank top, is supposed to be tight fitting but it's loose around her stomach. A lot of knee bone still in her legs, which makes me wonder how old she really is.

She folds her body into the corner of the car's backseat. "What's up!" she says in this guy-type way that's way too old for her. When she closes the door, there's a feeling of being vacuum-packed, the air sucked out as the door seal licks around the rim of the door. The radio's volume is ant-sized. I don't even get introduced. She's wearing blue sneakers that have orange shoelaces, socks that have Snoopy and Woodstock on them. Toby hangs his palm over the headrest, and she hooks fingers with him.

"So let's go *get* that drink already," she says, faking a twang. "Pitcher of Get-the-Hell-Outta-Here Juice."

Toby rubs his chin. "We could always drive to the Kove, Nate."

Good God. Not the Kove. I haven't even told you about the Kove. I practically contributed lambs and small countries to God hoping I wouldn't have to bring up the Kove. The fact that Toby's bringing up the Kove—a Toby museum exhibit—is enough to make you pity him until he turns into his own brand of syrup.

"Let's go somewhere else," I say.

"I was, shall we say, reminiscent," Toby says, more loudly, to the girl.

"I could be persuaded," she says, again, in a loud adult way that doesn't belong to her.

"Very well! But, to the liquor store first, captain!" Toby says.

The Kove? The Kove is this abandoned hardware store where Toby and his older friends who I haven't seen in years, people you'll never meet, used to drink vodka and wrestle each other unconscious in sleeper holds. Matt Sullivan, Mitch Keisler, Ryan Glasscock, last name actually Glasscock. They furnished the Kove with some sofa they stole from a curb, and some cafeteria chairs Toby stole from the high school. And, the other thing—the only guy who has the keys to the Kove's padlock? Toby. Glasscock gave Toby the key one night when he was drunk enough to think he'd lose it, before he went off to college and became a regional accounting manager in North Dakota.

I remember, one time, how Toby described sex: like a hammer covered in skin.

My car crackles over some gravel at some liquor store parking lot, and Toby gets out to buy a cube of Genny and a plastic thing of tequila. The light from the store makes Toby's girlfriend more visible from the rearview mirror. She frowns out the window.

Looking at her, though, I think, right then, she's someone who could help me do the first right thing I've done in some time.

"Do you really want to be with Toby?" I say.

She droops and glazes in the backseat.

"I'm taking the GED. He supports me," she says.

"Why would you quit school? You live in Pittsford."

"You try serving up ice cream at Abbott's, and having some ex-boyfriend that's at every show you go to."

"'I've known Toby for a long time,'" I tell her. "Has he told you why he brought you out here? Has he told you that out of boredom he tried to convince me my best friend was a serial arsonist? Has he told you this?"

She looks at the car's floor.

"Give Toby three months, he will bring you to a bar so his friends can lick tequila out of your navel. Give Toby three years, he'll shove aside the dinner you make. He will never have enough money to take you anywhere. We can Springsteen this car back home, while he's still in there. We can unkill the time we've lost tonight."

I let the crickets, the occasional car that breathes by, help my point sink in.

"Are you hitting on me?" she says.

Toby walks out of the store, silhouette only visible in the store light. He strains the shocks when he angles, ass-first, into the backseat next to his girlfriend.

"And we're off! Commander Spock, take us away!" he says,

holding the girl's hand. He cracks open a beer one-handed and opens the bottle of tequila.

I drive onto 104, which noodles out past towns like Holley and Albion that are maybe the size of a tic-tac-toe board on a map. Towns that have 1st St. or an on-a-whim 5th Ave., like they'd wanted to start a city, but only got as far as one or two lights on at night and maybe one smokestack, where a large, muscular arm of smoke might reach upward, until sunrise.

Toby says something into the girl's ear. In the rearview mirror, I see the girl stretch out, like she has to think with her body.

"Well, I guess there was one other guy," I hear her say. She murmurs something else, and pushes his sweat-shiny palm away from her dress. "I don't know. I'm not mean like you."

There appear to be steroids in the air. Toby gets bigger by the breath.

But when I pull into the Kove lot, there's a sushi restaurant in its place, dark inside and closed for the evening, with an awning that has some Japanese lettering, some tiny bamboo plants on the windowsills.

Toby gets out of the car, leaving the door open, just before I come to a full stop. The girl gets out after him. His voice sounds like it's been strung up and hanged; he grips his forehead-fat with his hands: "Oh no no no no. Oh no no no no. Come on. No."

Toby runs to the restaurant's door, stabs the Kove Key at the keyhole, and hurls the Kove Key across the street, where there's a gated-off dirt lot, further off, and a Home Depot that has large letters that spell COMING SOON across the windows.

It's late enough, and getting cold enough, to see our breath in the light from the street lamps. The girl plants one hand on her hip.

"What," Toby says to her. Their bodies are backlit in a way where you can see their arm hair from far away. I stay by the car, to give them the idea that I can't hear them argue.

"You didn't say it'd be this far out," she says. "I have to be home. I told you we have my parents' boat."

Toby jams the heels of his hands into both sides of his temples three times, audibly. She sticks her jaw out, like she's ready to yell, but Toby cuts her off:

"Oh my *GOD!* You always do this!" he says, spit leaping off his lower lip. "Whenever I make a wrong turn, whenever I write down the wrong address. I provide the money! I provide the car! That's something I do."

Toby pulls her in, arms like chompers on the back of a garbage truck. "It's just that I try so hard," he says, lips pressed into her scalp, "and all I want is to die all the time."

Since I'm calling this evening over, I twirl my keys around my index finger. But suddenly I feel a scrape on my knuckle and my keys are gone, because Toby has just yanked my key ring off my finger, hooked the girl's body with one arm, and opened the driver's side rear door and slammed it shut. He slaps down all the locks on the windowsills and immediately grabs the girl by her hair and facebombs her on the lips. I hear her gag and try to say something, and Toby's suctioning her whole face practically, and something creaks in the car, and a handprint smears on the window, and I see Toby's fist under the back of her shirt, and the girl's hair mats up against the glass, and Toby almost rolls into the seat well, and the car shakes when he palms the floor, and then I see the girl's hand, trying to push Toby's face away, and then I realize Toby's trying to rape her, and my chest clenches into a trash compactor, and every other building is closed, and I look down, and I find I'm poised, somehow, like a shortstop, but just standing there, knees bent, and all I can say to myself is Oh God Oh God Oh God, because the girl yells, "Please no!"—muffled by Toby's chest, and the glass begins to fog up, and she jams a thumb in Toby's eye, and, with a cylinder pump, Toby pins her arm to the seat.

I slap the windshield with my palms. I climb on the roof. I slap the rear window, through which I see—Oh Please God No—Toby bracing his legs against the passenger-side door, holding the girl down with his shoulder while he wrestles with his fly and, hooking his thumbs into his shorts, shoves them down his thighs.

She screams, over and over. Then, for exactly one second, my eyes meet hers.

Her pupils are tightened to the size of pencil pricks. I don't even know if she sees me. I think, maybe, three minutes before this, she was some girl who liked that band the October Project, or whatever short-haired lady did that song "Bohemia" that BER played when I used to station-surf while doing my homework.

Because, the nearest payphone is Godhowevermany miles away. Because, if I even try to call police, then I'm leaving this girl alone with Toby. I punch the window as hard as I can, and seconds later I open my eyes and I'm on the ground, doubled over my hand, nearly choking to death. I yell something that's not a word to nobody in particular. I give a half-running start, but I don't commit to it as much as I should, but when I extend my foot, I connect, and then a yardstick-sized spike of pain shoots up my right ass-cheek through my shoulder when I land on the gravel. When I look up, there's a heel-shaped crunch in the glass. Toby and the girl are sitting up, staring straight ahead. The doors are unlocked. No cars come by. It's so quiet above us. You can hear the mist in the air.

Future Nate is screaming at the TV: Take him to the police! But when I get in the car my brain is in a flooded crawlspace, and the only way out is to get Toby away from us. When I pull into his house's driveway, he opens the door, looks at us, looks to the sky, and screams the weirdest thing I've ever heard.

"Each one of us!" he says. "Each one of us, are two ballerinas, turning, falling, infinitely. Never knowing—when we'll land."

My headlights blare against Toby's garage. He slams the door and walks across his front lawn. In the grass, there's a wooden cutout of a woman in a bonnet bending over to garden something.

When I get back on 490, I shake my head, and hope Toby's girlfriend notices it.

"Sorry," I say.

I can hear her sniffling. On the highway, there's a pair of headlights way off on the horizon behind me, a pair of brake lights way off on the horizon in front of me.

"Any one of these gas stations has a payphone," I say. "We can call the police there."

"Don't condescend to me," she says.

Which I ignore. "Do you need anything? Police? Coffee?" I say. "I'm not tired at all."

At her house, she opens my car door as little as possible, slips out, and eases the door shut so that the latch barely clicks and my Door Ajar light stays on.

Here's something else, which is either terrific or another picture for the Failed Plan Hall of Fame Calendar.

Years later, at Eastview Mall, way after this story ends, I go into the Sears to buy a mini drain snake for my kitchen sink. My head is down when I enter the store, and a girl is just passing opposite me, walking out toward Eastview's main concourse. She almost walks past my blind spot when I realize, suddenly, who she might be. I turn around, and only see the back of her head. She's pushing a baby stroller. Some guy with a collared short-sleeve shirt and good triceps, sitting on a bench underneath a tree, stands up to meet her. He hangs his arm around her. I want to think she smiles here. Her orange and baby-blue clothing lead me to believe the girl is Toby's once-girlfriend.

I have a good track record of this, of going a long time without seeing people and recognizing them years later, far past the point after they've stopped recognizing me. It's her I'm seeing, walking past the display Kia Sedona being raffled off and the teenage girls wearing short skirts and the sunglasses kiosk and the hot-pretzel smell. I could catch up to her. I could talk to her, vaporize some guilt right then. I even stand there; I even debate myself over this, for a good four minutes. I even walk after her a few steps, before I lose sight of her completely. Afterward, I buy what I need and spend a half-hour at the pet store aquariums, looking at the neon tetras and the clown loaches. Bright-colored fish that begin dying the second you bring them home in plastic bags.

COSIMUS BELVENDE,
GEORGE EASTMAN

Walking out of the 3-Mezz elevator, way down the cinder-block hallway, there's a red door on the left labeled VENTILATION. Through that door, a large aluminum ventilation shaft, wide as a dump truck, angles gradually downward from the ceiling as I walk, a football field's walk, to where the shaft meets the opposite wall. In the three-foot space below where the vent meets the wall, on the floor, in the dark, I find a white blanket and pillow.

The pillow's stuffing is bunched up into three or four knots. If this were *The Proto-Stachening of Nate: The Movie*, this would be where I discover a dead body or a Grail. I fold the pillow in half and set my head on it. The heat from the vent is lint-scented, strong enough to warm the gray-painted concrete floor. I close my eyes, feel my leg twitch and my eyeballs crazy-dance—"Good evening, sir, welcome to Club Sleepybats," the doorman says, and unlatches the velvet rope.

On other days, I make more Sleepybats: to get through an hour when the conveyors are turned off; to beat back a

hangover until it's speck-sized in my head; to relax after the
10 a.m. canister rush.

Then, one morning, a Friday shift, I'm flung awake by a
noise that sounds like the entire building gagging up a house-
sized cube of iron.

Red lights, suddenly, go on everywhere. An alarm sounds,
apocalyptic, low, like an angry dial tone, loud enough to give
you a nosebleed. My cleansuit wedgies when I run down the
hallway. I can't hear my footsteps. "Nathan Gray. Please call
1184. Nathan Gray. 1184," the PA says. I harpoon my hand
to the doorjamb and swing around back into the chemical
recycling room, where canisters are backed up across the entire
length of the conveyor. "Nathan Gray. 1184." I plug my ear
with my right finger and, with my left hand, pull what canisters I can off the line.

Then, I hear a loud click, which echoes through 3-Mezz's
steel beams, and the alarm sound winds down, getting lower-
pitched and quieter. Yelling arrives from down the hall. Two
men who I have never seen before, in white cleansuits and
hairnets, jog toward the bag dispenser. I realize I have no idea
what color anybody's hair is here. One of the men, carrying a
clipboard, presses the dispenser's green Go button repeatedly,
and corkscrews violently toward me.

"What happened?" he shrieks. I can't tell if he has eyebrows. The boniness of his face makes his sweat extra shiny.

"Is the line stopped?" I say.

"Jesus *Christ*!" He wings the clipboard to the floor,
where it tumbles over itself and skids until it hits a pallet
of spare bag rolls. "I've never seen this. Never once in my

twenty-two years." The men swing their arms hard walking away.

"Colonel Hellstache," I mumble.

The clipboard man wide-strides back to me and points his nose down at my eyebrows. I feel my tear ducts squirming. "What did you say?"

"Nothing."

"The *fuck*, did you say?" His face is shaking.

"I didn't say anything. 'Crap.' I said 'crap.'"

He walks away, swiping his arm down to pick up the clipboard. I make a crossbar with my left arm and uppercut my right bicep into it to make a giant middle finger.

Because, I've started saying phrases to myself, mostly to get them back—Maverick Jetpants, Colonel Hellstache, Hashbrown Gargoyle. Because it's not my fault I hate my job. Not my fault I'm in this huge room, and can hurl canisters against the wall all twelve hours without anybody noticing.

After 6 p.m. relief, the locker room belt rack on the wall has belts hanging down that are almost as tall as me. Pictures of old Jordache models curl on the brown, blistering paint on the insides of men's lockers. Mustached men, who no longer care if anyone sees their dicks in the shower, shower.

I round the corner and Todd Vick appears. He puts his hand on my shoulder. "Nate. Could I see you a second?"

I remember that he hasn't talked to me at all since I started working here. His goggles are propped up on top of his hairnet. Without them, his eyes look like dots and parentheses. He waits for two men to walk by us and lowers his voice.

"Kodak has hired a consultant to assess our current

production model, and I'd like to squeeze in a performance evaluation with you on Monday before I meet with them," he says.

"I'm off Monday," I say.

"I know," he says. "Plan to be here anyway."

"I thought evaluations were in February. Is this because of, you know, today?"

He raises his eyebrows, like maybe he wasn't expecting the question, and draws a breath: "Building 17 conference room. 9 a.m."

I check my balance at the ESL ATM: $73. And, the way a python swallows a pig, I drive home and begin the slow, brain-dark work of worrying down the weekend until Monday.

And Mindy Fale: I don't even know what her problem is. She's gained twenty more pounds. She has not Brought the Funny since Bilingual Cock. She will treat you like every one of your mistakes was made on purpose.

Because, at home, Mindy Fale, already in pajama pants, has removed a back cushion from the couch and is using it as a pillow against the couch's armrest. CNN is on mute. I sit down next to her and lay my head on her thigh.

"I got yelled at today."

"Why?" she says, not running her fingers through my hair or anything.

I stick my hand between two of the couch cushions, which makes my knuckles smell like toasted fiberglass. "I stopped the line. Todd said I have to attend a performance evaluation on Monday."

Her leg muscle tenses. "What'd you do."

I clench my teeth. A whole Anger Montage of Fists steams through my head. "Nothing! I was tired. I take melatonin that doesn't work, and wake up at 4:15 a.m. to get to work by 5:30."

"Are you trying to get fired?"

I push myself up away from her.

"That's what they do!" she says. "They give you a shitty evaluation so they can make it easier to fire you."

"You could be a little more supportive," I tell her. "It's a million-dollar accident that happened. I really don't appreciate this right now."

Her eyes widen. "You don't appreciate!" She's almost laughing.

I go into the bathroom, dump maybe a third of her bottle of astringent into the sink, and run the faucet to wash down the smell.

The next day is the weekend, so Mindy and her friends from work or wherever go out to dinner at Eastview. Eastview is the only mall in Rochester that's actually getting bigger, in this way where I imagine the mall is some huge magnet that can pull buildings to it—Mexican limestone and Moscow onion domes.

Walking into the mall, I still feel the world's possibilities, like I can afford things like refrigerators and massage chairs. It's airy and white-tiled, a palace made of aspirin, with sky-lights the size of Olympic swimming pools. A mall-breeze goes through my Thurman jersey—NFL issue—because that's what I wear to the mall. Mindy Fale, though? She's wearing black work pants and open-toe high heels, dark, humorless brown lipstick that, like all lipstick on her, makes her look as if she's hated me all along.

The entrance of the restaurant faces the mall's concourse and has small, round, thick tables, each with a votive candle, stumpy wooden chairs and menus with wooden covers with the logo—J.T. Something-Or-Other's; Est. Whenever— carved into them. Mindy Fale stops holding my hand the second we see her work friends, already at a table.

She sits diagonally across from me, next to this bleach-haired guy with a hemp necklace, who you know totally owned a motorcycle in high school but whose bad-assery has since been whittled down to untucked button-down collarless shirts, like the one he's wearing now, and owning a parrot. Her other friend is some girl with muttony arms—blotches of pink like they've been slapped. I've forgotten about her before I can even remember her.

"This guy came in with headphones and poked a wand into the floor," the girl says. "He found the leak in two minutes. Three hundred dollars."

Which, that statement alone I will let speak for itself. The hamburgers here are $12. Labatt's are $4. I get paid $250 a week. But rent is due next week—$600 total, and Mindy Fale pays $400 of that, so minus $200 for my portion of the rent will put me at $123. But renter's insurance is due this week, so minus $30 or so puts me at $93. Mindy Fale pays cable, and groceries, and the only thing I have to take care of is the phone bill, which should put me at $33 or $23 at the very worst.

As if she has no idea how frequently I do try to math out my problems, Mindy Fale closes her eyes and leans her head against the guy, the Parrot King's, shoulder. Which, maybe they're just good friends.

"There was a lawsuit I read about, against PVC pipe makers in China," the guy says, squeegeeing off the sweat of his water glass with his thumb. "Front yards: dug up all across Mendon."

When the waitress takes our drink orders, Mindy Fale goes: "Can I get a Red-Headed Slut?"

"What's a Red-Headed Slut?" Parrot King asks.

A smile forms at the corner of her lip. "You can have a sip," she says to the Parrot King.

Parrot King waggles his head and smooths his collar-tips. Ham it up, asshole. "Sounds like a job for"—he turns his head away, swings it back around and shakes his goatee at her—"The Hedgehog!"

Mindy Fale cracks up. Suddenly the back of my neck is hot. I scan the restaurant's dimness for any girl with bare arms, any girl who would do me the charity of wearing shorts as the nights get colder. And I think about telling Mindy Fale that I'm sick of her multiple personalities—how she'll grow cuddle-fur when it's us in the apartment, but in public she transforms into Spring Break Avalanche, Night at the Stalls edition. I think about telling her that I know that men are supposed to joke down these situations, to charm her back to you when she's being hit on, but it gets so hard to think creatively around her.

"Colonel Hellstache," I cough into my arm instead.

Mindy Fale narrows her brow at me, mouth open and chin stuck out a bit.

"What was that you said?" Parrot King asks.

"Tell him, Nate," Mindy Fale says.

"It's just this phrase," I say. "It's stupid."

"Maybe I'll start saying that," the guy says, which is either earnest or the meanest thing anyone has said to me.

"Tell them how it's everything you hate," Mindy Fale says.

There's pressure on my cheeks; my ears are getting red the way Lip Cheese's used to when he was embarrassed. I wish I could have done everything differently. I've never explained Colonel Hellstache to anybody. Even worse, nobody, apparently, has cared before to ask.

"Basically, I think, me and Necro—a friend—rode our bikes all the way into the city one time. We saw a flier for this band, stapled to a telephone pole outside the Bug Jar. Astrojanitor Records Presents: The Black Arrows, and this other band, Dago Frogstache. That's where Stache came from, and we started putting Stache at the end of everything we said that day. Hell came from Hell, which became Hellstache, after me and Nec—this friend of mine—later that day got stuck in a rainstorm riding back to my house. Then, I guess, we just moved it up the ranks. General Hellstache. Colonel Hellstache."

But that can't be all there is to it. Mindy Fale's friends have finished their iced tea. "Oh," is all the girl says.

"But, yeah," Mindy Fale says. "I heard Chinese copper, in some of these new houses, can spring leaks like—"

"Don't interrupt me," I say.

She blares her eyes and relaxes her shoulders. "I thought you were done. Sorry."

Mindy Fale runs her hand hard against her scalp. Our drinks come. Mindy's is this pink-looking thing with no ice in a whiskey glass. She's drunk before she even drinks it. She downs the whole thing, turning her chin toward Parrot King, her tongue clearly at the bottom of the glass.

"Come on," I say. "I am right here."

I let her know it, too. I stare at her through the entire meal. Mindy asks the waiter for two checks—one for us and one for her friends—and she smirks when he sets the check booklet for us down in front of me. She plunges her hand into her purse—making a whole opera out of it—and takes out her credit card. So I drop the bill in front of her, throw my hands up, walk away, and wait for her by the host desk.

Outside the restaurant, I see the Bon-Ton at the opposite end of the mall and walk toward it. Mindy Fale stays about three feet behind me. Because I've figured this out now: I have nothing to wear in Mindy Fale's world of work. I need shirts and ties for this evaluation at Kodak. I need shirts and ties for the rest of my life.

A circular table at the Bon-Ton dress section, which I've never not been in without my mom, has a display of shiny dress shirts, paired with ties, and laid out fan-like in a rainbow color pattern. I sling a gray tie over my shoulder.

"What are you doing?" Mindy Fale says. "What is wrong?"

I flex my stomach muscles to keep from screaming. I also get pants, which, like everything else I do now apparently, is no longer funny. The cashier radar-guns the items and swipes my ESL card. The swipe machine makes a long, microwave-type beeping noise. She swipes it again; beeping noise. I slap at my neck. She folds a plastic shopping bag around the card and swipes again. Same beeping noise.

"This card's being declined for whatever reason," the cashier says.

Mindy Fale sighs, head rolling toward her left shoulder.

"Can you cover this for me?" I ask her.

People in line behind us hang clothes over their forearms and shift their weight.

"I can't do that," Mindy Fale says.

"My paycheck comes Tuesday, I swear."

I step aside from the line. I tell Mindy Fale: "You have no problem blowing $150 on your friends at Outback-freaking-*Fake*house!"

"That's different."

"It's not different! How?"

She looks past me, face completely flat expression-wise. "It's just different."

I hang the clothing on a rack of girls' pink winter coats and walk out after her. She throws a quarter in the fountain, this blue-tiled thing with a pile of plastic rocks that the water runs down. I flip up my hands.

"I was saying a prayer," she says.

"Jesus charges twenty-five cents per prayer? A prayer for what?"

"I'm not saying."

People walk past us: a man in a sweater tapping on a PalmPilot; a toddler in a pink dress holding the hand of a large, shaved-headed guy with a black T-shirt that says ALKQN in gold, medieval-looking lettering.

"Give me your purse," I say.

She stops. "No. Freak."

"I get paid next week. Just give me your wallet." Suddenly I'm cranky. I always forget that two pints at a restaurant makes you way more cranky than two pints at a bar.

"No. That's assault."

A chinfat man with a Flutie jersey. A red-haired kid with a shirt that says LOSER, who mock-punches a tall skinny kid in a Celtics tank top.

Mindy Fale starts walking. "Wait," I say. I reach toward her to see if she'll let me touch her. And on accident, I hook my ring finger and pinky into her purse strap. Her shoulder yanks back, she swings around, and her arms are thick and bullish and, on accident or on purpose, the heel of her hand flies into my cheek. "Damn!" someone yells.

The embarrassment dulls the pain. More than anything, I'm concentrating on standing up straight, trying to look as casual as possible: "We've got a live one here," I say, apparently, to everyone here.

She draws her fist back. I flinch, my shoulders seize. But she checks her swing, and when I open my eyes she's walking away again. Then I follow her to the car and she drives us home.

She doesn't say anything until we get on the highway, and she flips her blinker on to go around a truck. "I just don't think you understand how much of an insult it is," she says. "You think I like taking calls all day about property and casualty? I don't like my job either. But I still work hard so we can at least have money. I paid for your dinner, paid to get you drunk tonight, and you thought nothing of it. And you whine and whine about this job that was handed to you by your friend."

"I'm not whining; I'm complaining."

A Mustang with an undercarriage blacklight streaks past us.

"My dad gave Jamie $50,000—for permits, whatever, to open that rims shop," she says. "But he went out and bought trunk speakers for his Civic. Even after he sold his ring, he still owes me $4,000—credit card payments, a certain trip to a certain clinic he said he'd pay for. For you to have to borrow money, this quickly, is a bad sign."

Never mind that we're not married, so it defeats her point, so never mind.

"I don't know," she says. "Maybe you're just happier not working."

"That's not true," I say.

But it feels far worse than any complaint she could make about me. I already miss, like childhood, when she'd say "See you tomorrow Mister Natebones Gray" before kissing my head goodnight—the way it implied the future. I want so badly to get home so I can wash the dishes and pick my socks up from under the coffee table and throw them in the hamper, and then: I get the Idea. It hits me like a musical.

"I've got it," I tell her. "I have a Plan."

We get back to the apartment, and I leap down the stairwells of each floor and unlock our basement storage closet. I peel the blanket off the Cosimus Belvende Propeller and drag it up the stairs, angling it through our apartment door, scraping the floor, banging the lamp hanging from the ceiling above the dinner table and knocking a paper towel roll off the kitchen counter. I set it upright against the living room wall.

Mindy Fale, already in her pajama pants and on the couch, blinks six or seven times.

"Exactly," I go. "Exactly. But!" I tell her what Necro told me—about the government testing planes; about Cosimus Belvende, who came here from Italy, about tantalum oxide and camera lenses. I say Brownie Hawkeye.

"This is the last piece of the plane that invented Kodak," I tell her. "Museums will pay thousands for this. If I sell this, I could pay rent and groceries for you for years. This is the propeller from the plane that Cosimus Belvende, aka George Eastman, used to build this city."

The wooden propeller leans there, brown.

Mindy Fale, then, belts out this laugh. A smart anger-laugh, that rises for a few seconds into almost-joy.

"George Eastman was born in Waterville, New York, Nate," she says and starts laughing again.

I think: Did Necro, in his own way with his story about the propeller, completely tell me off one last time? Did he make all that up just to get back at me?

"Cosimus Belvende? You fucking retard. The Italian deer hunter? *Thee?*"

Later that night, she lies on the couch under a yellow and black Kodak blanket I got after my first month there. She watches the movie *Labyrinth* at least twice.

"Standing there and staring at me is not going to make this better," she says. Then she adds, "I *hate* that."

"I'm going to work on what's wrong with me," I say.

"What?"

"I know. I need to do better. I'm going to try to do better."

"Good," she says. "Good for you."

Because, when I go to bed, the heat's coming on. Listen to the radiator fizz sulfur under the bedroom window, the first hiss. Smell the leftover soot from the summer. It's been a warm fall, one I T-shirted most of the way through. These things are enjoyed more with women, Mindy Fale being a woman.

When I wake up, it's 9:31 a.m. on Sunday. My T-shirt collar is soaked, my pajama pants are damp on the backs of the knees, in a way where I know I slept the shit out of the evening. But Mindy Fale's not next to me. The sheets on Mindy Fale's side of the bed are drawn up to the pillow. When I look into the kitchen and living room, it's quiet. The Kodak blanket is folded on the couch's armrest. The sun is like a radioactive egg yolk through the windows. The silverware in our kitchen sink's dry rack glows like a condensed electrical fire.

"Hey. You here?" I say.

"Mindy?" I say louder, a wine glass ringing by the sink.

Her toothbrush is still wrapped in a piece of toilet paper on the sink edge. When I unwrap it, I press the brush to my lips; it's dry. The clothes she wore last night aren't in the hamper, the closet, her dresser. The orange Evening Tic Tac I set under her pillow last night—which I just made up so we could take them before bed and have a Thing we did as a couple—is still there.

I think, immediately, that I can't be here anymore—how

can I sit here and wait, if Mindy Fale went out after I went to bed? I think that, immediately, I need to go find Necro. I need to find Necro and ask him were you lying or not about the $40,000 Cosimus Belvende Propeller, because I am running out of money and I am running out of my sense of humor and I am running out of people.

But I've heard nothing from Necro at all. And Mindy Fale? I'll just grind my teeth at the back of her head until I die of rage at age fifty. I haven't kissed her on the lips in six days. Her skin tastes like Vaseline and grilled Avon. Mindy Fale is nothing but another fight.

So this is what I have left: the growing loudness in my head, and the sofa, and the shelves that me and Mindy Fale made from taped-together milk crates. And all I can say is I need to think; I need to think; it's all over and I need to go somewhere and think this thing away like wind smoothing out a rock for three thousand years.

And right then, I know what it is that I've needed to think.

I empty my milk crates of clothing and jam my T-shirts, jeans, underwear, toothbrush and shampoo into a trash bag. I take some leftover rope from the move and strap the Cosimus Belvende Propeller to the roof of the car, just in case I need to shove $40,000 in Mindy Fale's face at some far-later point in my life. In our basement storage cage, I unstack our plastic storage bins and unsnap their tops. I dig through the paper stacks—chafing my knuckles on stacks of old homework as- signments, a strand of basement spider web on my tongue— until I find the retreat pamphlets at the bottom that Fake Dad No. 3 gave me.

One pamphlet has a picture of clouds stretching outward from a sunrise and, below it, the address in King of Prussia of a place called Continual Center. On another pamphlet, a picture looking down from a cliff into a pond shaped like a human brain. On one of the pages inside, Fake Dad No. 3 has double-underlined a passage that says: "—not *at* the master, but *yet* the master. Yet" and that's it.

Outside, the apartment houses seem bigger and more evenly spaced than usual, paint jobs cleaned by the sunlight when I drive past. The trees are bare as capillaries, and the orange and yellow leaves on the grass are bright and wet and spaced like stars. I take the long way to the expressway, past Park Ave., my favorite street, with houses like tuxedos. Then down through 490, through the tollbooth, and onto I-90.

I unstick a cigarette from the orange coils of the lighter, and when I go over a slight, uphill curve the farmlands explode into view—green and tan velvet rising like stomachs; a red barn and, up in the woodland hills, a house, peach like a vitamin shard. CMF's wattage is surprisingly strong—it's always some little peppermint from Christ when you hear three good songs in a row—and "Bark at the Moon" throws some static punches at "Sussudio" from some Syracuse station and wins.

I pass the first interstate fast-food stop, which only makes me think of when Mom, before she gave up on it altogether, drove me during April break to look at the SUNYs and talk to people about colleges. On the highway, we stopped for gas. Already I missed home; I was so nervous, head-and-lungs nervous, about having to go to Cortland or Fredonia or Albany,

even just to consider living there. And I looked in the rearview
mirror at the gas station attendant unscrewing the gas cap—
this kid who was a more baked, stubbly version of me—and
I said to myself: I want to be that guy. He gets to stay here
tonight and not be nervous.

But now I am that guy! And that guy is asking me: Do
you even know how to *get* to King of Prussia? Did you even
call about a retreat registration? Don't you know Muler and
the T-Gods are playing the Bug Jar tonight?

But it's like when you watch a dog charge through an
electric fence—the collar box sending electricity through the
dog's neck, the dog hustling it through to freedom—and outside Syracuse, a static frenzy eats up one last Boston song (try
not to hear a Boston song on CMF—the Boston Challenge,
me and Necro called it!) before it's gone. And I haven't earned
a Muler concert yet anyway.

I get on I-81, only the second interstate highway I've ever
been on. King of Prussia: I know nothing about it. Maybe
I'll move there. And maybe everyone will finally ask: Have
you heard from Nate? I heard he disappeared; I heard his
apartment had no furniture and just a lamp on the floor
and he prefers that; I heard people just *listen* when he talks;
I heard he turned thirty in Cincinnati; I heard he turned
thirty-four in Arizona; I heard he's really mellowed out since
1999; I drove all the way out there to ask him how I should
describe the ocean or a nuclear power plant as seen from an
airplane, or the feeling of waiting for someone you love to go
to bed so you can be up, alone, and he said nothing to me.
Not a word.

But when I eventually do come back to Rochester, five days from now, one month from now, ten years from now—I'll let it be long if I need to—my brain will be so lean I won't even need to wonder. "How was King of Prussia? Are you different now?" everyone I've known will ask. And after I tell them "That's not a question," I'll never need to call anyone again.

I'll feel some lengths of forearm muscle do some unsung work when I shake the hands of the managers in the city, and at Kodak or Xerox or 4-H or Wegmans, my thoughts will arrive one after another through the turnstile, each task a present I'll wrap and send along. And, finally, I'll find Necro who, at that point, might be just Andrea, the way Toby is Toby Winter and Lip Cheese, all along, has been Kevin Posniak. And we'll both say, minds clear and boring, "Nothing much. Just working," and drink some Shea's and get tired early and go home, certain in the morning that we have nothing left to say.

Then someone will have the whole city to himself—to lick salt off margarita glasses at that new Mexican place, adopt a dog and name it "Dad," buy a Dryden Theatre film pass, sit alone, empty seats to the left and the right, and wear a pair of 3D glasses if they ever do 3D Movie Week again, smirking whenever a character turns to the camera and points a huge index finger into the eyes of the audience. Someone with taste for once, with a way of walking under banquet archways without smiling too much. Someone who waves off the trays of toothpick snacks and waits calmly for everyone to break eye contact—no need to scribble phone numbers on place cards or torn-off program pages. Someone who leaves as the staff removes the tablecloths, into the quiet night on East Avenue, one car left under the parking lot lamps. Someone named me.

ACKNOWLEDGMENTS

And with that, ten years of my life. Thanks go to my parents, for their enduring patience and sense of humor about all this. In Rochester, thank-yous to the original Winjas, responsible for much of my own sense of humor and more than a few private references in this book: Nick, Brad, Derek, Dan, Amie, Kris, Philippe, and Mike, who we have been unable to track down. In New England: Pete, Greg, Matt, Ben, Katie, Ian, Adam, Sabrina—I wouldn't have gotten into metal or read David Foster Wallace or looked up court documents without you. In Gainesville: everyone on Team Dora for, if nothing else, the clutch viewings of "Pelts."

Likewise, the Massachusetts Cultural Council came through when I'd given up. Thanks as well to Sabina Murray, Noy Holland, Sam Michel and John Wideman, who righted my brain fiction-wise. Infinite thanks to Leigh Newman, for her enthusiasm, criticism, insight and overall wonderfulness. And, obviously, thanks to everyone else at Black Balloon Publishing for believing in this book.

Bigger debts are owed to Grace Paley, whose writing profoundly changed mine, and whose story "The Little Girl" was in part a basis for the second-to-last chapter; Stanley Elkin, whose story "A Poetics for Bullies" I've been trying to write for years; George Saunders, Harold Brodkey and Amy Hempel, in general; and Judge Judy, for the line "I'm the boss, applesauce."

Parts of "A Thing to Invest" and "Home of Triscuit" originally appeared in a short story called "A Thing to Invest," which was published in *Pleiades*. Thanks to the editors. General information on Timothy McVeigh was obtained from articles published by *The New York Times*, *The Washington Post* and *The Los Angeles Times*. The excerpt of McVeigh's letter, as quoted by Bambert Tolby, was taken from a 1997 article published in *The Los Angeles Times*. The line "I've been tried as one," whose origins Nate cannot specifically place, is from *The Simpsons*.

Finally, thank you to Donna Wrublewski, for her very existence. In a book of in-jokes, my love for you is MegaBagelon-sized.